I0691853

FOUND GIRL

PROJECT ENTERPRISE 6

PAULINE BAIRD JONES

PBJ

ABOUT FOUND GIRL

She's an alien farm girl. He's a hotshot soldier. Can their love save an alien sanctuary from destruction?

Arian Teraz refuses to waste her life on a loveless arranged marriage and a rocky plot of farmland. So when a mysterious ship lands in front of her and invites her to take a chance on something else, she doesn't hesitate. Fleeing her planet, hostile forces open fire on her ship, and she has no choice but to send the ship through a wormhole. Clinging to life, she rockets out the other side... and plummets into the strong arms of a handsome soldier.

After months of staring into empty space, Captain Jackson "Coop" Cooper is itching for some action. He gets it when a wormhole delivers an alien ship into their path. He volunteers to make first contact, rescuing the ship with its injured alien beauty and her unusual shipmate. Before they can get acquainted, new threats send them on a wild ride through the cosmos and into a mysterious sanctuary with no means of escape. With little time to sort out enemies and allies, Arian and Coop must work together to uncover the secret behind her hidden destiny if they stand any chance of surviving their future.

Found Girl is the sixth standalone book in the spectacular Project Enterprise sci-fi romance series. If you like cosmic battles, human-alien love stories, and imaginative future worlds, then you'll love Pauline Baird Jones' high-adrenaline adventure.

Buy *Found Girl* to beam into a sexy interstellar romance today!

———

*I'd like to dedicate this book to my parents
who taught me everything I know
about never giving up.*

*Ann Gwynn Baird 1932-2016
Robert Nebel Baird 1927-2016*

I miss you.

PART I

1

IF DESIRE alone could carry her from this place, she would be gone already. So it was not a surprise when she opened her eyes and found her two feet still planted on the ground.

Fickle, elusive hope. Like the stars, it beckoned and tantalized and ultimately left her stuck still.

She gave a soft laugh that morphed into a sigh. She should not have come, even though it was the last night, the last time she could look up and hope.

She had known tomorrow would come, had known it since she had been old enough to know much of anything. Everyone got older. Everyone reached their age of majority. Knowing all this should have stamped out hope. Tomorrow there would be a formal day of ceremony to mark her coming of age, and at the conclusion, pact bonding with a man picked for her by the Government.

The end of privacy. The end of hope.

A shiver ran down her back as she considered the men who had visited the farm. Most had looked at the land, but one—one had looked at her as if he knew what she hid. Her mind and her flesh had shrunk from him, though he had kept the legal distance the whole time. If the Government chose him—she shuddered at the thought. Would even her thoughts be private from those eyes?

She had thought—she had hoped—her desire to escape would somehow be enough to open a path to freedom. She gave a silent, hollow laugh. As if willpower alone could free her from the laws of science that she was not supposed to know. Well, if sheer stubborn will could not set her free, then she must direct that stubbornness into finding a way to kill hope this night.

No space ship was going to drop out of the sky and scoop her up—

Her thoughts skidded to a halt as one of the bright distant stars did seem to be dropping out of the sky. She stared. Took a step toward it, then another. With each step, it seemed to come closer, grow brighter.

"It is not, it can not be for me," she murmured. She was just a farm laborer. A small cog in a large, indifferent wheel.

It continued to approach—it had to be a ship, not a star because its brightness dimmed as if its pilot knew it was using forbidden air space. It was something conjured from her hope, she told herself, but the hum of it felt real. It vibrated through the soles of her work boots, increasing in intensity until it rushed past her, almost knocking her off her feet as its backwash hit. She staggered from the force of it, then spun to keep it in view.

She thought she saw a black bowl-shape drop below the tree line. She tensed for impact, but none came.

She did not consciously decide to follow. Her feet moved, slow at first, then fast, and faster still, as hope broke free from restraints, propelling her through the darkest shadows. It did not matter that she could not see in the nearly moonless dark.

She knew every rise, every dip, every plant and tree of this trap she'd been born to.

By the time she reached the fallow field where the ship hovered—silent and dark a few feet above the ground—she gasped for breath. She was a farmer, not a runner. Bent, her hands resting on her knees, she studied the quiescent object, barely visible in the mix of shadow and faint starlight.

It was a starship. She knew this though she'd never seen any of the ships that carried the food produced on Bosakli to the other planets in the Consortium.

Her breathing still rapid, she jumped off the canal bank and moved closer, keeping to the shadows thrown down by the trees that separated this field from the others. It was unlikely anyone else was out this late, but she had not survived this long by being careless.

She stopped where what light there was began. *Be careful what you wish for*, her grandmother had told her many times. Was it here for someone else? As the thought formed, her mind, her heart rejected it.

It had come for her.

It felt as if all she had hoped for, all she had longed for throughout the long dreary years, had coalesced into this single moment of utter certainty. This ship was hers.

She felt no fear, no relief. Just a sense of something finally feeling right for the first time in her life. With her shoulders back, she stalked up to the ship as a ramp lowered to meet her. Something stirred in the depths, a soft clicking, then two eyes, yellow circles surrounding dark orbs, appeared out of the black depths.

Its height and position made her suspect it was not humanoid—which the Consortium claimed was not possible, but she had never believed them anyway.

For a moment she hesitated, but one did not reject a gift, just because it might contain a two-edged sword. Or nonhuman aliens. She jumped up on the ramp. Her boots thumped as she walked forward, and she heard a soft click of claws against metal as the eyes retreated, then the whir as the hatch closed her in...

2

Now that they'd boldly gone somewhere, Colonel Jackson "Coop" Cooper would have liked to do more than talk about how cool it was to boldly be somewhere.

The *Boyington's* geeks claimed they had passed the boundary into a new star system during ship night. He'd have to take their word for it. Looking at the projected view outside? All he could see was a whole lot of deep space on one side and even more deep space on the other.

He loosed a silent sigh. Probably not much chance of finding another hidden base full of advanced technology and weapons, no matter how far they got from the Milky Way. In his experience, the universe didn't repeat the good stuff. In the absence of a hidden base, he would settle for first contact with some actual aliens.

Where was the adventure they'd promised him as a consolation for the trip to Mars he hadn't got? Okay, so the secret expedition wouldn't be secret if they went to Mars where the Project Enterprise ships could have been spotted by who knew who—though no one had explained how they'd managed to get out of their system. And they wouldn't. He was a fighter jockey, the commander of the *Boyington's* air group, which meant he got orders, not explanations.

He leaned back in his chair and tried not to yawn as the head geek blah blah blahed about the results of their initial, deep system scan. Sure, he was ecstatic it had so much cool astrophysical crap and a big healthy sun. Who didn't like finding another sun? He needed to work on his tan. Or here's a thought. Turn him and his flyboys loose to go look at all of it. Flying sim-drills was not making any of them happy.

He glanced at Pappy, sitting across from him. Not General Boyette's real name, but the nickname came with the command of the *Boyington*. Pappy, hiding a yawn with a hand and a cough, met Coop's gaze and gave a slight shrug. Must be galling to him that they'd missed the battle in the Garradian Galaxy, then been sent here before things hotted up again. On the upside, the *Boyington* had been upgraded with a lot of the cool tech post battle, enabling it to go further than any of the other expedition ships.

Pappy's eyes narrowed. "Is it just our point of entry that makes it look like we came in on the empty side of the system?"

It did kind of look like they'd arrived in the system's boonies.

There was a concerted turn of geeks' heads as they studied their arrival point, then the cluster of planets huddled on the other side of the system. What appeared to be streams of debris fanned out, as if drawn toward the cluster.

"And what is all this?" Pappy's finger pointed to the debris fields.

"Asteroid belts?" one geek postulated.

"Not belts," another disagreed. "Not seeing any with a center of gravity."

There was a stir of excitement as someone zoomed in on the region.

"Some of the clusters do appear to have gravitational orientation," someone murmured.

Coop tipped his head to one side. Kind of reminded him of a pool table. Wasn't sure why that thought made him uneasy, other than the fact the *Boyington* seemed to be on the cue side of the table. He glanced at Pappy and found him frowning.

"Might be a good idea to do a risk assessment—"

Coop stiffened a half a second before the alarm cut off Pappy's words. He was up and headed for the hatch opening as the alert began its klaxon call ship-wide. It was, so his pilots claimed, his super power, this uncanny ability to sense trouble coming even before the sensors.

"Clear," he ordered, flattening civilians and other personal against the wall as he jogged past, headed for the squadron's hangar bay. Over his comm, the updates started to come in from Ops.

Unknown contacts.

Collision warnings began to blare as the space around them filled with multiple objects.

Unknown risk factors.

Other than the chance of getting slammed by multiple objects? "What do you know," he snapped into his comm. Lots of explanations, but nothing with meat.

By the time he'd donned his speed jeans and was settling into the cockpit of his *Dauntless*, Ops was reporting that at least one of the objects was a ship. One possible life sign on board. Low energy signature. Possibly an indication of damage, or it was a dead/dying ship. Or it was just had a low energy profile.

Amazing how fast things could go from "wow, this is so cool that we're in a new star system," to "wow, there's a bunch of UFO's and an alien ship and I think I just wet my pants." The civilians all looked wide-eyed, the military personnel, well, this was why they were here. If you were gonna go where no one had gone before, it was good to have guys and gals with guns around to respond first.

He fired his engines, hovered into point position at the open bay doors, and waited for the go command. When it came, he punched it, the force of it slamming him against the back of his seat as his ship passed through the protective energy shield. His squadron followed him out in tight formation. Once they'd cleared the ship, they spread out, assuming an attack profile.

What had been almost empty deep space now looked like someone had tossed a bunch of rocks into their path. Big ones. Little ones. The stream of rocks was denser at one end, thinner where his sensors picked up the ship. According to the data coming in, the objects at the front of the mass were moving faster than those at the rear, but all were oriented in one general direction. Like dice tossed on a table.

He adjusted course and speed to match their bogey and began a cautious approach.

"Keep back and cover me," he ordered. If the universe was flinging rocks, he didn't want his whole squadron to get caught in it. At least all the bogeys were following pretty much the same course, if not the same speed. He threaded a careful path through the thinnest section of rocks he could find, closing on the ship.

According to the original sensor data, there'd been a bright flash of something, then the rocks and ship were just there. Geeks were still studying the readings from that. No indications of a familiar power source coming from the ship.

Unlike the lumpy rocks of various sizes and shapes, the bogey was a classic oval that widened out to a rectangular snubbed wedge on its back end. The single life sign reading was based on Garradian technology that might not identify all alien life forms. Truth was, they didn't know what they didn't know.

Yet.

So far bogey and rocks were behaving predictably enough for him to ease in closer, though he jigged as much as he dared on approach. No reason to make himself an easy target if there were hostiles on board. He kicked on his spotlight, light stabbed out, and there it was. A for-real alien ship among the rocks. Almost as black as the deep space around it, it spun or tumbled —he wasn't sure which—as he eased closer to take some further readings.

"Sure you want to get that close, Banshee?" his wingman, Tiger, asked.

Coop ignored the question, keyed his radio, "Home plate, you say you're picking up life signs from this thing?" Looked dead dark to him.

"Affirmative, first base, at least one possible life sign."

Which wasn't exactly an affirmative.

Well, he'd wished for this, and now he'd got it.

First contact with something.

He throttled back, matching speed with the bogey and activated his camera, then ran his light along it from stem to stern, recording the scan for the geeks to study, taking it slow—was that damage? Had it taken fire? Looked like it to him, but what did he know about what crap looked like out here? Some of the damage could be from impacts, but he could see something that could be scorch marks.

His light brightened, and it almost seemed like a feedback running back along it. He tensed, but nothing happened, and no warnings appeared on his screens. Had he imagined it? He ran a quick diagnostic and got an 'all systems fine' notice. Wishful thinking, maybe? No, his gut was twitching. Something was looking back at him. *D'oh.* There was that possible life sign in there.

Seemed like it was taking a long time for the geeks to get back to him. He keyed his radio. "What do you want me to do, home plate?"

His radio crackled. "Banshee," it was Pappy's voice, "our people have identified what appears to be a port. Do you think you could tow the bogey safely back to home plate?"

Coop hesitated. "You want me to tow this thing?" It wasn't just all the rocks. Just because the ship hadn't acted up, didn't mean it wouldn't.

"We'd like you to try. If you get into trouble, cut it loose."

Pappy's ship, Pappy's call. "Affirmative."

"You're not to risk your ship. That's an order, Banshee." Another pause. "They're sending you the location of the port." A pause. "Tow it to the aft bay."

Coop gave a silent whistle. Aft was the off-limits, super secret bay where it was rumored all the super secret alien stuff from the super secret Garradian base was stored. "Roger that, home plate."

He studied the image they sent, then did another traverse—there it was. It was gonna be tricky. It had rocks tracking along with it at varying distances, some a little too close for comfort. How had it ended up in the middle of that mess? He looked for a larger gap, did a silent countdown and slipped into the rock stream. Some of his sensors didn't like it and complained. He ignored them and activated his cable, sending it slowly toward the port. Of course, the bogey would have to accept the connection for this to work—it clicked into place, flashing green, an indication it was a solid connection. Okay then. Life sign confirmed? Maybe. Could be an automated response.

He'd done sim tows, but this was the first time he'd tried it in the real world of outer space with a bunch of rocks in play. He reduced the slack on the tow line, then began easing the bogey in closer to his ship. Good thing he knew his math. And had a computer on board. He calculated the distances, tried the line to get a feel for the timing between pull and movement —something the computer couldn't help with. When he was sure he'd got it, he eased his ship out of the stream of rocks. Once he was clear he waited and watched for the right moment —there it was. He tugged the ship toward his—it got bumped by one of the rocks and accelerated toward him. His sensors screamed as the bogey threatened to bump heads with his *Dauntless*.

In slow motion, he tried to correct, even as the bumped rock went on to bump another, causing a slow motion cascade effect as they headed off in different directions, including toward him and the bogey. Trouble was, he was moving slow, too. Sweat beaded his face as he jinked and tugged, trying to get both ships out of the collision zone. One rock tracked close enough to make his *Dauntless* cry like a baby and started some chatter from home plate and his squadron. He didn't have time to talk as another rock tried to cut his tow line—it twanged a bit but held. He had to speed up to keep the bogey from looping around and hitting him head on, though.

And then, just like that, both ships were in the clear—both those still following the main course and the bumped ones— continued on without them.

In the confusion, the line of rocks had ended up between him and the *Boyington*, but the line had an end point. He frowned. Kind of odd, that, them tracking along like a mute squadron, but he was glad to have a clear course back to home plate—

Something flickered on his com panel, so quick he thought he'd imagined it. Until it happened again. He opened his mouth to demand a systems check, but never got the words out as a message formed on his screen.

Thank you for your assistance, Banshee. Some systems on this ship are damaged. Pilot injured. Request emergency transit to your ship.

Coop had to clear his throat to get out, "You seeing this, home plate?"

"Affirmative, Banshee." A long pause. "Permission for expedited transit."

3

TRAJAN BESTER RETREATED to his ready room, but he did not rush to open a channel to his client. Instead, he paced slowly, considering how to frame his failure as a delayed success. It might be a bigger challenge than his few days on the backward Bosakli. How he hated being dirt side.

His client would not be pleased that the item had not been secured, but he was not an unreasonable...species. Or less than most, Bester amended. There were stories—but of more concern was losing his very substantial payment and future commissions from a collector with such deep pockets.

It had not been Bester's idea to integrate with the planet's society or to make such cautious approach to the item. If he'd been allowed his usual snatch and grab, the item would already be on its way. He also had not known there were competitors for the item. His client had neglected to mention that in his briefing.

Still, Bester had seen no sign of other, off planet interest during his time down there. None of the other pact bond males had shown signs of being more than the useful drones the Consortium had designed them to be. Not that he relied solely on his eyes, but he'd sensed nothing from them but interest in the farm. Most had barely looked at the item.

Almost, he'd agreed with them. Drab clothes, downcast gaze, a subtle sense of defeat in its posture despite the Consortium mandated erect posture. A female drone preprogrammed by the Consortium to farm and breed more drones. Then its lashes lifted and—briefly—he'd seen distrust and dislike in a gaze of surprising intelligence. How had that awareness survived Consortium screening? He watched it carefully after that, but it was no fool. It hid its loathing of the pact bonding preliminaries and him.

It was, he recalled thinking, a pity his contract required the item to be delivered intact. He could have had a little fun before he froze it for delivery. He preferred his partners unwilling, which it was. But it was not worth the risk. Nothing was more important than payment.

Curiosity was dangerous for someone like him, but he was not able to be completely immune, not since he found out there was competition. Why was his client willing to pay so much for this artifact? Who had out maneuvered both of them? He needed to know what he was up against, he told himself. He hadn't had to look hard. One could not kick around the galaxy grabbing artifacts for collectors and not have heard more than one of the legends of the Seven. Almost every species in the galaxy had a myth about them, ranging from the simple—they were witches who cursed the enemies of their friends, to the ridiculous—that they controlled some super weapon. He took care in his search, however. Pleasing his client was of more concern than hyped up legends of some ancient tangram.

Might as well believe in the return of the missing *Phoenicopterians*. That was the problem with myths. No way to know what was true and what had been corrupted by time and telling. Too bad the *Mycterians*—who were credited with causing the disappearance of the *Phoenicopterians*—weren't the ones who disappeared. That was a nasty species. If the stories were to be believed, they'd not been satisfied at driving the *Phoenicopterians* out of the galaxy. They'd spent the time since trying to find them so they could eradicate them. He'd managed to stay off their radar, but it hadn't been easy. He'd almost jumped into a swarm of them while heading for this system to collect the item. Still broke out in a cold sweat thinking about it. As he was coming in, they were going out, or that wouldn't have ended well.

If the task wasn't difficult enough, apparently there was a legend linking the Seven with the *Phoenicopterians.* How ironic would it be if his search for the lost artifact took him into a nest of *Mycterians?*

He strode over and poured himself a drink, tossed it back, welcoming the burn in his throat and the fire it put in his belly. The artifact was worth a lot to him, but the *Mycterians?* He shuddered. They liked to feast on defeated enemies while they were still alive. He poured another shot and took it with him to his station, dropping into his chair. He took a pull from his glass, and then pulled up the next report. According to this, his client had received similar artifacts from Bester's rivals—and occasional allies. It was a big galaxy. Sometimes the only people a mercenary could trust were his closest enemies. The people who hired him would never admit they knew him, let alone help him in a tight spot.

They hadn't been paid as much as he would be getting, he noted. Because the artifacts were in cold sleep. Lucky him. He got the one that was awake and able to fly away. He took another drink, just enough to take the edge off fear and leave him with his lust for the money. He had pride in his work, too. He always delivered the goods. The client knew this, had told him it was why he'd been hired for this artifact.

So how did he get it back?

He had Elfel, his best man, going over the scans from the anomaly. An anomaly that hadn't appeared in any data on the Consortium system. He'd like to shoot someone for that, but he was a fair man. The Consortium was a mostly closed system. Oh, they allowed pirates to operate in the fringes, to keep people in or out. And his ship had been in the wrong place for an intercept. All he could do was watch in frustration as the small ship came under heavy fire. He'd been sure it was doomed when the anomaly appeared. It wasn't clear if the ship took the out, or was pulled inside. Didn't matter. The result was the same.

It was gone.

Would the client blame him? Clients usually did. And what was he supposed to tell it? It did not like excuses, though he had good ones. He finished the glass and got another, tossing it back, too.

He had video. He had scans of the ship. He had scans of the anomaly.

He did not have the item. And he did not know where it had gone.

His comm trilled. It was Elfel.

"Yes?"

"I might have something, sir."

"What?" He had drunk enough that his hopes could not rise.

"The ship had a tracking beacon broadcasting on a specialized frequency."

He tried to form the question, then wondered why he bothered. One of Elfel's specialties was finding what others could not. Besides, beacons had a limited range because of people like Elfel.

"I thought it was beyond reach," Elfel said.

Bester straightened or thought he did. "Are you telling me it is not? That you can track it?"

"Yes, sir."

Hope bloomed, then dimmed. "How far?"

"We'll need to use an unregistered jump gate to get there. We don't have a handy anomaly to ride."

Bester did some math. Jump gate access was not cheap, particularly unregistered ones.

On the other hand, he had hard information to offer his client in exchange for...understanding about the delay.

4

HE'D ASKED FOR IT, Coop reminded himself. He'd wanted to meet some actual aliens, but when he'd imagined first contact it had not been with a lizard.

Hadn't he learned to be careful what he wished for? This was going to be hard to live down.

Almost he wished Pappy had ordered him out of the bay with the other personnel. Curiosity had long been Coop's curse. This time it had landed him in the super secret bay that didn't look that interesting, with a lizard and a security team in hazmat gear. He glanced around, wondering if he could leave now. Probably not. Bet the bay was locked down until they assessed the risk level of a lizard. They'd learned a bit about alien bugs and trusting too soon during their adventure in the Garradian system. Coop had left on his zoom bag, with his head gear in place, just for this reason.

The lizard didn't look worried. It had slithered into view not long after a hatch had opened on the snub-nosed end of the ship. It had stopped at the top of the ramp, and no one had moved or said anything for what felt like a long time. At this rate, the injured pilot would be dead before anyone did anything —though he did wonder what kind of help the lizard was hoping for. He didn't think there was a vet on board.

He glanced around. He wasn't wearing his red shirt, but he had volunteered to take the big risks. The fact that team had also agreed to this didn't seem to have moved the dial yet. With a quick sigh, he headed for the lizard, easing through the semicircle, pushing up one gun so he could pass. He strolled to the bottom of the ramp. Up close, the sight of the lizard was a bit unnerving. Not exactly small. He hesitated, but he'd come this far. He nodded in what he hoped was a non-threatening way.

"Hey." The single word kind of echoed in the nearly empty bay. He might have fielded a couple of looks from the team, for which he did not blame them. He'd just said "hey" to a lizard. This would be the main reason he'd not been picked for the First Contact Team—

I am a Draze Dragon, not a lizard.

Coop looked left, right, and then arched a brow in the liz— dragon's direction.

You may board this craft, Banshee. And someone with **human** *medical experience.* The lizard's gaze seemed to sweep over him and the team. *There is no need for your protective gear. I have sanitized the ship for your safety.*

Human? Coop glanced back at the team leader. "Did you hear anything?"

"Sir, no, sir." He got a better grip on his weapon.

Only you can hear me, Banshee.

"Okay." Coop hesitated. Looked like he'd been added to the first contact team by dragon default. He lifted a foot to the ramp. His comm pinged.

"Captain." Pappy's voice had a warning question.

"Someone needs to do something, sir." He unlatched his head gear and took it off, handed it to the guy closest to him.

"If you're wrong…"

Coop didn't say what they were both thinking. That first contact usually went wrong, so they might as well get it over with. If it was his day to be a red shirt, then waiting wouldn't change that. He looked back at the camera and lifted a brow.

The pause went on for what felt like long, then Pappy said, "Go."

"Can we get a medical doc headed this way, too, sir? For the injured pilot?"

"Affirmative."

Coop didn't wait for a doc. If something was going to go wrong, better it happen before the doc arrived. He started up the ramp and the liz—the dragon—turned, vanishing inside with a twitch of its tail. The click of claws against metal gave him a direction to follow. The craft felt bigger on the inside than it had looked. As a *Dr. Who* fan, he liked that, while admitting it also made him a bit uneasy. It wasn't *that* big, though.

The passage seemed to follow the curve of the ship's hull around a bulging bulkhead that lay directly ahead. The liz—dragon paused and looked back at Coop.

"What?" Had he done something wrong already?

Your shirt does not appear to be red.

"Not yet," Coop said. Because he didn't want to explain, he glanced around. "Your pilot?"

The dragon moved again, and a hatch opened, like a metal eye, in the center of the bulge, revealing a figure sprawled on the floor. Light fell on the dragon as it entered what he guessed was the bridge, mostly because everything he could see looked like a bridge. And, he wanted it to be a bridge. It was a fighter pilot thing.

Her restraints failed during the transit, which was…rather rough.

Considering the rocks they'd arrived with, this did not surprise Coop. He paused in the hatch opening and looked around. There was a pilot's chair designed for a humanoid pilot, and one for the dragon. The dragon's was a space age pet carrier with seat belts. Broken straps hung off the other seat, confirming the failed restraints.

The injured pilot, definitely humanoid, had landed between the metal supports for the two seats, one arm flung out, the other half trapped under her body. She wore a simple jumpsuit, one devoid of insignia, as far as he could tell. Sturdy boots, almost the same color as her jumpsuit, had bits of mud clinging to the soles. Her hair was brown, longish. Her skin was tanned, well, by Earth standards. Could be her natural color. At least she wasn't purple, like some of the Garradian system's humanoids.

The dragon scrambled up to its spot as if to get out of his way.

With the pilot down, it was almost standing room only, and the dragon did have more legs.

Coop crouched and studied her hand. It looked humanoid, was well shaped and strong, but the long fingers had callouses at the tips, and there were tiny cuts and signs of old bruising as if she had done some serious physical labor. He felt her wrist for a pulse, wondering if she'd have one and how he was supposed to know if it was normal or not. He'd had more than basic first-aid training before deploying with Project Enterprise, but there hadn't been a section on alien physiology. By their standards, her pulse felt strong and regular.

Her physiology is very similar to yours.

He glanced at the dragon, not comfortable with the idea he heard its voice inside his head.

It is the only way we can communicate. My physiology is not designed for human speech.

Dragon had a point. "Can anyone else hear you?" he asked, a slight movement from the pilot drawing his attention back to her.

Other than you? My pilot can hear me.

"That's going to be hard to explain." Doc was taking too long, but if her physiology was similar, Coop could do a quick check, maybe juice things along on the first contact front—he ran his hands along her arm, feeling for broken bones. When he found nothing, he cautiously straightened the limb to a more comfortable position. She didn't protest, so he scrambled around the dragon carrier and checked out her legs. He felt the flex of muscles under his hands, and she straightened them without his help, her back arching as if she were regaining consciousness. He went back to her head.

"Try not to move until the doc gets here," he said, then made a face at himself. She probably couldn't understand him—though the dragon did. And how was that possible? In the movies, there were universal translators, but real life—he glanced—he had a dragon. There was a joke in there somewhere.

She either didn't understand him or didn't care. She shifted her body into a less painful configuration, wincing a fair bit in the process and groaning once. Her lashes lifted, revealing eyes that were a mix of blue and green, not unlike the surf off the Virginia coast where he liked to sail when he wasn't boldly going somewhere. Her lashes were the same brown as her hair and thick, the dark brows arching over her eyes. Her lips were compressed into a straight line over a determined jaw.

For what felt like a long moment, she stared at him, confusion flickering in the depths.

"There was some kind of transit accident. You're on board our ship—the *Boyington*," he said, trying to sound reassuring, even if she couldn't understand his words. "Well, you're aboard your ship which is on board the *Boyington*." She gave a slight nod which could have meant almost anything. "Where does it hurt?"

She untangled her arm from the support and felt the back of

her head. Coop gently pushed her hand away and explored her scalp. Found a decent sized lump.

"What about your ribs? Any pain when you breathe?"

She shook her head. "Do I...who did you say you were?"

She spoke slowly as if the words were new to her and she had an accent of some kind. *D'oh*. The alien kind. "I'm Coop—Captain Jackson Cooper, ma'am. United States Air Force. And you are—"

Her chin dipped slightly causing her to wince. "Arian. Arian Teraz."

"Pleased to meet you, ma'am."

"The honor is mine, sir."

Coop had a feeling the words sounded weird to her.

You are correct. I am translating for her.

Coop glanced at the dragon. "Thanks," he said, though not happily. Still didn't like the idea of an alien dragon poking around inside his head. Not that he'd find that much in there—according to his last girlfriend anyway.

"I would like to rise," Arian said.

"Maybe you should wait for the doc," Coop suggested. He wasn't shocked when she ignored this suggestion. She might be an alien, but she was still a woman.

He helped her up, noting, even though he shouldn't, that she was very much a woman, with everything where it should be. Definitely closer to his idea of satisfactory first contact. Which was pretty much inappropriate to circumstances. Good thing a guy could be politically incorrect inside his own head. He shot the dragon a look. The dragon looked away. Had a feeling if it could have whistled, it would have. He tipped his head to one side. Kind of looked like a bearded dragon, now that he thought about it.

The dragon's gaze turned back toward him, something in their depths that indicated amused.

Draze Dragons are very similar in appearance to your Earth bearded dragons.

How did this dragon know about the Earth ones? Or Earth?

The dragon didn't say. Just looked away once more, as if its bank of instruments were the most interesting thing on the ship. Coop bit back the urge to demand some answers. Not his job. He turned his attention back to Arian. Found her looking at him with remarkable calm, a look that was almost ceremonial, he decided. It wrapped her like an invisible cloak. Impressive, considering she'd been bounced off the decking and woke up with an alien looming over her.

"How do you feel?"

"I believe I will continue to exist, thank you."

Okay. "That's good."

A silence formed, not a comfortable one. Not threatening, but her fixed, almost unblinking gaze made him want to shift from one foot to the other like he was back in school. Or boot camp.

"A bit tight in here." He spoke more to fill the silence than because he had anything to say, tugging at the top of his zoom bag and wishing he'd taken it off, too.

A tiny frown formed between her brows. "Tight?"

"Not big. Cramped." Was he hoping for a tour of the ship? Probably. It was his first alien ship and he had a feeling he wouldn't be invited on the tour by the geeks. This might be his only chance.

After a pause, she nodded. "That—yes, it is very efficient."

Another silence. He cleared his throat. "Looks like you took some fire on your way here."

"Fire?"

"Saw some damage on the exterior of your ship." He hesitated. "Looked like weapons fire? Somebody shooting at you?"

She stared at him for a long moment. "There was debris in the anomaly."

That wasn't exactly a no, I didn't take weapons fire. "Anomaly?"

We transited through an unstable space channel.

Her lashes flickered as if she'd heard this, too. Space channel? The geeks would love hearing about that. "Debris? You mean the big rocks?"

I thought your people called them meteors?

I'm not a geek. Coop turned back to Arian. Riding a channel —was that like a wormhole?—with that bunch of rocks would indeed be rough transit. "I'm surprised your ship made it through intact." He hesitated. "What was it like?"

Her lashes flew up. It almost seemed like she wanted to grin. "It was...very...interesting."

He'd wondered, looking at her, if she really was the pilot. She didn't have the look of one, but that sounded about the right amount of crazy to be a pilot. Odd the geeks hadn't mentioned any anomalies, channel or wormlike, during the briefing.

This particular one seems to come and go.

The dragon sounded a bit wry.

That didn't sound good. Not that he knew a lot about anomalies of any kind.

"Captain?" The voice was a little hesitant, and the deck vibrated slightly as someone—most likely the doc—stepped onto the ramp.

"Come on in, Doc." Coop met her gaze, holding hers with his. "My people will have questions."

She didn't flinch or look away. "I'm sure they will, Captain."

He grinned. "Call me Coop, ma'am."

The smile flickered at the edges of her mouth again. "Please call me Arian...Coop."

He liked the way she said his name but he'd always been a sucker for an accent.

———

Arian watched with interest as Doc fitted something over her arm and tightened it, the fabric making an audible—and most unusual—crinkling sound. She had never been this close to any male before, let alone two of them. The male presence changed the feel of the bridge, the energy in the room much different from the pact bonding visits. She stole glances at the two men through her lashes. Doc seemed younger than Coop. Fresh-faced. Nervous. A hint of something pungent clung to his person, a contrast to the clean, crisp scent of Coop when he'd leaned over her to help her up.

The obvious concern in Coop's eyes had helped smooth the shock of waking with a strange man looming over her. It had eased the chill she felt from laying on the cold decking, replacing it with an unfamiliar warmth. There was concern in Doc's eyes, not to mention curiosity, but it did not affect her the way Coop's gaze did.

You like him.

I don't know him. And he didn't know her.

Liking is an emotional reaction, not a logical one.

She glanced at the Companion. Emotion had brought her here, where ever here was. *Do you know where we are?*

Scanning is currently offline.

She knew how it felt to be offline. And he hadn't exactly answered her question. She considered this, then decided she did not mind not knowing where they were as much as, perhaps, she should. If the Consortium didn't know where they were, chances were good that no one else could find them.

You don't call this "found?"

She ignored this interjection, though she did shoot him an annoyed look.

Doc's hands shook some as he finished adjusting the device he'd affixed to her arm.

Is he frightened of me?

I think it has more to do with you being a female. And alien.

Interesting. In their eyes, she was the alien. Instead of unsettled by this, she was intrigued.

He caught her looking at him. Color tinged his cheeks as he smiled at her.

"This measures your blood pressure, ma'am."

But blood flowed inside the skin, she wanted to protest, as he turned her arm so that it rested on the supports of the pilot station seat. She braced for the pain to come.

"Try not to move until it's finished. There will be some pressure, but it won't last. Okay?"

It seemed late to ask her permission. But he seemed to need reassurance, so she gave a slight nod, trying to calm her breathing.

He did something, and the band began to tighten. As he had said it would, it quickly became uncomfortable, but not painful and there was no sign of blood being spilled for him to measure. Just when she thought she could not endure more, the pressure stopped, then began to ease. He stared intently at a screen on the band. When the symbols on the screen ceased to change, he seemed satisfied and removed the device from her arm. She gave the area a surreptitious look, relieved to see no blood.

"You have great blood pressure, ma'am," he told her, folding the device up and stowing it in the case he'd brought with him.

"Assuming her blood pressure is in the same range as ours," Coop pointed from where he leaned against the bulkhead by the hatch opening.

That earned him a slightly wide-eyed look from Doc. He looked the question at Arian, but she did not understand the question, so what answer could she give? Her stomach knotted, but her shoulders rose and fell in their usual slow rhythm. Her hands lay relaxed on the grips on either side of her chair.

"Do you...know what your blood pressure is? When it's normal, I mean?"

She gave a slight, noncommittal shrug of her shoulders. Doc did not seem to mind this non-answer.

What is his purpose?

He is a Healer, her Companion said.

The fingers of one hand moved before she could stop this tell-tale sign. She stared at Doc. Had he already begun the process of re-wiring her brain—

It is not his purpose to alter your mind. He is concerned only with your physical well-being. He came to help you.

Why would they do that when they do not know me?

Perhaps you should ask them that.

She ignored this and considered Doc instead. If he was a healer, then perhaps Doc was a designation of his purpose on this vessel, rather than a name. She stole a glance at Coop. What was his purpose on this vessel? What did the designation "captain" mean?

He is the pilot of the ship that towed ours to this hangar bay.

Pilot. He flew ships.

You flew this ship.

Into a wormhole. She thought she felt the Companion give a mental shrug.

What was done was done and could not be undone. She knew this without being told.

I wonder if they know where we are? A ruffle that could have been a snort fluttered through her mind. It was true that knowing their current location was only half an answer if they did not know where this was in relation to where they'd been. If she'd been alone, she might have shrugged.

Being lost was not the worst thing that had happened to her in the many seasons of her life.

5

COOP SHIFTED POSITION, his gaze moving around the bridge and then back to Arian. He wanted to ask her questions, but there was a protocol—mostly about letting the pros handle first contact, so no one started another war.

She didn't look like the type to start a war. But look what had happened in the Garradian system. No one saw that one coming. It was what you couldn't see that turned shirts red. And started wars. He'd always trusted his instincts over his eyes, particularly if his eyes liked what they were seeing. And they did, though heck if he knew why.

She sat there looking meek as a nun. He'd always had trouble reading women, but she was the most closed book he'd ever come across. And she didn't own the pilot's seat. Wasn't sure what that meant other than it bothered him. There was red mixed in the brown of her hair, and the angle of her chin sent a signal that was at odds with the statute calm she projected.

He'd like to see her smile. The random thought made him shift uneasily. The alien, he reminded himself. He'd like to see the alien smile because she was an alien. That he liked looking at. Because she was an alien? He could be that shallow. Except...

she was also a woman. Which didn't help make him less shallow. No, that thought made him feel like Captain Kirk. Not that he'd had a chance to have a girl in every system. Or any system other than his own.

If he'd thought about this moment, he for sure hadn't planned on a Captain Kirk moment with a girl in a space ship with a dragon for a traveling companion. Other than the dragon, the set up wasn't that alien. It was a bridge of a ship, so it had controls and crap. The smell of it was different though. He wasn't sensitive enough to parse the smells, just knew it didn't smell like the *Boyington* or his *Dauntless*. He knew some of it was her, which could have been nasty, but wasn't.

As if she felt him watching, she looked at him. Her gaze showed uncertainty, worry and yes, fear. Then her lashes swept down, and a bit of color tinged her cheeks as if she were embarrassed.

He felt the urge to remind her she'd ridden a wormhole here, probably under fire, and was now on a ship with a bunch of strangers. It was natural to be a little nervous. But he wasn't the guy in charge. He couldn't make promises. Not even if she hadn't come trailing signs of trouble. He considered the thought. What kind of trouble was she trailing? The usual kind that always came with women, or the intergalactic war kind? Would it follow her here? Only time would answer that question. Pappy —whose instincts were as good or better than Coop's—wouldn't be happy, oh no, he wouldn't.

As if Pappy had heard him thinking—which it sometimes felt like he did—his head set crackled.

"Report, Captain."

Coop came to attention, even though Pappy couldn't see him —not that Coop wasn't sure he couldn't. Pappy was rumored to have eyes on the back of his head. Eyes that could see through metal decks, too.

"Doc is still examining our guest, sir."

The silence was not a happy one. Even through all the decks that separated them Coop could hear the old man thinking.

"Report to my ready room, Captain."

"Yes, sir."

He straightened, pulling her gaze his direction. There was nothing in her face or expression asking for reassurance, so why did he feel the need to offer some? "I have to report to the, to my commanding officer." He wanted to tell her he'd be back, but would he? "The doc will look after you," he said, feeling awkward for no reason he could explain.

She nodded and, without moving, seemed to retreat to a place of resignation. For no reason he could put the finger on, he felt like he'd kicked a kitten. She's not harmless, he reminded himself. Oh, no she wasn't. She was a woman, and they were never harmless.

"It was nice to meet you, ma'am, Arian." He gave a half salute and left without looking back. With each step, he felt the pull to go back, felt as if he were the one on a tow line now. Outside, he ran into a wall of tense. He'd forgotten no one knew what was going on inside. The first contact team shifted uneasily just outside the security perimeter. The team leader—whose name Coop didn't recall—stepped forward.

"Captain?"

The old man would not thank him for briefing this guy first, so Coop kept moving, though he did tell him, "The doc is still giving her the once over."

"Her?" His tone was sharp with surprise.

"Her. Go on in," Coop turned back, hiding a grin, "she hasn't bit anyone. Yet."

He let that be his parting shot as the hatch slid open, then closed behind him. He made tracks for the lift. As usual, the old man knew how to time it so he came into the ready room on Coop's heels.

Pappy nodded toward a seat and sank into the one at the head of the table. When Coop didn't speak right away, he arched his brows. "Do we have a problem, Captain?"

Coop didn't rush into a response. The old man expected him to think before he flapped his lips. Then he shrugged. "Not sure, sir. She's—"

"She?" Pappy cut in.

Funny how they all acted surprised, despite the fact that they had women serving all over the *Boyington*. Maybe it was because the Garradian Galaxy had been so devoid of equality for women. It should have been reassuring, or something, that Arian had been piloting that craft—but he didn't sense anything like that kind of confidence from her. Was she coming home or fleeing trouble through that wormhole?

Under Pappy's gaze, Coop told him everything except the moment of lust. After a long silence, Pappy spoke.

"Do you we know how badly her ship is damaged?"

Coop's shoulders twitched. Not a question meant for him.

"She and her lizard could stay on their ship," Pappy finally said.

Coop felt the bore of Pappy's gaze. "It's pretty tight space, sir. But—" They'd must have lived on the ship. His mouth twisted. "We can wait for the First Contact Team to make an assessment..."

Again the pause was long. No surprise when Pappy pushed back his chair and stood up. He'd always hated waiting on the diplomats.

"How about you introduce me to your alien and her tele-pathic lizard."

———

Arian watched until Coop was out of sight, wondering at the odd empty feeling in her chest. She could not miss someone she'd barely met, could she?

My people will have questions, he'd said.

Questions that needed answers or, she suspected, their good-will would fade. She glanced at the Companion.

Answers can be interesting, he agreed.

Or dangerous.

"How do you feel?" Doc asked.

Almost she turned her hands up for him to study. He was not asking about that kind of feeling, she realized just in time. He was humanoid. He must feel the same way she did. His face was open, his curiosity unhidden. All he thought, what he felt, passed through his eyes. It was almost too much to process. She felt many things but...

"I feel well," she said, taking the answer offered to her by the Companion.

"Any persistent pain anywhere?" he asked.

After a moment's hesitation, she lifted a hand to the bump that Coop had probed, angling her head so that he could see it if he so wished.

The chill of the gloves over his hands soothed the spot.

"That's a nasty bump." He retreated, digging in his case for something. He extracted a rectangular object, ripping off a covering and then twisting it. After a moment, he gave it a shake and handed it to her.

It was cool like his hands had been. At his urging, she put it against the bump, and it numbed the pain.

"Better?"

She nodded. "Thank you."

"I could help you better if I knew more about your physiology," he said, somewhat diffidently. "Do you have medical records

I could look at? Or understand?" he added with a rueful smile that was rather sweet.

"I will...try...once the ship's systems are back online," she said.

My people will have questions. What questions? How did one prepare for an unknown test?

"Sounds good." He hesitated, then said, "I need to go report...some other of my people will probably want to talk to you."

She nodded. "Thank you for your assistance."

"It was my...you're welcome." The doc gave her a final half wave and ducked through the hatch. She heard and felt his steps vibrating through the metal decking as he left the ship.

And then silence. Not even a murmur of sound from those gathered outside penetrated into this space. She wanted to close her eyes and shut it out, to retreat to the safe place inside her head, the place that had kept her safe from the Enforcers on Bosakli, but she did not dare.

My people will have questions.

She could almost feel them waiting to ask their questions. She rested a palm on the control panel, not sure it would work until it did, bringing up the view outside the ship. Several people milled around, their purpose not clear. Their bright yellow clothing looked bulky and uncomfortable. They carried weapons and watched her ship warily. The emotion that came through the strongest from all of them was uncertainty.

You are unknown to them.

I have always been unknown.

Even to herself. She set the pack on the arm rest, rose, and spread her fingers on a strip of bare wall, pushing so that her palm fully connected with the cold metal. It was smooth and cool, like the pack she'd set aside. For just a second it seemed as if sparks of light flickered under the skin. She blinked, but if they'd been there, they were gone. She flexed the fingers, turned her hand over, then looked at the back again.

Nothing. She had banged her head. The last time she'd done that, stars had appeared before her eyes. She touched the metal once more, then looked up, her gaze tracking across the metal ceiling. She turned so she could take in the bridge. It was an odd feeling to be surrounded by metal, both on this ship and by the other one out there, after a life lived so completely on the ground.

She breathed in, then slowly exhaled to calm herself. Only then could she feel a faint vibration from the larger ship's engines throbbing against her palm. Her mind separated the sound into separate engines, learning their signature tones before she let her hand drop away. What purpose did it serve to learn the engines? They would not be the ones asking questions.

The space outside this ship was quite large, but there must be much more to see. A smaller ship rested off to one side. Behind it were several others in berths along the other side. Coop's, she wondered? It was positioned to have been the ship that towed them here. Directly ahead was an opening, dark with the faint glow of stars beyond it. A force field must separate in from out. How odd she knew that. As always, she knew more than she should, yet still not quite enough.

She turned around to face the Companion once more.

"Why?" she spoke aloud since they were alone. She felt amusement from him.

That is a child's question.

I feel young... She frowned. And also old. She'd always felt different, separate from the others on Bosakli, but that feeling had tripled since boarding this ship. Why? But she didn't give voice to the thought this time.

My people will have questions.

Arian returned to her seat. She had to focus on what was in

front of her. There was some relief in that thought. Questions led to answers—answers she might not like giving. Answers they might not like receiving. She glanced at the Companion.

I have questions, too.

He was the Companion, but she was not sure what that meant. She waited, but he did not respond to this thought. His eyes were solemn pools of knowing, or so they seemed to her.

"Do you have answers, Companion?" When he didn't respond, she looked at him.

What is it that you wish to know?

"Who am I? Who—" She stopped because they both knew she wasn't ready to hear the answer to that question.

———

There was a stir outside. Arian made herself relax and then slowly rose to face the hatch opening. Metal vibrated as more than one set of feet tramped aboard. Coop was the first one to enter. The relief she felt at the sight of him shocked her. Her gaze wanted to cling to his, but after giving her a brief, reassuring grin, he moved aside, tucking himself against a control panel to the left of the opening.

His elbow came close to an environmental control section, but she decided it wouldn't matter if he shut off the air when the hatch was open.

An older man entered next. He was bluff and determined with a detached, all-seeing gaze. She liked the confidence he exuded and the straightness of his back. He occupied space without overpowering it, but she sensed he could, had he wanted to. The scent he brought with him was different from the doc's and Coop's, but not unpleasing. It awakened an echo of some distant memory...

Could it be her father? She had no memory of father or mother, though she must have had both at one time.

Behind him was a thin, lanky man who had a wide open face. Did it not exhaust him to have all he felt on view?

Because hiding who you are is so relaxing.

Warmth tinged her cheeks, but she did not respond to this.

Of necessity, the two newcomers needed to stand close to each other. Neither seemed thrilled by this. Arian bit back words of apology. These were not guests she had invited into her space. These were the people with questions.

Her chin lifted, she studied both men once more and decided the older man was the one in charge. He didn't crowd the other man physically, and yet, the younger one huddled under the angled area as if to get as far away as he could, his head bent uncomfortably to one side. Their clothing was different. The older man wore clothing similar to Coop's. A uniform, she decided. The younger man's dark clothing was mostly plain, though there was a shiny strip of colored cloth that circled his neck and hung down the front of his chest.

Arian turned her attention back to the dominant male and felt a jolt of shock when their gazes connected. His gaze bored in, searching for something. She lifted her chin and met his gaze squarely, though it was not easy. She sensed it was important that she hold her ground through this first assessment.

When the intensity of the look decreased, Arian dipped her chin in greeting, then looked at Coop, letting her arched brow act as the question she did not know to ask.

"Colonel," Coop broke the silence, "this is Arian Teraz. Arian, this is Colonel Boyette. He is in charge of our ship, the *Boyington*. And this is Dr. Adam Derwent, head of our First Contact team."

"First contact?"

"With al—" Coop started to explain, but the first contact doctor cut him off.

"With new peoples."

Aliens. The Companion sounded amused.

They do not seem as alien as you did at first sight. She let herself process the realization that they had a team to meet aliens. Did they hope to meet many different peoples? Perhaps other species?

Arian placed her fisted hand against her heart, with the smallest finger outward, dipped her chin once more, offering the next level of greeting, then lowered her hand to her side. After a moment's hesitation, the new doctor mirrored her greeting. It rather amused her and confirmed her sense that he was of lesser importance. The Colonel didn't mimic anything. He nodded sharply, as if impatient to get past the formalities.

Derwent is a diplomat.

She'd never had dealings with the designation, but the Companion provided her with insight beyond what her eyes and senses told her. The explanation did not matter, except it helped for her to know that it was his job to smooth their first interaction. She looked at the Colonel. Could anyone smooth this man?

"You are welcome," she said, not entirely truthfully and was sure this Colonel knew it.

He looked almost amused, then glanced at the Companion and arched his brows.

A slight flush rose in her cheeks. "This is the Companion, Colonel Boyette," Arian said.

"The—" He stopped a shade of discomfort in his expression.

"He's a Draze Dragon," Coop put in, though Arian had a sense that this was not what the Colonel had been about to say.

They think I am a lizard.

This troubles him?

I suspect he is concerned by the telepathic link I have established with Banshee. And that I can communicate at all.

It was disconcerting when one was not used to it, she could have told the Companion, but she suspected he knew the telepathy was not the only disconcerting thing about him.

"Are you Draze as well?" the Colonel asked her.

Why would he assume this, she wondered. "No."

There was a pause as if they wanted more from her, but what?

They wonder if you are from this system.

Oh. It felt strange to answer a question they hadn't asked, but if it would help, "I am not from this system." Their gazes moved to her Companion. "Neither is my Companion."

She could not see that the additional information helped ease the uncomfortable silence that reformed around her words.

You should thank them for assisting you.

It seemed good counsel, so she did, finishing with another formal nod of her head.

"We are pleased we could assist you," the diplomat doctor said, his expression more worried than pleased.

Into another uncomfortable pause, the Colonel spoke. "The doc said you seemed to be all right, other than the bump on your head?"

"Yes." She resisted the urge to touch the sore spot, which, she realized now, was not as painful as it had been. Apparently, the cold thing had helped.

His gaze scanned the space. "And your ship? How is it?"

Your ship, he'd said. Arian felt pleasure at those words. Almost it seemed the ship twitched in disagreement.

"There are some damaged systems. I will need time to repair them." A bold assertion, she thought with an inner jeer.

"There's no rush—" the diplomat doctor began, but Coop interrupted him.

"Maybe we can help." His grin was genial, but the look he cast around was...interested.

Arian was not troubled by his interest in a ship so much smaller than theirs. It was different and therefore worthy of the attention of a fellow...pilot. *I am a pilot.* She half expected the Companion to dispute this. He did not, and even his silence lacked dissent. Her back was straight, almost as straight as Coop and his Colonel, but she found she could straighten if further. She met this Colonel's gaze as directly as she could. Despite this, she felt doubt they could help. Neither of them looked to be a mechanic or an engineer.

"Do you think so?" she asked.

"We can try," he said, with another grin.

"And we'd like to get to know you, your people...possibly share information about this system, or about where you come from," the diplomat doctor put in with a look that was both pleading and minatory toward the two other men.

Why would a healer diplomat be interested in such things?

He is a different kind of doctor, the Companion told her. *A man of learning, of ideas, not healing.*

This she understood, as well. She also longed to know more, to understand. Perhaps with understanding, she'd not feel so overwhelmed, so wearied by the unfettered emotions of these people. It did not help that she was tired and hungry. But it was uncivil to eat in front of, or with, guests. She felt guilty that she'd forgotten this basic hospitable offer of sustenance.

"I would like this as well," she said. "I regret the lack of seating..."

"She's right," the Colonel said. "Captain, get something set up in the bay, something private, where we can all sit down," he added, before turning back to Arian.

Coop disappeared back down the passage leaving an awkward silence behind.

"I am able to offer you sustenance," she said hesitantly.

The Colonel did not look grateful. The diplomat looked nervous, but he said, after clearing this throat, "Sustenance... that's very kind..."

Grateful for something to do, Arian edged past them to the sustenance station and activated it. After a few seconds, a panel slid up revealing two small cakes. Arian lifted the dish and extended it toward the two men. Her mouth watered, and she rested a hand on the wall as weakness wavered through her.

Both men looked dubious, though they tried to conceal it from her. It seemed wise, rather than discourteous, to be wary in the face of the unknown. She was impressed when each man took one of the cakes and studied it for several seconds.

"It is quite pleasing," she reassured them.

The Colonel took a small bite, his eyes widened, and he tossed it all in, chewed with enthusiasm and swallowed before he said, "That is very good."

With this stamp of approval, the doctor ate his. They both glanced at the sustenance station with looks of hope.

"It is not advised to eat more than one without waiting to see how it affects you. It is very concentrated for travel through space." Arian had suffered a most painful episode from eating three of them, so she spoke with conviction.

"Thanks for the warning." The Colonel looked almost friendly as he glanced around again. "While we're waiting for the Captain, could you give us the dollar tour?"

Her brows lifted despite her best efforts at controlling this telltale sign of weakness. "Dollar tour?"

"Would it be possible for you to show us this ship?" the doctor/diplomat explained.

What else did they desire to see? Did they sense...

"As space explorers, we are interested in technology that is different from ours," the Colonel said, easily.

As if he needed to ease the sudden divide, the doctor asked, "Do you have quarters? Where do you sleep?" A tinge of red crept into his cheeks as he added, "And do...other things?"

Other things?

He is curious about the sanitation arrangements. Once again there was amusement from the Companion.

Why would that embarrass him, she wondered, moving past them to activate another panel. "The pilot's sanitation needs are accommodated here," she said. She pressed a button, and a sanitation module came out. Both men seemed to flinch back. She turned back to find them looking...discomfited. Interesting. "The command position reclines for sleep."

They both studied the chair with a certain amount of sympathy. She could attest that it was not terribly comfortable.

"You'll need to repair those straps," the Colonel said, sounding less formal as he picked up an end and examined it. "Do you know why it failed?"

She picked up the other end. "I do not think they were tested for anomaly transit." The words were a bit rueful.

"Your ship sustained a fair bit of external damage," the Colonel said, something in his tone brought her gaze back to his. "Not all of it looks like meteor strikes, though." His smile was easy, friendly almost if she hadn't been looking into the cool eyes.

Her insides tightened, but she lifted one brow with outward calm.

"Looks a lot like weapons fire to me."

"Not all systems are...friendly. I stumbled across some... pirates..." the unfamiliar word provided by the Companion seemed to satisfy them and removed the necessity for explaining the pirates had not been the only ships pursuing them. "I was... outgunned...so when the anomaly appeared, I...took the opportunity to exit the space." It had the virtue of being the truth. Tell as much truth as you can, was a maxim learned early. This man, he would know truth when he heard it, she was sure.

His brows shot up. "You pointed this into a wormhole full of meteorites?"

Did wormhole mean the same as an anomaly? Arian reviewed her words and his, then nodded. "Yes."

He made a move that was almost a twitch, but more controlled. "Gutsy move."

Arian was not quite sure how to respond to this, so she remained silent, her gaze straying to the restraint, considering how to fix it. She would need it again. Strange how the idea of leaving did not make her as happy as it should have.

The Colonel lifted the Companion's strap, almost absently, then his gaze sharpened. "Your dragon has better restraints."

"Yes." She could tell he would not be satisfied with this. There was more than just truth at stake now. He was testing her somehow. "For longer transits, the pilot is supposed to cold sleep."

"Cold sleep?" The Colonel's tone was sharp. "You mean, cryo-sleep?" He looked around as if he expected to see the pod pop out of the wall like the sanitation facility.

She had to have the Companion translate this for her. She nodded, her wary hidden but very much there. *Why does this interest him?* Because it did. She could see it, though he tried to hide it.

"Does it work? Why didn't you use it?"

She stared at him, but even the Companion could not help with this question. So she told him the truth.

"I wanted to see where I was going."

His head jerked back slightly, then, to her shock, he grinned.

The Colonel opened his mouth, but before he could ask or speak, Coop returned.

"I've got us set up in the Master Sergeant's office." He looked at Arian. "He takes care of maintenance on our birds, our ships. It's not that much bigger than this, but it does have chairs."

From this, Arian processed one main point, possibly more, but definitely one thing. They did not wish to let her roam around their ship. A lack of trust was not unknown to her. She did not think she had trusted anyone in the whole of her life. Or been trusted by anyone, she had to admit, at least to herself. Which made it odd that the one thing she wanted to do was trust these people. And be trusted by them.

On this uncomfortable thought, she followed them off her ship.

———

Pappy strode toward the small office, scattering the hazmat team, and Derwent's first contact team, with a look. Derwent stayed beside Arian, so Coop took her other side, steering her in the Old Man's wake. She looked around her with what Coop assumed was her version of curiosity. Gal had a butt load of self-control. Derwent could take lessons from her. He couldn't keep the shock and awe off his face. He wasn't the only one giving their second, in-system alien a stare, though. Everyone left in the bay noted, with varying degrees of interest and maybe a bit of disappointment, how human she looked. The dragon had changed the expectations. As her gaze passed over them, they either looked away or gave her a respectful salute in greeting. She offered a somber nod in return.

As they passed his *Dauntless*, she stopped to study it with a bit more curiosity showing in her eyes.

"That's my bird," he said.

"Bird?" Her head tipped to one side, and she blinked slowly.

"My ship. A *Dauntless*. What I was flying when I towed your ship here."

She glanced at him. "I am grateful for your assistance."

"You are welcome, ma'am." He touched the brim of his cap. "Glad to help out a fellow space traveler." He grinned.

Her lips twitched once, then she turned, reached up and touched the side of his bird, her fingers spreading on the surface. "It is smooth." She glanced at him. "And well made. A fine ship." Now her fingers traced the words he'd painted on the side. "What is this pattern?"

Coop touched the words, careful not to touch her in the process. "*Ye shall know the truth, and the truth shall make you free.*" She looked at him then, an open question in her eyes. He hesitated, wondering if she could understand. "We all pick a thing, in case we have to fight, so we're fighting for something, something personal, I mean. We all fight for our country, and all that, but we need, well, some of us fight for family, a girl, home." His family was gone. Didn't have a girl. When he wasn't on his sloop, home was here on the *Boyington*. So he fought for the truth. "Every time I climb aboard, I remember why I fly. What's personal for me."

"The truth shall make you free," she murmured. "Which symbol means truth?"

He showed her, then added, "This one spells free."

She traced both words with her finger, before looking at him. "I have not found the truth to make me free. The truth was... dangerous where I came from."

He rubbed his chin. "The truth can be dangerous where I come from. Not everyone wants to hear it. Doesn't change what I do. Or why I fight."

Her gaze studied his, and his senses sparked off the light flickering in the blue-green depths of her eyes. Heat flicked lightly along his nerve endings as awareness arced between them. His nostrils picked her scent out of the metallic bay smells, exotic, ordinary, compelling. His attention shifted to her parted lips. The edges started to tip up—

"What's the holdup, Captain?" the Colonel's voice broke the moment apart.

With a rueful grin, he gestured for her to continue toward Pappy, but he was aware of something that felt kind of like regret that he'd missed her smile. If she'd been gonna smile. She glanced back at him, and he knew she had been gonna smile, and for whatever reason, she was sorry, too.

Derwent stepped between them, cutting off his view, directing her into the small room Coop had set up for their meeting. Coop held back. He needed to get a grip. Pappy wouldn't thank him for risking his detachment over a girl, no matter where she hailed from. Or maybe that was particularly where she hailed from. Which they still didn't know, he reminded himself.

"Is there a problem, Captain?" Pappy's dry tone cut into his thoughts.

"No, sir." He hastily entered the room, stepping carefully past Derwent and then Arian to reach the only empty seat in the corner.

Pappy's gaze was not stern, but curious. He lifted a brow in a silent question. Coop shrugged, shook his head slightly, and then, after everyone was seated, sank down, too. Arian glanced at him, then looked away. Her hands settled in her lap, one resting lightly on the other. She gave the appearance of calm, but this close to her—she was far from at ease. It was weird because he'd never been accused of being sensitive to lady body language. Almost felt like he'd connected with her. It was a new enough experience for Coop that he would have dipped his head in some cold water—if he could have. He looked around for a distraction, which was provided by Pappy, another one of the old man's super powers, Coop decided a bit wryly, as all

Coop's systems jolted back to normal in the face of his Colonel's chill stare.

Pappy had taken the seat behind the desk. He leaned back now, his hands clasped on his chest, his gaze sweeping the tray of coffee, juice, and sandwiches that Coop had arranged to be delivered. Coop saw Arian's gaze stray to the tray and leaned forward to offer her the plate of sandwiches. When she hesitated, he told her, "I asked the doc, and he said it was okay if you had a little something to eat, but to call him if you feel queasy."

One hand reached out, shaking slightly before she secured a triangle off the top. How long had it been since she'd had food, he wondered? With careful control, she took a small bite, her white teeth sinking into, and then through the white bread.

"Thank you. It is very pleasing."

Now her look seemed almost shy. He offered her a choice of beverage, and she appeared interested in the juice, so he poured her some.

She sipped it, then inched past sipping. "That is excellent, as well," she murmured, lowering the glass only when it was empty. "Thank you. I feel much refreshed."

Color crept into her cheeks. The edges of her mouth tipped up, in a movement that was carefully contained. What would it be like if she lost control? Was it wrong to hope he'd be there? He caught Pappy looking at him again and thrust the plate in his direction. Both Pappy and Derwent shook their heads decisively.

"That cake was very filling," Derwent admitted. "But good," he added hastily.

"I ate three the first time. It was most painful," Arian offered, her head turning toward the doc with a tone that was almost friendly.

Coop found it...annoyed him. "You had cake without me?" That got her attention off Derwent. He grinned, so she would know he was joking, relaxing into his seat.

Pappy cleared his throat ominously, and Coop straightened hastily. Derwent looked like he wanted to speak but was silenced with a look. The old man studied Arian for long enough to make even a senior officer shift in his seat, but she didn't. Her chin lifted a bit, but that was all.

"Don't take this wrong, young lady, but you're something of a problem for me." Derwent choked, but Pappy ignored him. "You see, we tried this first contact stuff before—with mixed results. We don't know you, you don't know us. So trust is—a work in progress."

He paused. Arian appeared to assess his words before offering a slight nod. "I understand."

"Do you? You pretty much popped up out of nowhere in front of us and your—" he stopped then, for the first time looking uncertain.

"My Companion was concerned for my safety."

"Right." He paused, but she didn't enlarge on this comment.

She was parsimonious with words. *The truth can be dangerous.* Well, there wasn't much more dangerous than first contact, particularly one against many. She didn't know them. And they didn't know her, he reminded himself. It didn't help as much as it should have.

"Your telepathic companion," he added.

"His physiology is not designed for human speech," she said. "It is the only way he can communicate with us."

"Well, on our planet, animals don't talk to us telepathically or otherwise."

She regarded him intently but didn't comment on this. It was kind of like being in a room with an expert witness. Or a lawyer, he decided. Could tell it didn't sit well with Pappy. He wanted her to chat, to relax and reveal enough to get a read on her.

"It can be disconcerting," she agreed.

"We're new to this neighborhood, so we don't know who all

the players are. While we're happy to provide assistance to someone in trouble, until we know more, we don't take sides or—"

He stopped and waited, his gaze fixed on her.

This silence was longer than the last. Pappy didn't look upset, so Coop tried not to worry.

"...trust without further data," she finished for him finally.

"That's right. Why should we trust you?" he asked bluntly, making Derwent wince.

"You shouldn't," she said, almost sounding wistful. "You don't know me."

Pappy looked disconcerted. "Are you a danger to my people or my ship?"

Her brows arched a bit. "I don't think so."

"Why don't you know?" he barked back.

"I don't know enough about your ship to know what is dangerous to it."

Coop had to hide a twitch of his lips with his hand.

"And I've obviously banged up my ship." She had a tiny frown between her brows, and she paused as if she were seriously considering the question. She gave a small sigh. "I probably wouldn't trust me."

"Of course, we'd like to build a trust, er, relationship," Derwent put in.

Arian turned toward him. "How?"

She sounded curious, not hostile.

"You could tell us more about yourself," Pappy said.

She turned back to Pappy. "What would you like to know?"

"Well, where you come from would be a good start?"

"Are you familiar with the Itraxis system?"

Pappy glanced at Coop. "No."

"Then how does that help you know me?" She frowned. "Trust is complicated, is it not?"

"Very." Pappy sounded rueful.

"Do you know anything about this system?" Derwent put in, trying not to sound like he was foundering, too.

"No."

"Wait?" Pappy straightened. "What?"

"I am unfamiliar with this system," she repeated.

"But you must have known something about it before jumping here."

"No."

Pappy looked a bit winded. "You don't know this system, or you don't know where you are?"

"Both," she said again, not sounding concerned.

"But the wormhole...you must have known where it would take you."

"It was not a mapped anomaly. When we came under fire, my Companion said there were rumors of an unstable anomaly in the region. There were also many meteorites that we could use for cover."

For Arian, all those words were like sharing a whole book, Coop decided.

"You were looking for an unmapped wormhole in a meteorite belt?"

A slight smile quivered on the edges of her mouth. "It was the only way to escape."

"But," Derwent choked slightly, "that must mean you're...lost."

Not all who wander are lost.

Coop jerked at the words in his head. How did this alien dragon know a quote from *Lord of the Rings*?

"I am not dead," she pointed out.

Coop wondered why she didn't add, "and not a prisoner," then realized why. For all she knew, she was their prisoner.

6

ARIAN WIPED her faced with her sleeve and looked at the Companion. "Try it now."

Claws clicked against controls from his specialized station. To her, he was an odd choice for a companion or co-pilot, but her curiosity about him had been trumped by the meeting with the *Boyington,* and Coop's people. Her Companion had assisted her with the language divide at first, but at some point, his voice had faded away and she'd understood, well, she understood the words. She did not always understand the meaning Coop's people gave the words.

Coop. She smiled to herself. Last night he had given her a somewhat limited tour of his ship. There'd been "dinner" on something called an MRE in a canteen. Canteen. She liked the word. From now on she would call the sustenance station the canteen, even though it was a slot, not a whole room. In a way, the cakes were also MRE's, since they arrived ready to eat, but there was more variety in Coop's MREs. There were courses. And dessert. The word fit the experience. She loved dessert.

After dinner, they'd gone to a lounge to watch a movie. She liked it, too. This view into his home, his world, and his life made her thoughts spin. It was, according to Coop, people pretending to act out a story, but yes, it was somewhat like real life, he had admitted. He'd struggled to explain the differences, but she had not paid that much attention. The story unfolding on the screen left her wide-eyed and with a warm flush on her skin as the male and female got to know one another and fell into something they called love. Her cheeks had heated when the clasping turned into coupling, and she was relieved when the scene changed. She felt Coop looking at her, but she could not look at him, at least not directly. All the way back to the ship, she'd peeked at him, wondering what it would be like to be clasped in his arms, to have his lips pressing hers as they'd done in the movie.

Love was different from pact bonding since the couple had taken the time to find out about each other. There had been talking and preliminary touching, she'd noticed. Now she felt hyperaware each time Coop touched her. His fingers lightly clasped her elbow as he steered her around an obstacle. Or just the brush of shoulders together as they walked.

Once a crowded corridor had forced them closer together. She'd stared up at him, felt his breath catch, and the dark centers of his eyes had dilated. The two of them had been surrounded by many others, but she'd felt as if they were alone. She'd licked dry lips and his breath had caught again. His hands on her arms had tightened and then he'd given her a rueful smile that made *her* breath hitch and warmth suffuse her body.

Longing had clogged her thoughts because she did not know what to ask or do. The crowd had pressed harder, forcing their bodies together. Her lips had parted and she'd felt aware of all of herself in a new way. Then a new shift of bodies had forced them to part. Even the brush of her own clothes against her skin left a restless longing, a tightness in her chest. It felt like hunger in some ways but in others? She did not know, but it grumbled inside her, becoming more insistent each time she was around Coop. And when she wasn't.

Why?

The need for an answer, and the lack of the words to ask it, had left her tongue-tied on the trip back to her ship. How could she explain the traditions and practices that had shaped the world she fled when she did not understand them? The two of them were as different as the food they ate. And the movie? There was nothing like it on Bosakli. There was work, there was eating, and there was sleeping. And after pact bonding? Thankfully she had not had to find that out, would never have to see Trajan Bester again.

Coop had been mostly silent on the walk back to the ship, though he had asked one question that she had been unable to answer. Considering it now, it was odd that the Companion did not have a name. As if the Companion sensed her attention turn his direction, his head lifted so that his snout was visible over the back of his seat.

Is there a concern?

"Do you have a name? Other than the Companion?"

He blinked slowly. *My given name is Rhubreak.* He watched her for several seconds, possibly for a reaction, then his snout retreated, and the clicking resumed.

"Why didn't you use it when we met?"

It wasn't relevant.

Because she was supposed to cold sleep, not drive them into an inter-system ditch.

His head lifted again. *A ditch?*

"I was remembering the first time I tried to drive the tractor."

Into a ditch?

She smiled. "Yes. My grandmother was not...happy." A pattern that persisted the whole of their life together. Now when it was too late, she wondered what the next day had been like for that formidable lady. The day after Arian disappeared with the dragon.

Are you worried about her?

Arian considered the question, feeling some guilt that she had not thought about it until now. Their relationship was so detached, it wasn't a relationship at all, based on what she'd observed here. But she did not wish for her grandmother to be punished.

"It's done, and I can't change it," Arian murmured.

You did not belong there.

The miracle was that she had survived with her mind intact enough to leave. That she'd managed to hide who she was for long enough to escape. How was that possible? Even from her first memories, she knew not to ask, not to question, not to show anything but a blank exterior to those around her. She'd never even asked about her parents. What had happened to them? Why hadn't she ever asked that question? She'd wondered that many times, but she'd never asked. She had never belonged there. She'd known that her whole life. But knowing that didn't tell her where she did belong.

Rhubreak lowered his head out of her sight once more.

Life support is working at seventy percent efficiency.

Arian hesitated, then accepted the change of topic. If he had the answers, he wasn't thinking them. "Is that good enough?"

For now.

"The ship needs a name, too," she said, under her breath.

Flivius.

Is that the ship's name? She hesitated at calling him Rhubreak.

Yes, that is this ship's name. And yes, please call me Rhubreak.

She nodded, aware that something had changed between them but not sure exactly sure what. She fingered the small laser she'd used to repair life support systems and finally said, "*Flivius* is not an inspiring name."

She liked the sound of the *Boyington* much better. Coop said it had been named after a brave man.

Flivius means "collector."

Arian frowned. "What is the word for broken?"

He didn't respond, but it felt like he chuckled. She went to the next panel and removed it. The damage here was minimal, thank goodness. They needed their long range scanners—their eyes Coop called them—up and running. She studied the configuration of wires and circuits, and in her mind saw how they should be. As she made her adjustments, the flickers of light appeared under the skin of her hands again, and for a brief instant, she thought they made a trail up her arm. She touched her arm, but they faded away.

Scanner and sensors are starting to come back online.

She shoved the panel back in place and stood. As if the ship had been waiting for her attention, it pulsed with an unknown contacts alert.

She dropped into her seat as Rhubreak activated the controls that put the information up for her to see. She waited tensely for the first report. The last time they'd experienced this alert, it had not gone well.

Ships.

About twenty of them. She needed more—as if the ship heard her, the data tightened into a closer view. Her first reaction was a sense of relief. They were not Consortium. She frowned. This flotilla had some aspects that were similar to the pirates they'd encountered back in Consortium space. But they could not have come through the anomaly, or they'd be almost on top of them. She blinked, and the scan deepened.

"Thank you," she murmured absently.

For what?

Arian looked at him, opened her mouth to explain, then closed it. Her hands gripped the arms of her seat as she felt the sparks inside her. Whatever they were, for now, they were helping her. She shook her head and studied the flotilla. Just because it had been pirates back then did not mean—

If it looks like a pirate and acts like a pirate—

"It is probably pirates?"

That would be my assessment.

What was the word Coop had used? "Crap."

Indeed.

"Do you think the *Boyington* sees them?" She tipped her head, listening, but could detect no sound of alarms in the outer bay. That did not mean they did not know.

I do not have access to their systems.

The communications between this ship and the scientists on the *Boyington* was limited. Their scientists had pressed for more and been turned down. She did not blame them for worrying about their secrets. She was worried about them finding hers.

She hesitated, unsure of the protocol. Surely they knew...but what if they didn't?

I would advise contacting them.

She activated the permitted communications channel. At least they were not one small ship against many this time.

* * *

Coop was on the bridge when the call from Arian came through.

"This is Arian." A long pause. "On the alien ship in your bay."

Coop smiled, but her next words erased the smile.

"Have your sensors detected the contacts that appear to be approaching this location?"

Pappy straightened in his command seat, his gaze slashing toward Coop. "Contacts? Do we have unknown contacts on tracking?"

The tech at tracking looked harassed. "Scanning...I do not show contacts of any kind approaching, sir."

Pappy frowned. "Ms. Teraz, would it be all right if we sent one of our geeks down to take a look?"

There was a short pause.

"The Companion can link your sensors if you prefer."

"Tell her we'd like to take a look first," Pappy ordered.

Coop relayed the message, with a bit more diplomacy in his choice of words.

"Go with him. Take Tiger with you," Pappy ordered.

Coop opened his mouth to ask why then remembered that word wasn't part of his brief. And he probably knew. He was to watch the geek, while Tiger kept an eye on him.

"Yes, sir."

———

Arian tried to tamp down the flutter of excitement. It was not wise to wish to see him. Once her ship was repaired, surely she would be invited to depart. *You are a problem for me, young lady,* the Colonel had said.

She made herself focus on the alert, initiating a series of deeper scans on the cluster of ships. She glanced at Rhubreak. "How odd to encounter yet more pirates."

The surprise would be in not encountering pirates. They seem to be the one constant of inhabited systems.

At least they were not one small ship against many this time.

She lifted her head as she heard the vibration of footsteps on the ramp. She turned as Coop appeared in the opening, his usual lazy smile marred by tension. He was not alone. Behind him was Tiger, a fellow pilot she'd met in the canteen. She'd liked the younger man, recognizing the same strength and confidence in him that she saw in Coop. He looked tense as well.

Behind Tiger was the geek that the Colonel had mentioned. She must have met him before because they did not introduce him.

"What you got?" Coop asked his attention on her data screen.

She gave him a quick update, watching his brows pull together in a frown.

"How far out?"

"Several of your ship days at their current speed and track," Arian said.

He cocked a brow at her. "Any sign they could move faster if they wanted to?"

"There are indications that increased speed is possible," she admitted, pulling up that data so they could see it.

"What makes you think they're pirates?"

Arian produced a somewhat blurry image of the lead ship. It was a fearsome looking thing, the sides heavily decorated with distorted faces and humans killing and torturing each other, and other species. The images were disturbing and violent.

"Whoa," Tiger said, giving Coop a comical look. "All that needs is the Jolly Roger flying from a mast. We going to go take them on, sir?"

Coop tapped his radio. "Colonel Boyette? Can I send you the sensor data we're seeing?"

Arian heard his radio crackle, but not the words.

"Definitely need-to-know, sir."

The geek worked out a way to transmit the data to the *Boyington's* bridge in a manner, she assumed, that was more acceptable to the Colonel than linking. While the geek worked her controls, Arian studied the stream of data on another screen, her unease increasing with each minute that passed. It was true the ships were several cycles out—

Even as she thought this, the flotilla of ships made a hyper jump that halved the time to intercept.

* * *

The tension on the bridge of Arian's ship had doubled since the incoming bogeys had jumped again, cutting in half their time to an intercept with the *Boyington*. Coop stared at the screen as if his attention was the only thing keeping the bogeys from jumping again—

Apparently, he was wrong. This jump halved the time again.

"Why the delay between jumps," he muttered.

The geek looked up. "It is possible their jump drive needs to recharge. Depending on their technology, the jumps can be a huge energy drain."

And they'd want to make sure their shields were at full strength before they got too close, Coop thought grimly.

Tiger listened to something on his comm, then looked at Coop. "They've upped the threat level. We'll have to head for the fighter bay if it goes up again."

Coop nodded, wondering if the bogeys would have fighter ships and what their weapons and defenses were like? Would they find out in time?

The data changed again. The flotilla jumped once more, and then smaller bogeys appeared to erupt from the ships, as if in response to his question.

"What's what?" Coop looked at the geek, but it was Arian who answered.

"It is a barrage."

"Why would they launch so soon?" Coop asked with a frown.

They wouldn't. Pirates make their profit with plunder. Scan the barrage.

Coop presumed the last request—order?—was directed at Arian because she began manipulating her controls. It was her turn to frown.

"That's odd."

"What's odd?" Tiger asked, coming to stand at her other side, and exchanging a quick, worried look with Coop.

"The explosive yield is very small—" She stiffened. "There is a high probability that this barrage is designed to disable your defenses without destroying your ship."

"How could they know our defenses?" Tiger asked, not sounding too worried.

He has a point, but we also do not know what these weapons will do.

The data changed again as the ships and barrage jumped closer as if something linked them together, once more halving the time to intercept.

Coop keyed his radio. "Red alert. Shields up. Incoming fire." His face was grim now. "I've got to—"

The klaxon call of alerts, both outside in the bay and on this ship, cut ruthlessly across his words.

* * *

"Now what?" Coop asked, pausing his half-turn away.

"The anomaly is opening again," Arian said tersely. "Multiple contacts emerging. There is not time to alter course. Some of these could impact the *Boyington* negatively." She looked up. "If your Colonel was to order the launch of your smaller ships—"

"They will interact even more negatively," Tiger finished for her.

"How long?" Coop asked urgently.

"Everyone should brace for impact." The anomaly had opened very close to the ship and was growing in size, like a golden whirlpool forming in the dark of space, though that could be how her sensors "read" the data.

"Brace for impact!" Coop snapped into the radio.

Arian heard the whir as Rhubreak activated his seat restraints. Arian glanced at her seat, but she hadn't gotten around to fixing those restraints and what would the man do? It seemed wrong to secure herself when they could not. *Can we brace the ship for impact?* If not, they were going to sustain much more damage when the exterior of their ship interacted with the sides of the *Boyington's* bay.

I will attempt to deploy—

The outer edges of the anomaly reached the *Boyington*. It shuddered. She staggered but managed to stay on her feet. The scientist was not as fortunate. Tiger reached a hand down to him, yanking him upright without ceremony.

"Hold on to something," he told him tersely.

"It is going to get worse," she told them. There were many rocks emerging from the anomaly.

"Brace for multiple impacts." The Colonel's voice was calm coming to them over the larger ship's communication system, a stark contrast with the blare of collision warnings.

Coop caught her glance and said, "Our shields are good. Gonna get bumpy, but we should be fine."

Arian appreciated his optimism and hoped their shields were better than hers had been. She'd been through an anomaly and was not eager to ride one again. There was also the question of how the shields would fare against the incoming barrage. She returned her attention to her screen, splitting it so she could monitor the anomaly and the incoming flotilla.

"They've jumped again." Her voice was a different calm, or so it seemed to her. And the things her fingers could do were not things she knew that she knew. It had been somewhat like that when they had been under attack in the other system, but this time it felt more. When one unpacked a file in a computer system, information became available. This was how it felt inside her head. As if data were unpacking and expanding. She glanced down and thought she saw those odd flickering lights under her skin again. She glanced at Coop, but he was staring

at the screens. She flexed her fingers and put them back
to work.

Her screen showed the perspective of the *Boyington*, so Arian
altered the angle, wondering what she could learn from seeing it
from the view of the incoming hostiles. Her gaze narrowed. It
was possible that the growing edges of the anomaly might inter-
fere with, or blunt, the barrage.

As if in a slow motion race, rocks of many sizes continued to
track out of the anomaly. If it were the only problem, that would
be good news, but in the spinning bands of energy, sensors show
rocks in many sizes. Something about the shape and flow of the
anomaly puzzled her. They had called it a wormhole, but she
did not think it acted like a wormhole. Knowledge not yet
unpacked teased at the edges of her mind. If only she had
the time...

But she did not. There was only time to warn her companions, "Brace—" She was not sure what to warn them to brace for.
The circular motion of the anomaly was very similar to the
movement of water. But that might be a sensor problem, not
reality. That part of her brain that was studying new knowledge
recognized many unknown elements in the situation.

The scientist grabbed the back of Rhubreak's seat. Coop and
Tiger grabbed onto the pilot's seat, Coop grasping her elbow,
perhaps in hopes of stabilizing her. She knew logically she
should get more secure, but her brain, her hands kept working
the controls. Her hands wanted to steer the great ship, but she
did not have this access. So she kept sending data to their
bridge in hopes someone there would make the correct
decision.

Her mind counted down to the next energy wave impact. She
softened her knees, hoping to stay on her feet.

Realized this wave carried many rocks—the *Boyington* began
to slew around as rocks slammed into the shields. Through the

soles of her boots, she felt the engines strain against the drag of the anomaly. So far the anomaly was winning.

One of her ship's panels blew, spewing steam, and the smell of something burning competed with the acrid smell of fear. She glanced back. The scientist was gray. And a bit green.

The data stream started to flow both ways. She was not sure if the lights, or she, had done that. The engines continued their fight.

The rest of the barrage was almost on them.

The outer edge of the barrage slammed into the curving edge of the anomaly, multiple flashes lighting her screen. This light appeared to travel around the mouth of the anomaly.

"Five seconds to impact," she murmured, softening her knees and widening her stance. Even as she braced, she tried to force her sensors to break through to the flotilla behind the barrage.

...two...one...

These hits were different. Energy pulsed through the *Boyington* and her ship, crackling on metal and frying some circuits in her ship. She could only imagine what they did to the larger ship. One of her screens flickered and went dark. She split the screen that still worked, but now the data came through in fits and bursts and was filled with static.

"Shields are down forty percent," she said. "One engine offline..."

Despite this, it looked as if the *Boyington* continued to make headway against the gravitational pull of the anomaly. In random pulses, it seemed as if the light from the barrage continued to track along the ringed edges of the anomaly. Had it connected? The anomaly appeared to pulse, then double in size, increasing the pull on the *Boyington*.

This has happened before, she realized. They'd chosen not to fight against the anomaly because it seemed the lesser of two evils, but now she wondered if they could have pulled clear had they wanted to. Did weapons fire increase the size of the anomaly? This felt important, but there was no time to worry this either. She'd think about it later.

If they survived.

"The *Boyington* is entering the anomaly," she said.

"What?" The scientist's word ended on a high-pitched shriek as the *Boyington* lurched from more impacts, then the spin of the anomaly applied spin to the ship as the engines began to lose the battle.

Her fingers flexed, but she'd done all she could from here.

"Shields are down to fifty percent and dropping," she intoned. The spin increased, centrifugal force building.

Multiple impacts from the rocks in the anomaly could not stop the inexorable and increasing rotation. Coop shouted something, but the words sounded slow and far away. There was a sideways yank as the anomaly engulfed the ship. More circuits popped, and her screens all went dark.

She felt Coop's arm go around her waist.

They both staggered, as they fought the pull toward the outer wall.

The spin increased.

Someone slammed into them.

She felt Coop stagger, felt him fight to keep them upright.

He couldn't.

His arms wrapped around her as they went down. She felt the jolt as they hit the deck. Felt her legs lifting over her head as she somersaulted toward the wall—

7

_____

NOT ALL WHO *wander are lost.*

For some reason, the words were there in Coop's head as he woke to pain, darkness, alerts clamoring for attention, and the sense of being tangled with other bodies. And it felt like his face was mashed into a wall.

He cranked one eye open and found his face was half mashed into a wall. The other half was mashed into Arian. Her eyes were closed and blood dripped from her chin onto the metal floor they were also mashed into.

"Arian?" He didn't know how to get untangled without hurting her. Or himself, he had to admit. At least one arm was bunched uncomfortably under there somewhere. He kind of thought he was bleeding, too, if the warm trickle from his scalp was his and not hers.

She gave a soft groan and her lids lifted. She stared at him in confusion, but it faded fast. As if she knew what he was going to ask, she said, "It hurts everywhere."

"Same here." Though it wasn't all bad. They were also mashed together in a way that made up for the bad. He felt disinclined to change bad to worse by moving. In fact, it would be pleasant to close his eyes and just hang on to the girl—

Smoke drifting in the air, burned into his nostrils, mixed with the smell of fried stuff and fear. Funny how it always smelled the same. There was a groan, possibly two behind him, and Coop felt limbs being pulled away from what he realized now was a people ball. The pain ramped into the unpleasant zone, so once he could, he rolled to his side and sat up, leaning against the wall while he caught his breath. Easier said than done. Might have a broken—or bruised rib. Since both hurt like a son-of-a-gun, it didn't matter which unless he moved too much and punctured something. He carefully probed the spot and decided he could get up, then wondered why he was in such a hurry when what he'd already done had set his head spinning—or maybe the ship was still spinning. Either way, his stomach did this thing he didn't much like. Be embarrassing to toss something on the deck of her ship. And give them something to slip on if things got gnarly again.

Then he remembered what had been going on before the wormhole arrived and he struggled upright. He had to steady himself against the wall for a minute before he looked around. Looked like her ship was as unhappy as they were. The emergency lights pulsing didn't help his head any. In fact, they stabbed into his eyes like knives. He took a breath—didn't want to start crying—reached out, and helped Arian up. Okay, that hurt. He let the geek and Tiger get themselves upright, hoping it was the lighting that made them both look green. Only one who seemed to have come through it mostly intact was Arian's companion. That was some good pet carrier.

Coop tapped his radio. "*Boyington*? Colonel? Anyone?"

Arian moved unsteadily to the pilot's seat and sat down. She blinked a couple of times to clear the blood from her gaze, then started playing with the controls. At least it didn't seem like anyone was shooting at them.

Like he'd know with all systems dark.

"We need to see beyond the ship—" she said, letting him know she was worried about the same crap he was.

Had the pirates got hosed by the wormhole? Or were they coming through after them?

She gave a frustrated sound, then glanced around. Spotted a tool of some kind and grabbed it. She knelt in front of a panel, cleared the blood from her eyes again and opened it up.

"How can I help?" the green geek asked, staggering over next to her.

"When I tell you, try the controls just above where I am," Arian said, her voice, muffled but still matter-of-fact.

He could admit to himself, he'd been impressed before and he was now, while also trying to figure out why she seemed different from their first meeting. And then he gave it up as not worth the increase in his headache.

"Want me to go check out in the bay, sir?" Tiger asked. He leaned against the hatch jamb, but his color had improved.

Coop hesitated, then nodded. "Grab a first aid kit, too. There are probably several in the lockers."

Tiger headed out, using the wall to keep upright. There were at least two guys—guards—out there in the bay, Coop recalled. "Check on the guys out there," he called after him and got a "roger that" in response.

He turned back to the bridge in time to see Arian sit back and look up at the geek. "Try it now." She scrubbed at her face, smearing the blood around. She looked at her hand, then wiped it on the leg of her coveralls.

The geek bent over the controls and started doing stuff.

"Nothing yet."

Arian's head disappeared inside. "Try again," she said.

After more tapping, and what felt like a long time, the screen flickered.

"It's trying, but not—" the geek said, "no, wait, here it comes."

Coop helped Arian climb to her feet, and she joined the geek at the controls. He noticed she braced with one hand, while she studied the data. No surprise she might be a little dizzy when blood still tracked down the side of her face. He leaned against the wall on her other side and tried to process the data. The good news, there didn't seem to be a lot of bogeys around the *Boyington*. Some rocks were still tracking along with them, but no ships that he could see. Then he looked closer.

"Where'd everything go?" He was no geek, but he had a bad feeling that they weren't in Kansas anymore. *D'oh, wormhole.* They'd gone through a wormhole. Thinking it didn't help him process what his eyes saw. He repeated the words to himself. They'd gone through a wormhole from where they were to somewhere else. He rubbed his face, and the hand came away sticky and red. Maybe he was hallucinating?

"We're..." the geek swallowed. "...not where we were. We're... somewhere else."

"Where?" Coop asked.

"I don't...know. Somewhere. Could be a long way from..." Panic had filtered into his voice. "No way to know..."

"Well, at least we're not dead," Coop reminded him.

The geek blinked a couple of times and then nodded. "Right."

"I feared the anomaly would tear the ship apart," Arian said. "When the barrage interacted with the anomaly, it increased its size and gravitational pull."

That seemed to worry her more than the change in location. Of course, she'd done this rodeo once already.

Coop thought he heard the geek mutter under his breath. "Not dead is good."

Maybe if he said it enough, they'd all be convinced. Tiger came back with a first aid kit.

"They're both down, but breathing. Don't think they broke anything, but I'm not a doc," he said. He dropped the kit on the empty seat and opened it. He studied each of them, then said, "Line up for some first aid."

———

Coop sat impatiently tapping his boot on the floor while Tiger mopped him up and slapped a bandage over the spot. Didn't seem to be a big deal, but now that he knew it was there, it hurt. As if he figured that, Tiger handed him a couple of pills. He glanced over his shoulder at Arian, his gaze admiring. It wasn't the first time they'd noticed the same gal, but it was the first time Coop wanted to punch out his friend. Because he was a grownup, he could get past it. Besides, he needed to get a grip. Focus on the big problem. The really big problem.

They were lost. Lost in space.

He'd never liked the movie, he sure didn't like having it in his reality. *You don't know how lost we are,* he reminded himself. Just because the geek looked ready to cry...he didn't know either. They didn't know what they didn't know yet. Once they knew...

"We need to get in contact with the bridge," Coop said.

The link between our ships is still active.

"So they should be able to see what we're seeing?" Coop asked the dragon.

He hesitated. *There are many reasons they might be unable to see or respond to hails.*

"Ship is probably on emergency power." Coop blew out a sigh, then wished he hadn't. His ribs didn't like it.

Arian braced herself on the wall and closed her eyes, her head tipped as if she were listening to, or for, something. For just a second it seemed to Coop that little lights flickered under her skin. He blinked, and they were gone. Man, he'd really banged his head.

Her lashes lifted. "The power source does feel different, less than what it was before."

Coop exchanged a look with Tiger. How could she tell that?

She is what you would call a machine whisperer.

Coop was pretty sure he hadn't, and wouldn't, call anyone any kind of whisperer, but okay. He even got what the dragon was telling him. She was a good mechanic.

She is much more than that. The dragon sounded amused. *But you already sense that, do you not?*

I have no idea what you are talking—thinking about, Coop said, not out loud, because he was not stupid.

"Many systems are offline." She dropped her hand and sighed. "There is much...clamor around the ship."

He hesitated, considering the question he wanted to ask. Wasn't sure how Pappy would feel about it. On the other hand, Pappy wasn't in a position to object. And he expected his people to act in emergencies, not just sit on their hands.

"Do you think you could get the engines going again? Maybe help restore communications?"

Tiger's eyes widened. He knew Pappy's inclinations, too, but he didn't protest.

Arian didn't look surprised or much of anything. As always, she considered the question before answering. "It depends on the type and severity of the damage."

"Will you try?" he persisted.

"Of course," she said, this time with hesitating.

She was profoundly pragmatic, he decided. She had to know it wasn't going to be easy—and was likely to be dangerous—

working their way through a distressed ship, but she hadn't hesitated. Of course, her fate was tied to theirs now, but it didn't feel like that. Impression he got from her, it was...sensible. Even the way she bent to collect her scattered tools was practical. Drama-free.

Though it wasn't appropriate to the circumstances, his brain coughed up that moment in the passage when the mob of crewmen had pressed them together. Really pressed them together. She'd felt it, too. He'd seen it in the way her pupils dilated and the way her breath hitched. When she'd licked her lips, he'd almost lost it. If they'd been alone—they wouldn't have been pressed together, he reminded himself. He massaged his aching temple and looked around, at anything but Arian.

He saw one of her tools at his feet and handed it to her, wondering if it was what had bruised his ribs. Kind of looked like his rib felt. He turned to the geek. "You stay here and help—"

"Rhubreak," Arian said. "His name is Rhubreak."

Really? "Okay, you help Rhubreak with this ship, maybe try to figure out where we are—" Would the dragon be able to communicate with the geek?

I will use the screen to talk to him.

The geek looked like Coop had just asked him to be a red shirt but, after an uncertain look at the dragon, he nodded. A spark of geek-like interest in the alien ship pushed more of the panic from his eyes. He went to push up his glasses, realized they were gone and started looking for them.

"You say the impact of the weapons increased the size of the wormhole...?" His tone had already lost some of its fear as his geek wheels started to turn.

Coop exchanged an amused look with Tiger.

"There is a problem outside this ship," Arian said, erasing any signs of amusement.

Coop spun around and found her with her palm against the wall again. "Problem?"

Coop glanced toward the open hatch door and noticed a faint red pulse of light coming from the bay. Tiger's eyes widened in alarm. "The bay shield."

As one they turned to Arian. "Can you do anything?"

"I can try." She slung the bag of tools over her shoulder and headed out.

He looked at the geek. "Might want to work on getting the door of this ship closed while you're messing with stuff."

The geek's eyes went wide again, but Coop didn't have time to hold his hand.

Outside in the main bay, the red alarm lights pulsed. Based on the gap between flashes, it was counting down to failure. As if it had been waiting for them, it added an alarm to the mix. Would have been nice to do that sooner...

"You should help those men onto the ship," Arian said, her gaze scanning the bay. "Where are the controls?"

Coop pointed them out, then turned to help Tiger move the two downed guards onto the ship. It did not feel great when the door of her ship cranked up with them outside. Dragon could have waited until he was sure Arian could get the big doors closed in time. What would happen to the ships in the bay if it decompressed?

"Let's see what we can find in those lockers." Maybe there were portable oxygen kits in there. And some way to anchor themselves? As they headed toward the lockers, Coop saw Arian run a hand over the panel, then dig into her bag and extract a tool.

The red lights pulsed faster.

They were running out of time.

He grabbed a locker door and flung it open. Then another and another—there they were. He tossed Tiger an oxygen kit and grabbed two more, one for him and one for Arian, and a big flashlight. "See if there is anything else in these things we might need," he ordered Tiger. "Like some way to anchor ourselves."

She had the panel open now. He reached her side. "Oxygen."

"If the shield fails, we will be sucked out into space, will we not?" She didn't so much ignore him as stayed focused on the task in front of her.

"You might want to hurry," Coop said. He turned on the flashlight and shone it into the guts she'd exposed. "Maybe we should ask the dragon to let you on the ship, Tiger—"

The flashes got seriously closer together. In a way bad for them.

He looked back at the ship, wondering if they could make it now?

The huge doors began to close, but moving slowly. Coop turned Arian around and fitted the mask over her face. "Hold on."

He pulled a mask over his face and looked around. They'd need something sturdy to hang onto.

Tiger appeared out of the murk carrying harnesses with hooks. The door slid closer and the lights pulsed faster as they scrambled into the harnesses.

He pushed the hook over a bar and got a good grip on Arian, even though he knew it wouldn't help them when the cold of space rushed into to take the place of the oxygen and their exposed skin turned into chunks of ice. The red warning light turned solid, and an alarm shrieked—

He felt the tug from changing pressure—

—and the doors locked into place.

It felt colder than before. Despite this, he dabbed at the sweat on his forehead, and leaned against the wall to support legs that felt like rubber, He yanked off the oxygen mask. "That was close."

Tiger lifted his mask. "Let's not do that again for a while. Or ever."

"That would be best," Arian said, pulling hers down. Then surprised him with a sudden smile.

If this had been a movie, he'd have kissed the girl right now. A pity this wasn't a movie. For a lot of better reasons than kissing a girl, but for sure that one.

8

"I HAD a feeling you had a sense of humor," Coop said, something different in the smile he directed at her, something that replaced cold with warm.

Did she? Arian blinked. What was that?

The ability to perceive humor or appreciate it.

So it is a positive?

Yes.

She felt *humor* from Rhubreak, but she ignored him because she liked the look in Coop's eyes. The warmth that filled her felt like basking in the high hot sun. There were urgent things to do. She knew this. But they'd almost just died. Surely for one moment, she could be happy to be alive and smiling up at Coop? Tiger cleared his throat and Coop jumped and turned toward him, a tinge of color staining the top of his cheeks. She glanced at Tiger and caught him grinning and shaking his head.

"Man, you got it bad."

Because she did not know the proper response to his comment, she turned toward the hatch that would give them access to the larger ship. "Should we..."

"Yes," Coop straightened with a jerk, then looked startled.

"Surprised my legs are working. That was quite the shot of adrenalin."

"Yeah, adrenalin," Tiger jeered, but he followed them to the exit door.

Her legs felt different, less stable, too, as she followed the two men. Coop tried the control. It was not a shock when the hatch did not move.

"No power?" Tiger asked.

"There should be a manual override," Coop said, examining a panel next to the door, then looking at the other side.

Arian studied the walls on either side, as well, noting a place where there could be handles or access notches. She inserted her fingers in the spots. She tugged, and after some resistance, the panel released.

"That would be it," Coop said, reaching past her to force the handle down.

It did not appear easy. There was a loud click and the hatch slid part way open. The two men tossed packs through, then forced their way through the gap. Arian handed her sack of tools to Coop. Then squeezed through to a passage that felt unfamiliar with strips of dim lighting running along the floor. Warning lights, placed at intervals, pulsed near the ceiling, but did not offer additional illumination. Instead, they increased the murkiness by throwing red shadows onto the walls in strange patterns.

She reached for her bag, aware of the muted pulse of emergency power through the soles of her boots.

"You sure we should head for the engine room? What about the bridge?" Tiger asked, the odd lighting making his expression challenging to read.

Coop hesitated. "Was thinking we'd head toward the central core and see how it goes." His gaze, meeting that of his friend and fellow pilot, was sober and filled with worry. "We might not be able to get to either."

"The central core?" Tiger appeared troubled by this. "Wouldn't it be quicker to work our way down from here?"

"The engine room is more exposed, and so are all the routes there from here. If there are hull breaches or collapsed passages…" Coop ran out of words for several seconds as he tried to order his thoughts. "If we got stopped, we'd have to work our way back."

Tiger nodded. "Okay. Let's do this."

They fell into step beside Arian, but Tiger kept looking at Coop, she noticed.

"You're not thinking of doing what I think you're thinking of doing? Are you?"

"What's that?" Coop asked. He shone his light on the symbols that told them where on the ship they were.

"The central core. You're not thinking of trying to climb down that way?"

Coop shrugged. "If the power is off, it's the fast way down. We're only three decks up."

"Do we know if we'll know if it's off? Just because the engines are off, doesn't mean—if it's still active and we pop a panel, all that will be left is some crispy pilots. And possibly no ship."

Coop glanced at Arian. "Could you tell by doing your touch thing?"

Her touch thing? Arian looked at her hand, then let it drop to her side. "Perhaps." What had the girl in the movie said? *Don't make promises you don't know if you can keep.* A promise was serious, not something to be offered lightly. "I can try."

Coop's grin turned a bit crooked. "Well, let's find out." He looked around as if getting his bearings. "Let's try this way. If I remember right, it's quicker through the medical bay."

The corridors looked, felt, and smelled different from other times she'd been allowed off her ship. The air was thick, a bit smoky, and carried the scent of singed wire and burning chemicals.

It was a relief to her when they found that they were not alone—there were other survivors on the *Boyington*. They started passing people in various stages of recovery. Each time, the two men paused to assess, offer assistance, and ask if anyone had contact with the bridge of the ship.

Arian watched and added mental notes to the other things she'd observed about these people. Deeper into the ship, the injuries became less, so the stops became shorter. But she noted these other groups were working to help others, to open stuck hatches—doing what needed to be done. They were shaken but focused.

As they drew closer to the core, she became concerned. If these people were typical, then those in the engine room would also be working to repair the engines. That they had failed was troubling. Either there was no one there able to effect repairs, or the engines were seriously damaged. Or it was taking time, which left another question for her to ponder. How long did they have before they succeeded? She had not missed the part about how simply opening a panel could kill them. If her "touch thing" did not work, they would die, and perhaps cause other deaths.

Planning to risk her life in this way was new to Arian. She'd taken risks when she left the house to gaze at the stars—life-threatening risks—but a risk with low odds. Getting on the ship with Rhubreak was also a risk, and when they were attacked, well, that was do or die. No thinking involved. But moving through this ship, she had time to wonder why she had not hesitated to come with them.

The dangers must be obvious to Coop, but he still pressed forward, his expression growing grimmer but somehow more determined. It was his ship, of course, but the task at hand was not part of his skill set. She watched them muscle open a jammed hatch and added *they do not quit* to her mental notes. It was, perhaps, at that moment that she realized that she was not just observing and learning about them. There was something more there, a truth that was not comfortable.

She wished to be like them. To be less...alien. To be less of what it was that made her so different from them. And all the people in her life, she added somewhat wryly. Was this the place she'd been searching for when she left Bosakli? Could she belong here? Could she and Coop—her thoughts stilled. She was unsure what that would involve. Love is hard, they'd said in the movie. If they found it hard, how much harder would it be for someone who did not know what it was?

She trailed a hand along the wall as she followed the two men, trying to be subtle in her attempt to monitor the ship's engines. But, in the midst of her thoughts, she forgot to keep her touch light while they stopped work on breaching another hatch. What she learned got clearer as they got closer to the heart of the *Boyington*. It was a ship as bold and brave as its name, she decided—she realized Coop stared at her and yanked her hand back.

There were the strange lights under her skin again, and they were clustered in her palm—the part of her hand that had pressed against the wall.

Coop appeared not to notice the lights, even as he put her hand back against the metal. His grin was crooked, but it pushed out the pain and worry.

"Keep on whispering. And tell me anything I need to know."

She nodded and was sorry when his hand fell away from hers. In a life where everything had felt wrong, the touch of his hand to hers was the something that felt right.

The lights did not show on the back of her hand now, but

when she flexed her hand and looked, they moved under the skin of her palms. None of the people they passed paid her too much attention. Most were grim and intent, or—still too dazed and shocked—to care about anything but giving or getting help.

They passed through a space with reflective walls, and she realized that right now she did not look so different from them. They all had blood-smeared and smoke-grimed faces that hid their differences.

They came to a hatch that did not open, even using the manual release.

"Is there a way around?" Tiger wondered, stepping back to shine a light on the identifying numbers painted at junctions throughout the ship.

"This is the shortest route," Coop said.

A group of people approached, some holding long metal bars. "You need to get in there?"

Coop nodded.

She could not tell what their designation was. It did not seem to matter. They all combined efforts to open the hatch, which had been knocked out of true, or so it appeared to her, but the door was no match for the suddenly formed team.

Arian was thoughtful when—after the hatch gave way—and she followed Coop and Tiger into yet another dim passage. *These people do not quit.*

Then she would not quit either.

———

Coop worried that the time they'd used to breach the hatch was time better spent going around. It didn't help that he didn't know how much time they had, even as a clock ticked down inside his head. Made it worse, in a way, that he didn't know if they were already out of time, or if they had enough. Each footstep forward felt fast and slow. They breached a hatch, rounded a corner, and there it was.

The central power core of the ship.

Coop didn't know how it worked, just knew that the cylinder that housed it stretched from the engine room almost to the top of the ship, one end stopping just below the bridge and the other landing in the center of the engineering section.

"Three decks down." Coop half sighed. "So it might be active in there, in which case, we pop the panel, we die. Quick, but we die."

Arian nodded, her expression sober, but not panicked. Yet. She approached the wall, spreading her fingers across the metal in a way that was becoming very familiar. Her lashes drifted down.

"And the second problem?" she asked without opening her eyes.

"If it's not working, then that's what they are trying to get going. It could start up at any time while we are in there."

"We should try an alternate route," Tiger objected. "Three decks..."

"Rhubreak might be able to tell us if there is a clear alternate route," Arian offered absently, most of her attention still focused on the wall of the central core.

Coop jerked, but not as much as Tiger, who didn't know the dragon's mental reach. He hesitated, then shrugged. Pappy would already be pissed at giving them access. In for a penny, in for a pound.

Let me see what I can do.

It was unsettling to realize how deep the dragon could have gone into their ship, if it had wanted to. Or had already gone?

I was not invited into your systems until now, Banshee.

Coop flushed.

I am not offended. But I do not know how to reassure you.

Well, Coop said wryly, *maybe wait until we all survive. Then we can figure it out.* He felt humor from the dragon and something else. Sharpened attention?

There is some radio traffic now. If it is accurate, the engine room is currently isolated from the rest of the ship.

"So there are people alive in the engine room?"

There are signs that efforts are focused on getting the central core back online.

"Great." He looked at Arian. "We need to hurry." *What about the bridge? Any radio signals in or out of there?*

I regret to inform you that there is no contact with the bridge as yet.

Arian got to work on the panel—this one would be a lot harder to crack, he guessed, while he and Tiger assessed the supplies they had left in their packs, shifting items Coop thought they might need when they reached engineering.

"I could try to climb up while you head down," Tiger offered.

The silence from the bridge was troubling, but...

Coop shook his head. "No point in all of us dying in there. See if you can put together a team to make a try for the bridge. And keep trying your radio. For sure we aren't the only ones worried about them."

"I am ready, I believe," Arian said, "but I do not think it will stay open long."

Tiger moved closer. "Show me what to push, and I'll try to hold it for you both."

She shifted her pack to the other shoulder and showed him what to do, then positioned herself next to Coop, a determined look on her face. "I must go first so I can open the next hatch."

Coop almost objected, then nodded. She was right. "Pop it, Tiger."

The hatch hissed open. Coop stepped forward, boosting Arian over the edge. The hatch twitched, but Tiger managed to keep it back. Coop flung himself in. Luckily each hatch opening had a small platform, so he didn't dive the three decks. The hatch slid closed, brushing against his back as he got all of himself pulled inside.

It was dark and cold, a sullen yellow glow from below.

He realized Arian had already started down and made haste to follow her. The core filled most of the cylinder, with just enough space to work around it. They reached the next deck without incident, then the one after that.

"One more," Coop said, as his feet settled on the platform. Arian was at the top of the ladder when the warning lights began to pulse, signaling that the core was coming online.

9

Arian stepped back, ripping her bag off her shoulder and grabbing the tool she'd used to open the panel above. At least she had a better idea of what worked—

"Do you know how long we have?" she asked, surprised by how calm she sounded. There was that sense once again, of something expanding inside her head, new knowledge and skills appearing.

"Not a clue." Coop's voice was calm as well. He'd pulled out his portable light and shone it on the panel for her.

She was grateful she had the small platform between her and the bottom of this place. She had not realized, until she started down, that she might be afraid of heights. She'd not had occasion to be high before this, so how could she know?

She popped the panel cover, feeling a moment of dismay at the sight. These controls were somewhat different. But she had no time to comment or feel concern. No time to stop when the warning light pulsed faster. If it was like the ones in the bay, the timing between the pulses was a signal that the core was close to turning on.

The hatch slid open, but when she moved her hand from the hot spot, it started to close.

"You must hurry." She was aware as she said it that she might not make it through. What surprised her was how very much she wanted Coop to survive, to live.

He dove through and scrambled up, his hand reaching out for her when something else over-rode her temporary control.

The hatch slid closed between them.

Shutting her in with the core at the brink of restarting.

————

Coop slammed his hand against the hatch, then punched buttons on the control panel. Nothing. He beat at the opening again. He wasn't an engine—or anything else—whisperer, but one deck above the engine room, even he could feel the rumble as stuff tried to start up. He pounded on the hatch again, harder now.

"Arian!"

He'd lost men and women in battle, but Arian wasn't a warrior. She was a civilian who was in there because he'd asked her to help them. And—she mattered in some other way, too, a way he'd like to have time to figure out—

The sound below him built and built—then died away with a shudder of metal. He paused, felt it try again—and fail. With his fist a few inches from the hatch, he froze, and then it slid open and there she was. She might have been pale. Or it could be the dicey light.

"Are you all right?" he asked the question even though she looked fine.

She nodded with her usual calm.

"Let's get you out," he ordered, holding out his hand.

She stared for a moment, then shook her head. "I can go down—"

"Not without me," he said.

"It is unnecessary—"

"They won't let you near anything without me," he said, urging her back and scrambling over the edge.

She nodded. "We must hurry. They will try again." She started to turn away, but he caught her shoulders, his touch light because, well, if he tightened his hold he might not be able to stop himself—

"Thank you." He didn't know why it felt right to bend and touch his mouth to hers. It just did. He didn't linger, even though he could have. If they'd had more time...

Her eyes were big and there was something in them that was new. Happy? He hoped so. He turned her back to the ladder and gave her a gentle push, then followed her onto the ladder. It felt longer than the two decks they'd just done, which made no sense, but being lost in space in a busted-ass ship didn't make a lot of sense anyway. He dropped onto the ramp right over the heart of the core, where the sullen glow gave off some heat and a lot of warning. He felt no relief, just a rising anxiety about what they were doing on the other side of the hatch—

Arian worked at the panel, but before she could open it, it opened on its own, putting him face to face with a startled engineer. His gaze traveled from Coop to Arian and widened some more in a grease and sweat-grimed face.

Coop pushed him out of the way as he scrambled out, then he turned back and yanked Arian out—with a major protest from his sore ribs. Funny how he'd forgotten his ribs until now. And now everything he'd injured started sending complaints to his brain housing group. He pushed his arm against the ribs and looked at Arian, his mouth opening to ask—he closed it again.

She didn't look like she saw him or anyone else in the room.

Her gaze traveled over the floor-to-ceiling control panels that controlled the core and the engines. Like someone in a trance or a moth to a flame, she drifted toward them.

The Chief engineer stepped in front of her, and she stopped but continued to look past him.

"She's an engine whisperer, Chief."

"A what? Who is she? Not the—" He stopped and might have reddened under the streaks of oil and grime.

Coop looked around. Appeared that about half the Chief's team was down. "Seems like you could use help, any help." He arched his brows and added, "She's good."

With visible reluctance, he stepped aside.

"You in contact with the bridge by any chance?" Coop asked, other worries bubbling up now that they'd reached this goal.

"Your bridge is intact but devoid of power," Arian said absently. Maybe the sudden silence pulled her attention from the engine controls. She glanced back. "Rhubreak and your scientist got our scanners going. There is damage but no hull breaches. Most of the problems, other than power loss, seem to be localized damage from impacts and the anomaly."

"Injuries? Can he tell how many down?"

Arian shook her head. "There are life signs all over the ship, but no way to tell how many are injured or how badly." She hesitated as if listening. "There are people alive on your bridge."

That was promising if only Rhubreak could tell them who.

"What about the systems?" the Chief asked. "We are worried about feedback from damaged systems even if we get the engines back online."

"You have emergency power running." Arian's attention had returned to the controls. The hands at her sides flexed.

The Chief nodded, looking a bit bemused—a word Coop didn't think he'd ever thought before.

"Where are those controls?"

He pointed, watched her walk over and spread her hands on the controls in her whisper thing, saw the computer or whatever it was starting to talk back to her, data scrolling onto the screen. The Chief started toward her, then stopped and looked at Coop with something that might be awe in his eyes.

"Can I keep her?"

PART II

10

BESTER'S CLIENT had not been as understanding as he'd hoped. His body was coated with sweat from the encounter. At least he got extra time. And a warning.

"Deliver or be dead," his client had said, his many eyes and tone blank and cold.

Almost, he wished he'd listened to the warnings about getting involved with this client. But the payment had been triple his usual fee. It wasn't in his account yet, but he could see it there. The numbers were piling up to that day when he'd have enough. He was not certain when that would be or what that number was. Each time he thought he'd made enough, he found it wasn't. But someday he would.

A pity the tight timeline meant they had to use an expensive jump gate—which had cost more than usual.

"A *Mycterian* fleet came through and shot us up." The jump gate station manager had no color, but he was not dead. "Grabbed a few of my people and left."

Bester didn't ask why they'd been grabbed. He already knew.

Unregistered gates couldn't ask authorities for help, and the truth was, help wouldn't have gotten there in time anyway. They tended to be set up in big, empty, hard-to-find spaces, so the authorities didn't shut them down. And if anyone wanted to use it, they had to pay a premium. No place to complain about that either.

The manager's eyes had widened when given the coordinates, which were the same ones the *Mycterians* had used.

Bester frowned. What target was there for the *Mycterians* in that empty region of space? They couldn't be after the same ship, could they? But why send a fleet after one ship? As far as Elfel could tell, there was nothing out there, but he thought the data was strange. The signal was coming through on a thin beam, as if through a keyhole break in a cloaking shield.

Ghrym, his ship captain, pinged his station. "We are preparing to exit the jump gate, sir."

Bester strapped down for the turbulent exit. Unregistered gates lacked the technology to smooth out going in and out. This one was particularly bad, possibly because of the *Mycterians*. They hadn't destroyed it because that would close their retreat route, but they liked to do some damage, for whatever reason.

After transit, Bester learned that the space station on this side had also been attacked. And the news got worse, now that they were tracking along the same course as the signal.

When would he learn to let his instincts rule his desire for more?

"Let me see." Elfel popped the data up on his personal screen. It was worse than Bester had thought. It wasn't just a fleet. It was an invasion fleet, but what were they invading? What was in that region that would warrant such a show of force from the *Mycterians*?

He glanced back as if he could see the way home from deep inside his ship. He pulled up the record of his account credits.

He'd been thinking of the credits as already in there, so the amount was...disappointing.

Perhaps there was an upside to the *Mycterian* presence. They might prove to be the perfect distraction while he slipped in and got his artifact back.

11

———

THE BOYINGTON WAS RETURNING to normal, well, a new normal. At least the critical systems were online, and they'd been able to look over the new neighborhood a bit more. The high-level military staff were grim, some sporting injuries, as they gathered for a post incident briefing and assessment.

Of course, there were ship-wide injuries—ranging from minor to serious—but no fatalities, which seemed like a miracle. And Pappy was not happy that the bridge had been the last to come back online. Coop was glad he'd not been there during that time. Pappy moved stiffly into his place at the head of the conference table. He'd bruised one side of his face and had cuts and abrasions.

Coop wasn't sure why he'd been invited to this particular party so soon after getting a few strips burned off his hide for giving Arian and her dragon access to the ship's systems. Old man might have been down, but he was not out. At least he didn't hold a grudge. Coop knew better than to defend himself. Pappy wasn't as angry about that as he was about being lost.

Lost in space.

They were all trying to wrap their brains around this new reality.

To find a way to get found.

As the meeting progressed, if felt like everyone circled the big question so no one had to be the one to say it out loud.

Where were they? And how far was that from home?

After all the reports had been presented, a silence fell over the room.

Pappy's laser gaze tracked slowly around the table, pinning each person in place for what felt like a long time. When Coop's turn came, he held it but felt like he'd been sliced and diced again when Pappy finally moved on. He blinked and exchanged a wry look with the Chief.

Pappy flicked the edge of his computer with a finger. "These reports are helpful, and I appreciate the work that went into preparing them while you also dealt with the aftermath of the incident." He leaned back in his chair and studied them all once more. "Shall we deal with the elephant in the room? Where are we? How do we get our people home?"

Odd that these, the hardest questions to answer, finally broke the tension.

Typical of Pappy that he focused on his people and getting them home. That would be why they'd take a bullet for the old man, even when he regularly burned strips off them. Coop didn't grin because he wasn't stupid, but inside? He might have. Pappy's gaze flicked his way, and he sobered all the way through. Might have straightened in his seat, too. Didn't relax when Pappy's Basilisk gaze moved on again, finding the head geek and stopping.

"We don't know, sir." The geek did a decent job of not melting into his chair.

"What do we know?" Pappy asked, his tone at odds with his expression.

The geek perked up. "There are several inhabited planets in this system." He did something on his computer that put a view of the system on the big screen. There was a general shifting in the room, as people adjusted position to see.

Pappy studied this data like he hadn't seen it before. "And we know this how?"

"Concentration of heat sources, indications of a power grid, orbiting satellites—"

"Satellites?" Pappy snapped.

"Yes, sir." The geek pulled in the view. "They are not dissimilar to ours and could indicate some level of space capability, or that the indigenous people are heading that way."

"So they can see us?"

"It's possible. I mean, they probably have telescopes, so yeah, if they are looking, we could be...visible. We're not exactly hiding."

Silence.

"What about radio signals?" asked Pappy's number two.

"We are picking up radio signals," the geek admitted, "but we have not been able to translate them." He blinked twice. "Not unlike our world, there appears to be a range of, um, languages. At least, that is the general consensus."

Dr. Derwent, the first contact team leader, cleared his throat, then probably wished he hadn't.

"You have something to share, Dr. Derwent?"

His gaze shifted one direction, then the other. He cleared his throat again. "Our linguistics specialists have been having trouble translating the signals."

"Trouble?" Pappy shook his head. "What kind?"

"Even in primitive people, there are...well, we usually had ways to find a starting point, something familiar. They..." he hesitated and Pappy made an impatient sound. "Well, they sound like...birds."

"Birds?"

"That's what they sound like to us, too, sir," the main geek said.

"Birds," Pappy said the single word flatly, but the two men still flinched.

"If the species in the system are avian-based, it could complicate communication," Derwent stated the obvious. "We encountered the same problem with, well," he faltered some, "the Draze Dragon that traveled with the alien young lady. He uses telepathy to communicate with, um, well, that's what he uses, because his anatomy is quite...dissimilar from ours."

"Something about the shape of the throat," Coop added, then wished he hadn't. Pappy's gaze pinned him for a few seconds, then shifted back to the screen.

"How much of scanning data is from our scanners?" he asked with deceptive mildness.

"The...the..." the head geek faltered, perhaps sensing the trap, "the alien ship has better scanning than we do."

"Even with the Garradian boost?" Pappy arched a brow.

"We are a long way from those planets, sir." The geek tugged at the neck of his tee shirt.

"In the Garradian system—"

"—signals were boosted by the outposts, sir," the wing geek put in. "They were all over the place."

Pappy tapped his fingers against the desk for what seemed like a long time. Finally, he asked, "And we're sure this is accurate?"

The head geek looked at his wing geek, then back at Pappy. "Well, yes, I mean, not one hundred percent. Not without getting eyes on...things."

Pappy leaned back and studied the data again. "Can we do that? Can we get eyes on without being detected?" He turned back to the table.

The head geek did a pretty good job of holding his ground. "Well, if we used the Garradian shuttles, maybe." He turned to the screen. "We could send a team or teams, but we don't know..."

"...what we don't know?" Pappy made it sound like a question, but it wasn't. Not really.

"Yes, sir. I mean, no sir. I mean, pretty much, sir."

"Okay." His gaze did another traverse of the people in the room, but there was more worry in there now. "What do we know? And what do we need to do to move the dial in the direction of knowing more?"

Silence. Coop hoped he wasn't supposed to answer that.

Pappy tapped the table top with the fingers of one hand. Stopped. "We're out here because some very smart people not only looked past what seemed possible but did something about it. They moved the dial, turned a 'what if' into this, into Project Enterprise." Another pause. "You are part of the smart people, or you wouldn't be on my ship. I need to you to think past this moment, to kick on the afterburners and get from 'what if' to 'how can we do this?' I need you to help me get our people home."

Another silence formed, but this one was more thoughtful, less scared.

"And I think we need a risk assessment."

"A...risk assessment, sir?" the wing geek asked.

"What are the risks of another wormhole opening up while we're sitting here thinking? I also want a threat response worked up." He glanced at Coop now. "We ran into hostiles in the last system. Using what we learned from that, we need to upgrade our responses. We also need," he paused and blinked several times, "a rationing and resupply plan." He looked at them again, but this time it was his 'we can do this' look. "We may be here awhile. We need to survive and thrive. We need to live long enough to get home."

Coop saw nods and notes made.

"And don't just check off my list. Put your heads together and make your own lists. What will it take to find out what we need to know? Work together. Work alone. Get as many of the crew involved as you can. Keep them busy, keep them focused on solving problems. We don't need panic. We need solutions." With a hint of a grin, he added, "Make it so, people. Make it so."

A laugh ran around the table, breaking even more of the tension into pieces. Pappy rose, and everyone hastily followed suit. "Dismissed."

As the room slowly emptied, Coop caught Pappy's glance, read it correctly, and waited until they were alone. Pappy showed Coop his back—his unhappy back—shoving his hands in the pockets of his pants while he studied the data screen—or appeared to.

"You think I need to bring them in."

Coop didn't ask who he meant or answer the question Pappy hadn't asked. Even though he'd been in the room with the smart people, he didn't assume Pappy considered him one of them.

"Do you think the lizard knows where we are?"

"He might. I haven't asked him, sir." It wasn't in Coop's job description, as Pappy had made clear earlier.

"Could they have caused this?" Pappy swung around to face him, his expression hard. "Or contributed to it?"

Coop considered the question, not because he thought they had or because he had any way of knowing. Mostly he didn't want to get dressed down again.

"Did you talk to the geek who came down with me and Tiger? What does he think?"

Pappy sank into his seat again. "He doesn't think they did

anything, but he can't be sure there wasn't an accidental connection."

"They did help us, sir." Coop didn't like saying it, but...

"I haven't forgotten. I'm also aware that right now, their fate is tied up with ours." He stared at something Coop could not see.

Coop considered the trip through the damaged ship. Finally ventured, "Arian didn't have to do what she did, sir. I—" He stopped, not sure what he was trying to say. Women, alien or not, weren't easy.

"Chief says things weren't going well when she showed up. That she made a difference." Pappy suddenly swiveled to face Coop. "If she's so good, why is her ship still down?"

Coop hesitated. Pappy had a point. "We don't know that it is, sir."

"Then why are they still here?"

"It's a big universe. Maybe they are lost, too. Maybe...they had two wormhole transits. Maybe they are tired." Or hiding from someone? "We don't know what they are doing out here." It was a small ship, though. Feelings were not his skill set and yet... something was odd there, even beyond the telepathic dragon. He spoke slowly, "Rhubreak seems to have a kind of code. He told me he hadn't been invited into our systems, but that he couldn't prove he hadn't been nosing around." And he had gotten in far enough to talk to Coop when he needed help.

"Rhubreak?"

"The dragon, sir."

Pappy's eye may have twitched. "And the girl? What's your assessment of her?"

He had to get this right. "She's...profoundly pragmatic, at least, that's how she seems to me." He felt a cold chill at the memory of that hatch closing her into the central core. She'd been pale when it opened, but had still insisted on finishing the mission.

"Pragmatic?"

"She didn't hesitate climbing into the core, even after she knew how dangerous it was." He frowned, considering. "She wasn't scared, but she wasn't brave." Not their version of brave anyway. "Just..."

"Pragmatic." He nodded slowly. "I wish we knew what they wanted."

"Have we asked them, sir?"

He made a gesture. "Not really. I let Derwent handle that, might have been a mistake. We don't have time to be diplomatic anymore. We need to know." He shot Coop a look. "She was right about one thing, though."

"Sir?"

"How do we know? How do we trust them when she didn't seem to know what the word means?"

Coop hesitated. "I think she knows now, sir. She's had a good look at us, at how we roll. I don't think she would have helped us if she weren't part of the way there." He frowned.

"What's the problem, Captain?"

He looked up. "We could lose her trust, too. Where she comes from, I don't think it was a picnic."

Silence for a long minute. "You think we should ask for their help."

"They might know more than we do. The dragon seems to know something about Earth, based on a couple of things he's said to me."

"Then why haven't they said anything?"

"We haven't asked. I think it's that code thing. Maybe it's a kind of prime directive."

Pappy considered this and nodded, then looked at Coop again. "There's something odd about the two of them."

"Yes, sir." They were aliens, but he knew what Pappy meant. There was something odd about them and between them. And he wasn't sure they knew the right questions to ask to get the answers they needed.

"But you think I should talk to them?"

"Well, we are pretty screwed, sir."

Pappy gave a slow, reluctant nod. "Here or there?"

Coop knew what he'd prefer, keeping them both on their ship, but— "Here, sir." He met Pappy's annoyed gaze. "At least we—you can sit down."

"We, Captain. The lizard talks to you, after all." Pappy gave a reluctant, almost grin.

Coop thought about mentioning Arian could relay, then figured that Pappy knew this and didn't trust her. He nodded.

Pappy sighed. "See if they will both join me here in—" He looked at the time. "—let's say half an hour?"

"I'll see what I can do, sir."

———

"Did that do it?" Arian asked, letting her hands drop to her sides, her head resting on the decking. She kept her tone neutral but noticed that the hand she lifted to push back an errant piece of hair shook, the sparks of light under her skin dimmer this time. She was tired, but...

It is functioning within acceptable parameters now.

She scrambled out into the corridor, took a breath, then rolled over, and gathered up her tools. Only then did she stand. Out of the corner of her eye, she noted the green lights indicting acceptable parameters. She started to turn away, then stopped, her chin down.

"Was there any damage..." She stopped.

No.

Too bad. She headed toward the bridge.

Rhubreak had managed to deploy about half their stabiliza-tion hooks, which had not been enough to keep them from slamming into the *Boyington's* hull several times during the encounter with the anomaly. There was impact damage to some of their less obvious systems, including the one she'd just repaired. She pulled a cloth from a rear pocket and mopped at her damp face. Next up, she needed to work on internal temper-ature controls. It kept ramping up because the outer bay was still cold

Banshee is approaching this location.

Coop. It had been several days since she'd seen him. She moved toward the hatch, stopping just out of sight to watch him cross to the ramp. The sight of him made her heart leap in her chest, then beat faster. At her sides her fingers curled into the palms, so that she wouldn't reach out to him. They'd almost died. It seemed...urgent...that they press lips once more. That she tell him...something. The words lodged in her chest, getting hammered by her swiftly beating heart. It felt that, if she could touch him, the words would be freed.

But would they be welcome?

He moved loosely, his stride confident, his gaze clear and direct as he looked around the bay. He stopped, frowning. Based on where he was, it was the new damage to her ship that he looked at. She saw worry in his gaze, but not suspicion or distrust. He must have secrets. Everyone had them, did they not? It was the nature of the secret that mattered, surely? If she was... repulsed by what this ship carried, how would he, or his people, feel if they found out?

She did not try to shut this thought off from Rhubreak but was not surprised when he had no comment to offer. He must have felt her reluctance—for possibly the first time in her life—to effect the repair. It was the thing that they both pretended was not there. That the machinery that kept the two pods very, very cold, and their contents, did not exist.

She took a long, slow breath, seeking for calm, reaching for the place that had helped her escape the Enforcers for so long, then stepped out of the shadows as Coop reached the foot of the ramp.

"Hey," he said, stopping to smile at her. It did not completely reach his eyes. But perhaps her answering one did not as well.

My people will have questions, he'd said, but this time, he was the one with questions in his gaze.

"You are welcome here," she said, automatically, her gaze clinging to the sight of him, against her will. "You are weary."

She almost flinched at her words. It was out of character to make a personal comment. To mind someone else's business.

You are changing.

Was she? She longed to be different, to be someone these people could trust, to be someone Coop wanted—

Since her return to this ship yet again, she had not let herself think as much about his people or the things she'd learned. When she'd gone through the ship with Coop and Tiger, she'd felt one with them, but once she'd helped get their systems up, the divide between them had opened once more. It seemed that what had happened had not been as big for them as it had been for her. It felt as if the more she tried to fight free of her past, the more it held her captive.

Because she did not know how to change enough, she'd kept herself too busy to think or feel. Now waves of thoughts and emotions tried to break free, so much she swayed, and had to steady herself with a hand pressed on the frame of the hatch.

Was it her longing to belong that had fooled her into thinking she did belong? Was she once more star gazing, longing for that she could not have?

But you did escape to the stars.

Ships were not people. Ships were...ships. Ships did what they were told. If she felt dissent from the ship, she ignored it. People...were not that simple. So she veiled her longings behind her 'good citizen of the Consortium' facade and stepped back so Coop could enter. But he did not.

His smile turned rueful. "I'm tired. We all are." He hesitated. "The Colonel would like to speak with you and Rhubreak, if you can spare the time?"

An order wrapped in a polite request. Tell him I will be pleased.

Arian felt her lips thin for a moment, at Rhubreak's assumption that she would be happy to speak with Coop's Colonel—who had made his distrust of her very clear. Of course, she would for Coop, but—

You are weary as well.

How very much it annoyed her that he thought her reluctance flowed from weariness. Even if it probably did.

"Rhubreak is coming," she said, relieved her voice was devoid of annoyance—indeed it lacked all inflection. It was a lesson she'd learned well.

"Thanks," Coop said, a small crease forming between his brows. "This a good time? I'm not interrupting you, am I?"

Did he sense—her gaze met his and she knew he did.

Interesting.

In a good way? Or a not good way?

Her dragon did not respond.

"I could use a respite. The ship's repairs are proving to be tedious," she said, and wondered why that made his brows draw together for an instant. "It is not well pleased with its damage."

Coop stepped back and looked at the ship. "Not pleased, aye? You make her sound like she's the boss."

Arian looked back at the ship, too, and smiled as if he'd said something humorous. Instead of something true.

12

RHUBREAK'S CLAWS clicked rhythmically against metal as Coop led them through unfamiliar corridors, many still showing signs of damage. The air felt chilly to her and damage scents lingered as systems worked to scrub the air clean once more.

There was less curiosity in the eyes of Coop's ship mates that they passed. Some almost seemed suspicious.

They are afraid.

Of us?

They are lost. Their fear needs a focus.

They were the outsiders. Arian felt her outer shell harden, but she kept her chin lifted. They passed a room just as a door opened to let a crewman out, giving her a glimpse of people relaxing in chairs. The open door released rhythmic sounds into the corridor. This was not the same room she'd been in with Coop where they saw the movie, nor was it the canteen. She craned to look in as they passed.

What is that sound?

Music.

It was pleasing, insistent enough that some of the people in the room tapped a foot or nodded their heads in time to the sounds. She was sorry when the door shut the sound in.

Music. Why had her world not had music? What would it have cost the Consortium to soften some of the edges of their lives? This ship was all hard edges. Bosakli had been soft in appearance. Unnatural. Natural. She'd come from a community, had lived in one in the most natural of settings, but it had never felt normal or natural. This ship of metal floating in deep space felt more of both of those things. It was...ironic.

They had a clear chain of command, were required to obey orders, to do as they were told. Their clothing indicated status, just as on Bosakli. There was a hierarchy, differences in function and importance. They were afraid—

But not of each other or those over them. They were afraid because they were lost, but this challenge drew them together, not apart. They trusted each other. And themselves.

Trust.

She understood it better now but did not understand how to acquire or give it.

As they paused at an entry point of some kind, Arian touched the wall with her fingertips, relieved to feel the regular pulse of most of the engines far below. At the moment, it seemed the engines were more accepting than the people. She had felt —hoped—the Chief was a new friend. He was busy, she told herself. There was so much still to do.

The events following the anomaly impact seemed like a strange dream now. Had she helped them because she wanted to, or because she'd been conditioned to serve? That was the question she kept asking herself. Was it delusional to think it had been a choice? She'd changed even before meeting Coop. A kind of blooming had happened inside her head. The lights under her skin appeared more and more, too. The bump to her head, the wound on her temple were almost gone. All the injuries, the old scars from her work on the farm, were also gone. Erased as if they'd never been. How was this possible?

As strange as it all was, it also felt...natural...like blood returning to a limb after it had been cramped too long in the wrong position. Since walking onto her ship, or *the* ship, it felt like waking up from a long sleep. When she'd touched the controls deep in the *Boyington*, she'd "seen" what was wrong with the engines and how to fix them, like a movie inside her head. She still lacked the conscious knowledge to understand all she'd seen, but she...remembered.

How could she remember something that had never happened to her?

The return to her ship, the downward slide of emotion from the high caused by the danger had left her restless and frustrated. The smaller issues, the smaller engines on her ship bored her. Or—did she want her ship to be repaired? If she did, would it leave? Would she have to leave with it?

She did not want to go.

She faced this, though it terrified her to once more be at the mercy of others. Why had they been summoned by Coop's Colonel? Did he fear—

Did we cause the anomaly?

I do not believe so.

Can we prove we did not?

She did not wish to get booted out into space by Coop's commander.

I will do what I can to avoid that outcome.

Rhubreak did not point out that they would not have this problem, nor would they be in this fix, if not for her. He did not need to emphasize this obvious point. He was the bigger... dragon. Her lips twitched and her gaze intersected with Coop's. He arched a brow and gave her a reassuring smile. She had smiled more, been more relaxed around him, but now she felt uneasy. She slowed her breathing, trying to dive deeper into her safe place.

They stopped in front of the lift, the small box that lifted one up or down. It's doors slid back, allowing two people to exit, then Coop ushered them inside. She rested a hand on the wall, waiting for that odd sensation in her middle as Coop pushed the button and the lift began to rise.

"Beats climbing, doesn't it?" Coop said with a grin. "Artificial gravity is clingy."

She managed a chuckle. "I believe it would have increased our difficulty had it gone offline, too."

He made a face that could have been agreement. Arian noted signs of tension around his eyes and mouth, and he flexed his fingers as if something bothered him.

Her muscles tightened, and she struggled to keep her breathing even. Then she wondered why she tried so hard when these people didn't seem to notice or care? Or when Coop seemed able to sense her feelings. Was there some clue in the question? Was it possible that hiding how she felt created a barrier with these people?

It does make it harder for them to trust you, to relate to you.

It made a certain sense, she decided, recalling how the diplomat had tried to mirror her greeting. She took a deeper breath and tried to float free of her inner cage of calm. She shivered. The air felt cold out of that safe place. She flexed her fingers twice. Glanced down, but no sparks appeared under the skin this time.

"This is a fine ship." She spread her palms on the metal wall. It was easier to smile naturally when she was connected to the engines.

"She took a beating," Coop said, with a wry grin. "But she's still flying."

This was not the first time he'd called a ship "she." It was the first time it was a ship named after a brave man. Why?

Ask him.

What if he does not answer?

Then you will be where you are right now.

The logic of this could not be disputed, so she cleared her throat and asked. Coop looked both surprised and amused.

The movement of the lift stopped, and the door slid open. People waited for them to exit before boarding the lift, the door sliding closed once more.

"Ships are always she, always have been, no matter who they are named after." He kind of glanced around, then grinned before he said, "I think it's because ships are more like women than men."

His last comment had the feel of a confession but did not provide clarity. Did he believe males and females were different? The Consortium claimed there was no difference, but men had more freedom of movement and more choice in pact bonding. She followed Coop down the corridor until he punched in the code to open a door.

Inside her gaze was drawn past a seating area to the view beyond that gave her a glimpse of the outer ship. She wished she could go look out, but the Colonel stood there, his brooding frustration a live thing in the room as he turned to offer a courteous sounding greeting belied by his expression. He indicated the seating area with a sweep of one hand, then crossed to a seat opposite them. He did not desire this meeting, so why were they here?

Needs must when the devil drives.

She had to bite back a chuckle as Rhubreak scrambled onto one of the seats. She took the seat next to him, noting that Coop and his Colonel sank into the two facing them. The low table was not a large divide, but she sensed it could be. Rhubreak's snout turned toward the Colonel, and his beard flared black for several seconds as if he too felt this divide.

A silence formed in the space between them, an itchy silence that made her want to shift in her seat. Her first instinct was for stillness—which she was trying to change, she reminded herself. So she gave into the need and adjusted her position in a small way. This brought the Colonel's razor gaze to her. It took a struggle to let him see her worry and fear.

His expression softened very slightly. "Thank you for your assistance with our engines," he said, finally.

"I am sorry I could not get them all running."

"Chief says you worked a miracle." Suspicion flared in his eyes. "I guess you've worked on engines like ours before."

The truth shall make you free. "I have not." His gaze darkened. How did she explain something she did not understand? Her smile felt crooked. "I do not know why or how. I just do."

"Rhubreak called you an engine whisperer," Coop said.

Arian did not know what this meant, but it seemed the Colonel did, because nodded.

"Whatever you did, Chief would like to hire you for his crew."

"It would be my honor to assist in any way I can."

The Colonel nodded, but he did not accept her offer.

"There might be another way you can...help." He brought the word out very reluctantly, but this time he looked at Rhubreak before he looked at her.

"If we can..." Arian stopped, sensing caution from Rhubreak.

"Your scanners seem to see further than ours." He hesitated, then added, "You saw the pirates before we did."

Arian was puzzled. "We continue to share our scan data with your scientists."

"Do you?"

"I don't understand."

The Colonel glanced at Coop, and she sensed a passing of the problem to him.

"It's not just scan data we're interested in. We wondered if you had information in your databanks about this system?" Coop asked, angling so he could look at both of them.

Arian's fingers moved as if on keys, something they seemed to do when presented with a question, but the knowledge of what to do did not come to the front of her mind this time. She turned to Rhubreak and arched a brow.

His snout moved from her to Coop and then finally to the Colonel.

It is possible there is further information in the databanks.

There was a hint of resignation in the admission.

"You haven't looked? Surely that is the first thing you'd do," Coop said. He glanced at his Colonel and repeated what Rhubreak had said.

Rhubreak's beard flared black, then subsided. *The databanks are not a...Google search. They are designed to assist the ship's purpose.*

Now she sensed frustration from Rhubreak. She looked curiously at him.

"What is your ship's purpose," the Colonel asked, with a slight frown.

Collection.

Arian's stomach tightened at this word, but it did not seem to trouble Coop when he shared this with the Colonel.

The Colonel's frown deepened. "But surely, at some point, you would need access to the research information the ship collected?"

That process occurs at the end of the collection.

She frowned. Did that mean he wasn't done? Or that his mission wasn't done until he returned to where he'd come from?

"Have you tried to find the information?" Coop persisted.

I have tried.

This was new information to Arian.

So far without success. The ship was designed for me to operate so I can manipulate some systems, but I am a conductor, the Companion only. I believe, I hope there is a protocol for when something goes wrong. Once the ship is repaired, it may try to repair the...aberration.

"Aberration?" Coop seemed startled by this word.

The course alternation. I believe the ship would see the anomaly transits as aberrations. But I do not know this for certain. It is not part of my, er, brief.

"You've never gone off course before?" the Colonel asked, incredulously.

Arian looked toward the window and wished she could escape. Rhubreak shook his head slowly to one side, then the other.

The Colonel frowned, processing this exchange. "I thought you were the pilot," he said, looking at Arian.

"I am the pilot," she said. "I sent it off course."

The Colonel's gaze narrowed sharply. "Why?"

She stared at him, her eyes wide and dry. This man would know if she lied, but the truth, she did not think it would make her free. In any case, it was stuck in her throat.

"Collection," the Colonel said slowly. "What does it collect?"

Arian licked her lips. "It collected me."

———

Pappy stiffened, his gaze tracking to the dragon. Coop didn't even dare tug at the neck of his uniform shirt.

"It collected you? Why?"

"I do not know."

Arian had been different, less closed, but now she slammed shut like a door caught by a gust of cold wind.

She glanced at Coop. "You said the truth would make me free. I speak the truth. I do not know. Does that make me free?"

"Who does know?" Pappy cut in.

Arian looked at the dragon.

I don't have access to that information either.

Coop gave a slight shake of his head for the Pappy's benefit.

"Is she a criminal?"

No.

Coop did not like the relief he felt. He shook his head again.

"If you don't know why you collected her, how do you know she's not a criminal?" Pappy snapped.

Rhubreak felt startled, perhaps concerned—Coop wasn't certain.

"He did not capture me," Arian said. "I willingly boarded the ship at his...invitation."

Pappy studied her for a long moment, then turned to Rhubreak. "Why did you...invite her aboard?"

I was sent.

"Because?" Pappy prompted.

That information is not need-to-know.

Pappy scowled a bit. "Not exactly proof she's not a criminal, but," his shoulders rose and fell in a deep sigh, "you don't strike me as a bounty hunter or cop."

Coop hid a grin with his hand and a cough.

"He did not try to stop me when I declined the cold sleep," Arian offered. "Nor has he complained that I drove us into the ditch."

Pappy looked a bit something. "Ditch?"

"I was...I am a farm laborer. I said I had an affinity for engines. This is true. I was very young when I drove my first machine into a ditch."

Pappy's jaw might have gone a bit slack before he caught himself. "A farm laborer. And a pilot?"

She shrugged. "I have always pushed my...boundaries."

Which was probably why someone wanted to collect her. He could tell Pappy had figured that out, too. Would that someone try to find her? Oh yeah. And whoever it was would want their ship back, too.

"Had I not diverted our ship—"

"You wouldn't have come through the wormhole, and we'd still be here," Coop put in, "with our engines down."

A tinge of color returned to her cheeks.

He could see Pappy didn't entirely agree. The Chief might have got them up eventually. But at what cost? Getting their power online sooner rather than later had saved lives for sure.

"How do we know you didn't cause the wormhole?" Pappy asked the question. Coop wasn't surprised by that or that it drove the color from her cheeks again.

"I don't think we did." She didn't look away, which Coop knew, wasn't easy when Pappy was on one. "But I don't...know." Her lips twitched. "I had just finished scanning when we spotted the pirates and," she stopped to consider, "yes, I was doing deep scans when it opened."

"Could those scans have caused it to open?"

Instead of defensive, she looked intrigued by the idea. "The anomaly did increase in size when it interacted with some of the barrage weapons fire...but it seems unlikely. I do not believe we emitted sufficient energy to cause it to form in the first place."

"Would you be willing to let our engineers and scientists examine your ship?"

Her shoulders straightened as if bracing for incoming.

"Yes."

Pappy stared at her for what felt like a long time, before nodding slowly. "Okay. When we have the resources available, we'll send them down." He relaxed some. "We are off track from the big question and the reason we asked you here."

Now she appeared puzzled. "The real reason?"

Coop turned to the dragon. "You've been to Earth. Or you know about it."

The dragon's snout moved in a way that could be agreement.

"So it's possible that the location of Earth is buried in your non-Google database?"

Again, the non-committal something.

"We can't get home unless we know where we are. And where here is from Earth. Can you answer those two questions?" Pappy asked, looking right at the dragon.

If I can determine where we are, if I can get useful access to the database, it might be possible to fix Earth's location and plot a course.

"What's the catch?" Coop asked.

The "catch" is, how far this system could be from your Earth.

Coop passed this along to Pappy, who didn't like it anymore than Coop. Though it had occurred to all of them.

Pappy sat frowning in silence for a while, then he looked up. "There are things we need to know about this system, if we are going to be here...for a while." His lips thinned for a few seconds. Then he sighed again. "The Captain thinks you might could help with that?"

The dragon's beard flared, if he could look startled he would have.

Me?

"With your ability to talk mind to mind. Near as we can tell, the species in this system speak bird," Coop told him.

"Do you speak bird?" Pappy asked him.

13

WHY WOULD they think I speak bird?

Rhubreak sounded a bit outraged, and a tiny bit flattered, as they once more boarded their ship. For her, it seemed like all paths led to this ship. It did not feel that the truth had made her free. Or ever would. Though the Colonel hadn't kicked them out into space. Because he needed them. Or he needed Rhubreak. For now.

"Because you could speak to them, I suppose."

They do not speak bird. I do not speak bird. It is quite different.

"I think they noticed." She had the oddest sensation in her chest. A sort of tickle that traveled up and came out her mouth. The sound was not one she'd ever emitted before, and it left her feeling relieved and somehow more relaxed.

Rhubreak turned to look at her. *I have not heard you laugh before.*

"Is that what it was?" She rubbed her chest.

What is funny?

"Funny?" He was funny, as was his reaction to their request, but she wasn't sure *he'd* think it was funny. "It was just...the expressions on their faces and you, you were so shocked. And now you're annoyed. It's...funny." She frowned as a non-funny thought hit her. "What if, while we're attempting to speak with the birds, another anomaly opens up? Shouldn't they be thinking about changing their position?"

Perhaps they wish to be sure what they are moving toward. And if we are the source of the anomaly, moving will not help them.

"Do you think we did it?"

I do not believe so, but...

She felt an impatient huff blow through her mind.

I did not think I would ever miss Google.

"So you have been to their Earth."

Not necessarily. I received a memory upload before beginning this mission. One of my kind was on their Earth... He was silent for a moment as if considering. *It could have been me.*

How can you not know?

The upload mingles memories. It is difficult to sort out which are mine and which are not. They all feel real.

That felt similar to what she was experiencing, only not the same. The non-Bosakli memories did not feel "real," they felt alien. Could she have received an upload, possibly upon boarding this ship? She felt cold. What if the upload had been the time on Bosakli? What if her memories of that weren't real? Not that she'd have minded missing it, but why make her remember that? This made her head hurt. "So the information really could be in this ship's memory banks?"

It is possible.

He didn't sound happy about that. "Don't you want to find Earth?"

It is not that which worries me.

"Well, what worries you?"

What I said at the meeting. How far did the wormhole take this ship from their Earth?

"What do you mean? Remember I'm just a farm laborer."

It has to do with distance. This ship could have been flung several lifetimes from their system, their planet.

"You mean..."

It is possible that they will never get home. Or if they do, so much time will have passed that everyone they know will be long dead.

————

Coop watched Pappy with worried eyes. He'd been pacing since Arian and the dragon left. Finally, he stopped and faced Coop.

He straightened. "Sir?"

"You realize that even if we find out where we are and where Earth is..."

"We might not get home?" Coop rubbed the back of his neck. "I figure anyone who has seen *Lost in Space* has figured that one out, sir."

"You don't seem too worried about it."

"It's the dragon, sir. If he's been bopping around, collecting useful people..."

"Then he might know a faster way to travel?"

"It's possible." He half grinned. "Or another wormhole might open up and take us back where we came from."

His mind kept returning to the wormhole, but if Arian's ship had caused the wormhole, it didn't seem to be working for them. And he was a flyboy, not a geek. So why did he think he knew anything about any of this? He should be out boldly going not—

"I wish I shared your optimism." Pappy paced away, then back. "I want you to put together a team to...assess this system for resources and allies."

Coop straightened. Now he was talking. "What parameters..."

"Initial foray will be eyes only. First contact? We have time to figure that one out. Not a lot, but some. But we need intel." His expression cracked, letting his exhaustion show for several seconds. "You can use one of the Garradian shuttles. You'll need cloaking and jump tech—since the region of inhabited planets is so far away." This came out a bit bitter. "But even so, we'll need to close the distance."

Moving closer to the region with the inhabited planets upped the chance they'd be seen, but it had to be done.

"The hyperdrive online yet?"

"Chief got it going last night." Pappy paced over and stared out the external viewer. "It's not ready for big jumps, but he says it can do what we need it to." He looked at this watch. "We're making the hop at oh-thirteen-hundred."

"Sir, how do we know it wasn't our drive—" He stopped. It hadn't launched wormholes in the other systems. Could a system be inclined to wormholes? He wasn't a geek, he reminded himself again.

Pappy turned around. "I guess we'll find out."

14

THE BRIDGE of the *Boyington* was abnormally quiet, with an air of suppressed excitement. It wasn't toward home, but it was movement. Boldly going.

The geeks had been working on the computations, which were complicated by the amount of the debris littering this section of the system. The head geek believed that the debris was a result of the erratic wormhole. There may have been planets in this sector that were destroyed by incoming rocks. Or the junk had just been tossed in and left. Or the wormhole chewed up planets. Whatever the reason for the debris field, it did discourage one from wanting to linger.

The planned hop would take them just outside the debris field—and hopefully out of range of the next wormhole incursion. While the idea of a wormhole taking them back where they started was appealing, the reality is that it could take them even further afield. Or drop them back in the middle of a pitched battle with the pirates.

Play the hand you're given, not the hand you wish you had.

Coop wasn't a big poker player, but he hung with guys who

were. The clock was ticking down to the hand they had. They'd jump in sixty seconds. He glanced at Arian, sitting at an unused station at the back of the bridge.

Pappy had invited her and the dragon to the bridge for the hop. Only Arian had accepted, so he'd stationed a couple of geeks down there to observe and report. A wise precaution, according to the dragon.

So far the only real good news was that there'd been no pirate sightings.

Yet.

The clock ticked down, the numbers called out only when they reached a ten count. It felt both fast and slow.

Five...

Four...

Three...

Two...

One...

The *Boyington* gathered herself up and in, the hyperdrive kicking on, though it felt like it tossed her forward—

The short hops were different in a big ship, but he still felt that from-the-belly-button jerk forward, and then the slam back. Sometimes people left their cookies on the deck after a short hop. And some of the long ones. Depended on the stomach in question.

"How did we do?" Pappy's voice was the calm force that pulled his people out of the moment of disorientation.

Reports came from the various stations. So far so good.

Coop cast a discreet look around. No one had barfed. He took a couple of breaths, and his stomach settled back down. Arian looked a bit wide-eyed—which would have surprised him before she'd admitted to being a farmer.

A farmer.

That was harder to believe than her claim to be a pilot. She did not look like a farmer. Of course, he wasn't sure what he thought she looked like—other than a woman. She glanced up and managed to smile.

"Your stomach will settle down in a minute," he said, with a grin. His gut gave a warning kick. He stiffened. "Something's wrong—"

She gripped the sides of her seat. "We are being scanned."

Coop swiveled around and saw the rim of green light tracking across the bridge. As it came toward them, it didn't look like it was knocking anyone out or anything, but he still braced for it...

It passed him like a puff of pressurized air, and then moved on, exiting out the other side of the ship.

He glanced down. Looked like all of him was still there.

"Find the source of that scan," Pappy ordered his calm voice cutting across the babble.

"It came from off your port bow," Arian said.

"What?" Pappy swiveled to face her.

"Approximately point oh-oh-oh-five light years."

Pappy turned back to his view screen, and as if the ship that had scanned them had been waiting for them to notice, it dropped its cloak. And then three more ships dropped their cloaks.

They were surrounded.

———

The good news? None of the ships had opened fire.

The bad news? Just because they hadn't, didn't mean they wouldn't.

"Assessments?" Pappy's calm voice once again cut across the babble and consternation. "Recommendations? Tactical?"

"Recommend we raise shields, sir."

"That could be taken as a hostile act," someone else objected. A mild argument arose as crew members took sides.

"They'll be studying the data acquired during their scan," someone else said.

"And then what?"

"They aren't scared of us," Coop said, "or they'd already be shooting." But they had arrived prepared to engage them. If their scan data was correct, all four ships were heavily armed. Four to one told him maybe if they weren't aggressive by policy, they'd had problems in the past with visitors who were. How often did the wormhole dump ships here, he wondered? And how had the *Boyington's* scans missed these big ass ships? "They sure are pretty," he murmured.

Each of the ships was about two-thirds the size of the *Boyington* with the sweet lines of a yacht or a sloop. The skin color was a bit odd. There was a side argument going on about whether they were out and out pink or more in the gold range of pink. Other than the whole pink thing, they looked to be four sweet rides.

"They are attempting to open a communications channel with us," a tech said, the words cutting through the arguments. All eyes turned to Pappy.

"Open a channel," Pappy ordered.

Attention turned toward the video screen, but it stayed blank. A restless stir flowed around the bridge. Coop glanced back at Arian. She hadn't moved. He walked back and sat down near her.

"You okay?"

Her head turned slowly toward him, and she blinked, like someone waking up from something.

"Arian?" He touched her arm. "Are you all right?"

She blinked again and nodded, looking around as if she weren't sure where she was.

"Did something happen to you?" What if she was possessed by the other aliens or something? How would they know?

"That was very strange," she admitted, a frown furrowing her brow.

"What's strange?" He glanced at Pappy, wondering if he should give him a heads up, but he was a bit busy right now.

"Rhubreak was attempting to do as you ask, to talk to them."

"And?"

She pressed her fingers into her temples. "So many sounds."

"Sounds? Not words?"

She nodded. "But..."

"What?"

"Hearing them, it was almost as if..."

"As if?" he prompted when she stopped.

"I remembered..." She sighed and shook her head. "But it is gone." She lifted troubled eyes to meet his gaze. "How can I remember something that did not, that could not happen, where I lived?"

"You're sure it is a memory?"

"No. It was indistinct and...incomplete, like a dream." She frowned. "It is very frustrating."

She is valuable, the dragon had said. Was this a clue to why? Or just some new weird to go with the old weird of boldly going somewhere they hadn't planned? She stiffened and glanced uneasily at Pappy. "Rhubreak believes he has translated their message."

"Really?"

"It was very short."

"What did they say?" Coop asked, forgetting he should be speaking with Pappy about now.

"They want to know our intentions."

———

Coop had a simple answer for the aliens. They were here because of a Charlie Foxtrot. He didn't know how to translate that into diplomatic speak. Good thing that wasn't his job.

At least, for now, the aliens were being patient. They'd sent their question, and it was up to them to serve a response.

In bird.

Or something like bird. At least, that's what it had sounded like when it came through the comm. Twitterings or squeaking. Not something the humans on the *Boyington* spoke.

It was a good day to not be in charge. When Pappy ordered him to take Arian into the ready room, Coop was happy to comply. He steered her to a seat facing Pappy's desk and sat down next to her. She hadn't gone statue on him, but she was pale, her gaze troubled.

He hesitated, then reached over and took her hand. It was icy cold, so he tried to massage in some warmth. After a few minutes, he realized he was exploring her hand like it was a new world. Maybe it was. He turned her palm up, wondering what a palm reader would learn from the lines there. Her fingers were long, the tan fading from her soft skin. Something twitched at the back of his mind, and he felt sympathy for her memory struggles. But even that faded fast as his fingers stroked across her palm and her skin quivered. He'd seen these hands touch metal, fingers spreading as she learned the machines.

Now her hands turned palm to palm with his. What was she learning now? Did she feel his heart speeding up? His breath shallowing? The heat stirring in him? Her hands warmed, and color crept into her face as her lashes lifted, her gaze connecting with his.

He couldn't help what his other hand did. Touching her chin, then her cheeks, the fingers spearing into her silken hair. Her pupils dilated, and her free hand lifted, one finger tracing his mouth. The wonder in her eyes turned heat into fire under his skin.

"Why do your people touch lips together?" Her lips parted, and a pink tongue tracked the edges.

He blinked, trying to clear his vision. *Pappy's ready room, Banshee.* He repeated the words, but they didn't have much meaning as his blood flow changed directions, leaving his brain seriously deficient.

"We..." his voice had a husky edge, "call it kissing. Don't your people...when things get...intimate..." He stopped. Her utter innocence was terrifying. And a total turn on. What kind of sick bastard did that make him? She started to lower her hand, but he caught it, held it against his chest, trying to think through the fog.

"I do not know," she admitted. "I was scheduled to pact bond, but I left with Rhubreak the night before the ceremony."

"Pact bond?" He watched her lips form words, was sort of aware of the words, but was mostly wondered if she'd liked it when he'd kissed her by the core and if he could do it again. So wrong, especially in Pappy's space, but it was the first time they'd been alone since the last, far too brief kiss.

"When we reach the age of accountability, we are pact bonded to a suitable male."

"Suitable? Who decides that?" That helped cool the heat some. Not much, but some. He realized his hand was stroking the back of her neck...

"The Consortium controls everything."

"The government picks who you...marry?"

A small frown formed between her brows, but the hand he held turned to feel his heartbeat. "I do not know what is marry, but we live with them, have offspring together."

"You can't say no?" Repulsed was a jets cooler.

She considered this question. "They said we had a choice, but only males seemed to have it." Her lashes lowered, fanning across her pale cheeks. Then she looked at him. "The night Rhubreak came, I was out in the dark trying to...reconcile myself to the loss of privacy."

"Privacy?" Crap, how innocent was she?

Now she smiled, though it was not a happy smile.

"I know that...more than privacy was at stake. I have observed animals coupling. I needed not to think about that or I would have turned myself into the healers and let them erase who I was."

"Erase?" His voice got grim. His gaze might have been, too, because she looked worried. He made himself smile. "What was his name?" Her brows arched. "The guy that made you want to get your thinking rearranged?"

"Oh." A slight shudder shook her. "He was called Trajan Bester." She frowned.

"What?"

"If I had not known it was impossible, I'd have said he was not of Bosakli, but he must have been to be considered for the ceremony."

"Arian?" She looked at him. "Trust your gut."

"You think I was right to distrust him?"

"Yes." And not just because Coop wanted...to kiss her. All over. He freed one hand to rub his face. *Pappy's space*, he repeated to himself several times. She still looked a bit anxious and somewhere-else.

"Arian?" He called her back again. "You left. You won't have to see him again." His grandma would have called him out for that. Would have told him to never say never, because that removed the never. Created bad vibes. But this was outer space. You couldn't just accidentally run into a jerk tooling around.

Still wished he had some salt to throw over his shoulder. Or some wood to knock on.

He turned her face toward his and smiled. "Kinda crazy that being lost in space with us, and surrounded by some possibly hostile ships, looks better than what you left behind." Certainly put in perspective why she climbed on a ship with a dragon. Didn't explain the dragon, though.

"Arian, are you sure his motives are...okay?" Almost without thinking, he lifted her hand and pressed his lips to skin that was softer than he'd have thought a farmer's hand would be. He meant to lower her hand, but he couldn't. The taste of her skin was unexpectedly sweet. And the look in her eyes...

She licked her lips, her gaze focused on his mouth. "Who?"

"Um..." He forgot the question, instead he tugged her up with him and pulled her into his arms. Nothing seemed to matter but that. He'd been waiting forever for this, for her. She didn't resist. Might have tried to help. Her chin lifted in an unconscious invitation that it would be rude not to accept...

She kissed better than the last time. But he already knew she was a fast learner. And yeah, the girl knew how to use her hands. Her head fell back naturally as he traced a path along her jaw and found the tender skin where a pulse beat wildly, let his mouth linger there until her hand tugged him up so their mouths could meet again...

He gathered her closer, inhaling her, tasting her, teaching and learning...

Some survival instinct or just his gut kicking pushed them apart. She stared at him, her lips plumped and pink, her gaze dazed.

"Someone's coming." By the time trouble got here, he might even remember their names...

Color flooded her face, and she turned away from the door,

her shoulders rising and falling. Coop pulled up every ice cold memory he could. It helped to remember where he was and who was probably incoming. He gave himself a shake and turned to face the door just as it swished open.

Pappy stalked in. That's right. Pappy. The Big Boss of the *Boyington*. Lucky for them, he was deep in a scowl and didn't notice the tension in the room. He rounded the desk, went to sit down, and realized they were there. For a minute, Coop thought he was going to order them out. His gaze tracked between them for what felt like a long time. Coop used the moment Pappy was looking at Arian to sneak a look, too. She'd pulled herself together pretty well.

With something between a grunt and sigh, he gestured at the chairs and dropped in his, leaning back to rub his face. He lowered his hand and looked at Arian again.

"Apparently they are...willing to host a small delegation on their planet. The impression your...dragon has is that we'd be wise to be willing to be hosted. If your...if he is translating correctly. He thinks they said something about dinner." His gaze traveled between them. "He's not sure if the invitation is to eat dinner. Or be dinner."

Arian's eyes widened.

He relented some. "If they wanted to eat us, they wouldn't have to invite us down. Four ships? We couldn't hold them off for long. Since your lizard is the only one who can talk to them, he's on the team."

"He will need a voice, Colonel," Arian said.

She was back in pragmatic.

"I can be that voice," Coop protested. Pappy arched a brow. "I wouldn't ad lib, sir." Much.

"I'll need a pilot, Captain."

He was better at flying than talking. "Yes, sir."

"I can't order you to go," Pappy said.

"You do not need to order me." Arian hesitated. "I am not one of your people, but I wish—to help."

For the first time, Pappy's gaze softened as he looked at her. He nodded. "Thank you."

15

ARIAN STUDIED her image in the reflective surface affixed to the wall. Bosakli did not have many of these surfaces, so she had never seen herself with such specificity before. It was somewhat unnerving. The device was about as merciful as an Enforcer. She tipped her head to one side, then the other. A thin face. Unevenly cut brown hair. Her eyes looked too big for her face and sad. She tried a smile. That helped some, but the eyes. Is that what Coop—

At the thought of him, the eyes brightened. Other than leaving Bosakli, his kisses were the most pleasing thing she'd experienced. No wonder her eyes looked sad.

She touched her lips, traced the outline, remembering. Color flowed under her skin and the lips curved under her finger. The eyes turned dreamy. Curiosity had been satisfied, so why did she feel not satisfied? It became difficult to look at herself when longing replaced dreamy in her eyes.

If she could see this, surely others could? Could they tell that she had been kissed? Did her mouth look different? How could she know when she had not seen it before? She tried straightening her lips, but as soon as she relaxed, they curved up again.

It had been so very...wild and terrifying and yet she'd felt safe in his arms. The scent of him reminded her of the land after rain. Fresh and earthy and...pleasing. Unlike the first time, this time his touch, his mouth moving on hers was more familiar, increasing her pleasure. His heart had pounded so hard. A contrast to the gentle, teasing exploration. He'd invited her to enjoy, to relax, and when she had, she had been rewarded.

When mouth against mouth had not been enough, her hands had touched him, explored where she could reach. Strong shoulders, powerful neck, and skin. She touched her neck. His skin was not like her skin. Her hands had crept into his hair, crisp at the base of the neck, and soft and thick past his ears. She'd used touch to fix engines, but this was...different touching. Very different. She'd not felt this longing for any of the men who'd come to look, had not felt it for any of the other men she'd met on this ship.

It seemed she felt this only for Coop. Did he feel this for her? Would he want to kiss her again?

What did he see when he looked at her?

She touched her hair, fingering the strands. The women on this ship arranged theirs in so many different ways. In the movie, the woman had talked about a "bad hair day." What did that mean? She had always had the same hair day, as far as she knew, though now she noticed the ends were not as even as those of the other women. Her grandmother had tried to keep Arian's hair the regulation length, but even the Enforcers could not make hair grow evenly.

Now she touched her cheek. The color had faded again. The woman in the video had put something on her cheeks so that color remained. And her clothes were bright and well fitting.

Color, her grandmother used to say, was for nature, not for people. At first, she'd thought these people were the same, but when they stood down from their tasks, their clothes got brighter and more individual. She studied the uniform she'd been provided. It was not bright and colorful. But she preferred it to her her overalls.

The undershirt was soft and comfortable, the trousers and jacket were sturdy and did not obstruct movement. But most important, these clothes helped her look like one of them. She shook her head at herself. Still, you want to blend in, she told her reflection. This time it was not to be safe but to belong. To feel less alien. Which rather ironic, in that they were venturing out to meet...aliens. She sighed. She did not wish to be eaten by alien birds, but it was still a better fate than pact bonding with, well, with anyone. And her mind, her thoughts would be her own until she died.

She knew this did not fully explain why she'd agreed to do this mission with them. It was not because of a kiss or even the clothes, though she could not deny they were a factor.

She wanted to be with Coop.

There she had thought it, admitted it to herself. Around him, she felt like more than her past. These reasons were not enough, but it did not matter. Doing this felt more right than all the reasons the Consortium had given them for spending their lives in service. And these people had not used the word "serve." They had asked for her help. They hadn't demanded or expected it.

She chose to do this.

Her chin up, she picked up the matching cap and positioned it on her head, studying the effect. She made a small adjustment, trying to mimic the way the others wore theirs. Satisfied, she gathered her things from the shelf over the sinks and left this place they'd called a head. Though truly, it looked more of a backside place, if the line of sanitation stations were any indication. Outside, her escort waited.

"I can take those to your ship for you, ma'am," the woman said, holding out her arms.

Arian resisted the urge to tell her to lose them. If she'd had anything else to wear, she would have already pitched them into outer space. Instead, she managed a smile. "Thank you." She looked uncertainly around.

"I'll escort you to shuttle bay four, ma'am."

The woman tucked Arian's bundle under her arm and gestured down the hallway.

This was a different part of the *Boyington,* though it did not look that different from the areas where she'd been. So she studied the people who passed them instead. Now that she was dressed as they were, they appeared not to notice her. If they still felt fear over the situation, it had found another focus than the alien among them.

She looked closer, noting that they did not look as afraid as they had just after the incident with the anomaly. They moved with purpose through the ship's corridors. Purpose and something more? It was another attribute sadly missing on Bosakli, and not fully understood.

Bravery.

They appeared brave. And resolute. United in...purpose?

The Consortium claimed they had achieved perfect unity, but they lied. Unity was only a strength when people did not fear one another, when they had a common purpose when it was by choice. She had a choice, she realized, a real choice this time, to embrace this way that felt better, even though still imperfectly understood, or to stay shackled by her past. Deep inside her, something stirred—the something that had kept her fighting assimilation, she wondered?

It was possible, but it felt like more than that. There was remembering or the beginning of remembering. Bosakli was fading, becoming almost indistinct and out of focus. What was replacing it was also out of focus, but she was changing from the inside out. Right now they were almost superimposed on each other, but this "other, " the someone she'd truly been meant to be, was emerging from the shadows.

No lights showed on her skin, but she felt them inside her. Perhaps they were not real, but her mind creating a symbol for how she felt? Her worry was that others would see them faded some. Now she studied the women that passed and then her guide, watching how they moved. They knew who and what they were, and it showed. She tried to mimic their movement and the way they held their heads. Her guide glanced at Arian, her eyes widening. Arian smiled uneasily, but all she said was, "We're almost there, ma'am."

"Thank you." Arian hesitated, then could not help herself. "May I ask you a personal question?"

The woman hesitated. "Of course, ma'am." Her tone was polite but wary.

Arian glanced around to make sure they were alone, then lowered her voice. "How do you signal to a male, a man that you wish to be kissed?"

The woman grinned. "Just pucker up, ma'am. Hard part is to get them to stop."

"Oh." Arian considered this. She had not wanted Coop to stop, but he had. Had he sensed the Colonel approaching? But if a man would kiss any woman he was alone with... "So it is not something special when he kisses you?"

Now the woman seemed to really look at her. She was quiet for a few seconds. "It can be. When two people truly care about each other, kissing can be more...intimate than sex."

"How do you know which it is?"

Her guide blinked several times, then grinned. "Well, if you ask them where they think the relationship is going and they don't run away, that's a good sign."

"In the movie, they spoke words of affection," Arian said.

"That's a movie, it's like made up. You know that right?"

Arian nodded. Coop had explained that all the people were actors pretending to be the real people in a story written by someone else.

Her guide's brow creased in worry. "Sometimes guys will say things so they can, well..."

"Couple with you?"

Her face turned quite red, but she nodded. "Yes, ma'am. We call it sex. Or making love."

Arian filed this away for further consideration. "How do you know the difference?"

This appeared to be a most difficult question because the crease in her forehead deepened.

"Well, you..sometimes you don't know. You find out when they leave." Her eyes turned sad. "Or when they don't leave." Now her mouth curved in smile and her eyes softened as if she saw something—someone?—not there with them.

She'd been hurt. Arian sensed this from her, but she was better now. "I see." Or thought she did. She'd wondered what power Coop might have to damage her. This might be that power.

"They say love is a leap, ma'am. You don't know how it's going to end until you jump."

She would not have understood this analogy before climbing down the power core. There had not been much up in her life until now. "You take the risk, or you don't," Arian said thoughtfully.

"Well," her guide looked wry now, "sometimes you do it because you can't help it. Attraction can be a bitch."

The guide smiled, so Arian smiled back, sensing this was a mild joke.

"If your gut is telling you to run? Then do it, ma'am. It will hurt but not as much as if he walks away."

Arian placed a hand over her gut. It had told her to flee Trajan Bester, she recalled, but it was not telling her to flee Coop. Mostly it was tight from worry about the birds. And getting eaten.

"You have given me much to ponder." Not that she needed anymore, but she did desire to be kissed again. If all she had to do was pucker up, that did not seem so hard.

"Good luck, ma'am."

"Thank you." Arian filed this word away for later, too.

They stopped at a large hatch, with—she'd learned—the symbol called four painted on it. Her guide swiped her card, the hatch rumbled back. Her guide indicated Arian should enter, curiosity in her eyes.

"I believe the Captain is already here, ma'am."

"Thank you for your assistance. And advice."

"You're welcome, ma'am." The guide hesitated. "If love works with a guy, it's worth the risk."

And if it didn't work? Arian wanted to ask. Was it still worth the risk?

The door slid closed between them, but she would not have asked this anyway. Her guide could speak only for herself. And, Arian suspected, it was an answer that would depend on where one was in the leap. She tried pursing her lips a couple of times, then turned to seek Coop, but stopped in her tracks at the sight of the shuttle on the exit ramp. Her breath stopped in her chest, sound roared through her ears.

She knew this ship, knew it better than the one that had brought her here. She forgot her military stance, forgot everything as she drifted up for a closer look. She hesitated, but could not resist touching. Her fingers spread, meeting only slight resistance from the somewhat abrasive surface.

It was not beautiful. It had been designed for function. And to look less than it was. She walked along the side, dragging her hand along the surface. It was, how did Coop say it, what was under the hood where the good stuff happened.

This was not whispering. This was not learning from the machine.

She did not need to learn what she already knew.

The wonder of how floated into her head, but she did not have time or patience for how or when. She belonged to it, and it belonged to her. She turned so that both hands rested on its side, closed her eyes, and mentally went inside. It was big—in the mid-range of shuttle craft. It had a large upper deck with nicer fixtures and wide view screens. Seating for thirty people, as well as a service unit at the rear. Below the executive deck was a smaller passenger area that was part of the flight deck. The entrance to this area was by a ramp that lowered, much like the ship that had collected her. A hatch could be closed off from the cockpit.

She inhaled, her nostrils filled with the memory of metal and materials. Remembered it...new and fresh. Her breath caught on another, deeper scent. What...the sea. She sucked it in, knew it thought she had only caught a glimpse of an ocean as they left Bosakli's atmosphere. It was her first and last sighting that she knew of. But that did not matter. With her eyes closed, she felt sand between her toes, the salt tang mixed with the damp air, heard the gentle lapping of the waves, and wind whispering across her skin and tugging at her hair...

In her mind, she turned from the sea and walked up the shuttle's ramp. On the flight deck, there were benches and seats, storage compartments for ten to twelve passengers. There were also two science stations, but the co-pilots position could also do the functions of navigation and weapons control. At the front, in the blunt nose, were positions for the pilot and copilot. A wide-view screen took up the top half of the cockpit with banks of controls in front and along the sides. She felt the hum as the engine fired. Her hands flexed, working those controls. She'd flown this ship and next to her—

"Arian?" Footsteps clattered on the ramp.

Arian dropped her hands and turned as Coop jumped from ramp to deck. Pucker. She'd planned to pucker, but she could scarcely breathe, let alone pucker up.

"You okay?" There was concern in his voice, but he did not move closer.

He glanced up, and she realized the bay was most likely monitored. A good thing she had not puckered for him. What had they thought of her touching this ship?

Her cheeks warmed. She looked at the ship instead of at him. "I am well," she said. "It looks a most serviceable craft." She touched the side, but lightly this time.

"She's not a *Dauntless,* but she'll get us where we want to go."

She could do more than that, Arian thought, amused. "I am sure she will." She flashed a smile at him, inviting him in on the faint joke of calling this shuttle a *she.* He gave her a quick grin.

"The Colonel isn't thrilled about us using it for this mission, but, well, it's his call."

Arian looked at him, wondering what he had chosen not to say. "If the meeting does not go well, then it could be lost." It amazed her how calm she sounded, how calm she felt. Somehow she knew she'd faced death before. She did not fear what she'd already—she refused to finish this thought. It was a field too far.

"Yeah," Coop agreed, his gaze still on the craft.

Despite his agreement, she did not think this was the reason for the Colonel's reluctance. He was most likely concerned about the technology that might be lost. How had they secured this craft? She might not know where or how she had encountered this ship, but she knew it was not here, that these people had not been around. The sea...in her mind she saw the waves and hovering above it were two moons...

She took a breath to steady her thoughts and asked, "How does she handle?" adding to herself, *for you?*

"She's a bus, not a fighter."

She opened her mouth to protest this, then closed it again. She could not explain how she knew this was not so. And she did not *know.* She only felt she knew. For several seconds, disorientation threatened, her brain grappling with what was true and what was not. Both realities went once more out of focus...

"You ready to roll?" Coop asked.

His voice called her back from the edge. Thankful he had not noticed, she followed him up the ramp, stopping just inside. She needed to be here, to be now. She needed to keep her promise.

It was as she...remembered. Even the colors were the same. The spiral threatened again. She took a steadying breath. "Where do you wish me to seat myself?" She badly needed to sit down. She avoided looking at the cockpit, her fingers curling into her palms at the sight of controls she *knew.* She felt the controls, felt the pressure required to manipulate them, knew how this ship would respond...

She couldn't look at the co-pilot's station, not here and now. If she saw...her mind would splinter...

"Rhubreak seems to think you should plant yourself here at the rear station," Coop said, gesturing to the front seat on the left, just behind the cockpit.

The alien course corrections will need to be translated.

Arian saw her dragon now, in the seat next to the one Coop wished her to take. She had no sense that he'd heard her thoughts or seen her lapse into that other place. But she avoided looking at him as she slipped past him and sank into the seat.

Her fingers shook when she uncurled them and placed them on the controls. She did not allow herself to actually push anything. Not yet. The one thing she had learned on Bosakli was patience.

She took two calming breaths before asking, "Will there be others on the mission?"

"Yeah. Where are they?" Coop checked through his headset, as he headed toward the cockpit, dropping into the pilot's position. "They're incoming. Gonna fire her up."

Outside there was the sound of voices, footsteps approaching as the engines began to hum up through the soles of her borrowed boots. She pulled her hands back and shifted so she could observe who entered.

Of course, Dr. Derwent was their first contact expert. She smiled a little at the memory of his first contact efforts. Perhaps it was because he'd not been the first to have contact with her that it had not gone well. Dr. Gessner...it took her a minute to pull up his name. He'd visited her ship a couple of times. Had seemed more interested in Rhubreak than the technology, she recalled. Two soldiers behind them—too similar in aspect and build for her to tell them apart—and Tiger, Coop's wingman. He slanted a grin her direction, tapped a finger against his temple in a small salute, before joining Coop. It was almost a relief when he dropped into the co-pilot's seat. The...apparition she could not quite see vanished like smoke. Why did she fear and long to see the face in her memory?

Both doctors stopped, looking irresolute, in the center aisle. Were they troubled that she and Rhubreak were going?

"Park it, docs," Tiger said.

When they didn't, he tapped on Coop's arm. He turned, glanced from the doctors to Arian and said, "Arian needs to translate the instructions from the birds."

Ah, so it was the position they coveted. She could not blame them. She was the stranger, the alien among them.

Neither looked happy, but they did settle into the seats across from her. Dr. Gessner gripped his knees as if he needed a place for his hands if he could not have the controls. The two soldiers took seats behind the doctors, and the hatch began to close. As it sealed, low lighting came on along the floor and at seat height.

"Strap in, people," Coop said. He tapped communications. "Home plate, this is Alpha flight ready and waiting for the aliens to transmit course data."

Arian pulled the straps across her chest and secured them in the lock. These would hold much better than the ones that had failed on her ship. Only when she was secure did she allow herself to activate her station, her first action, opening a communications channel so they could receive transit instructions from the aliens. Then, with a careful glance sideways to make sure she was unobserved, she started exploring the ship's memory and databanks.

Of course, she remembered those weapons, and there was cloaking technology. She studied the settings. They'd found that the cloak could do more than just hide the ship. It could also project a weapons-free profile. It would not have much of a chance against the four ships out there, but the element of surprise could give the *Boyington* time. That was just in the first and second layers. She dived deeper, but could see no sign that they had reached this level of penetration into the systems. That was interesting. While the time and date stamps were not familiar, there were many of them.

As she explored, part of her was amazed at how natural it felt, how familiar. She knew this ship, but did *she* know this ship? Could there be a record of her somewhere in its memory banks? Did she know what this record would look like?

She flexed her hands, turning them over for study. Her hands had always been her conduit to knowledge. She'd used them to breach Consortium databanks while in her learning environment. Had hacked in to adjust her personal data when at various times. Had used them to learn machines...but she'd not used them to find herself. And if she did? What then? What would it mean? The timing was off. She needed to focus on the mission, but what if this was her only chance?

Longing and obligation waged a brief, almost bitter battle inside her head but before a winner could be declared, her screen flashed a warning of an incoming message. She firewalled the message and began to decode it with Rhubreak's assistance. There was regret, but there was also relief. Perhaps it was better not to know...

"We have our transit data from the aliens," she said, "I am sending it to your station, Captain."

"We have our transit instructions, home plate," Coop said into his radio. "Are we go, or no-go?"

"Alpha flight, you have a go. I repeat the mission is a go," a voice intoned over the intercom.

Tiger grinned. "Kick the tires and light the fires, Banshee. Let's go meet us some aliens."

16

THE SHUTTLE ROSE, then Coop accelerated through the containment shield and into deep space. Once clear of the *Boyington*, he banked for their intercept with the small flotilla of alien craft that would escort them to the planet. Wasn't in his *Dauntless*, but flying was flying, and at least it wasn't a sim.

Their course threaded them through an area between two of the big mothers positioned around the *Boyington*. His gut twitched like Derwent's eye was twitching right now, but nothing he could do about it. His job was to fly right and not talk unless absolutely necessary. Couldn't say Pappy didn't know him. Their scans claimed the alien ships were smaller than the *Boyington*, but from where he sat, these two looked plenty big enough to swat the shuttle into next week without much trouble. Times four, the ships would give the *Boyington* some trouble, too, if the aliens decided to bump heads with them.

He steered the shuttle along the length of the two big ships, noting what were probably weapons ports. All the ships were, according to scans, heavily armed. Tiger gave a low whistle but didn't say anything, his attention on making sure they stayed on course and could respond if they suddenly came under attack.

As they tracked along, he wondered about the ships and the neighborhood? Just how dangerous was it? Did they need the big ships or did they like having them? Civilizations didn't necessarily stop when they had enough weapons. There was always that impulse to do it better and better.

Might not be about the normal galactic neighborhood. Could be the wormhole. How often did it drop ships into the system? Based on the pirates that had been shooting at them, probably a good idea to keep a fleet positioned here. But where were the space going activities—if there was enough traffic to justify four big ships? Sure as hotel hadn't been any sign of anything around the planets.

He might have tensed a bit until they pulled clear of the big ships. He glanced up, using the rear viewer to check their passengers for signs of stress. Pity they couldn't have brought more Marines since it looked like the mission was going dirtside. Not Pappy's fault. The aliens had limited the delegation numbers. Sucked to be in the coyote position, howling at the out-of-reach moon—or for their home system. So eight people max and only five allowed to leave when they were alien planet dirt side.

Tiger, his co-pilot, and the Marines would remain onboard, but with their radios on box, so that Tiger could monitor the meeting. Assuming that was possible. Aliens could have blocking technology. Their cloaking tech was FM—f-ing magic —which meant a whole lotta unknown going into this meet with, hopefully, their new best friends.

So who did get to leave the ship? Derwent was the first contact dude, a role that was also turning out to be the hot seat. Gessner was the closest they had to a bird expert. Coop wouldn't call either man excited at this opportunity to excel. If Gessner gripped his knees any harder, he wouldn't be able to stand up when the time came.

He studied his two Marines. Big, square, tough, and had probably forgotten how to have expressions. Wished they could be at their back when the time came. At least they'd be in on the extraction if things went south. Assuming there was anything to extract.

The dragon? No way to tell if he was fazed by the upcoming meeting. He always looked the same. Right now he looked asleep.

Arian. As glad as he was to have eyes on her—and he wished that included lips on her—he would have been happier if she missed this party. Strong odds it was gonna be a Charlie Foxtrot with all of them playing the part of red shirt.

Pappy, well, he hadn't been happy about sending any of them. But they needed this meet, needed these aliens way more than the aliens needed them. Which was not at all. Unless it was as an entrée.

He'd have left Tiger on mother, too, if he could have. He'd never been able to shake him off, he thought with a grin. This wasn't his first rodeo as Coop's wing man, he just hoped it wouldn't be their last.

He half shook his head. They were an odd group. The geeks, the soldiers, and the dragon. He studied Arian again. Which group did she belong to? In ABU's she looked like a soldier, but her expression was all geek. Either way, she'd fit in until she started talking bird, assuming that she got the chance to talk.

His gut was tight, but not twitching. Just uneasy like.

The dragon, well, he didn't seem to be a geek, just the odd dragon out. Another check for the weird box on this mission, and he didn't mind admitting his fun meter was fully pegged.

The dangerously interesting Doc Clementyne had once told him it was her mantra in life to expect the unexpected. Had she expected to end up married to an alien—a Garradian? And what would she think of this setup? Wouldn't have minded having her along for this one, just because she was known for pulling the impossible out of her back pocket. They could use an expert in impossible right now.

He activated his comm. "Home plate, this is Alpha Flight. I have eyes on our escort. Will update when we have contact."

"God speed, Alpha Flight." It was Pappy's calm voice over the com.

For some reason, that made him think about the look on the old man's face when he asked the dragon if he could speak "bird." That would go under the heading of things he never thought he'd hear from his CO.

It was unusual for me, as well.

He glanced at the rear view camera in time to see Arian's lips twitch, but she kept her gaze on the monitoring equipment. Coop shifted uneasily, wondering how much of his musing had been overheard by either of them?

I am, um, only looping her into information relevant to her tasks.

So we're talking—thinking—through you?

That is correct.

He wondered what the dragon was filtering out from Arian's end, then felt guilty about thinking it.

"How long until our intercept?" he asked.

"Thirty of your minutes," she said, after a pause.

"When we hookup, then what?" he asked, wondering why this hadn't come up before. "Do we all jump together?"

"According to them, we move too slow. They will give us an assist." Arian met his gaze in the mirror. Something was oddly reassuring in her gaze.

"An assist?" Derwent looked more alarmed, something Coop would have bet was not possible.

Arian looked at him. "They have a, well, they call it a jump sling. I believe. We'll ride in that. We should be planetside in under an earth hour if our translation is correct."

It is.

Dragon was getting a bit cocky. Hoped it wasn't over confidence. "Did they send a dinner menu?" All he got was a mental chuckle and a choke from Arian.

"No, but they did send an adjusted approach vector. Sending it to your station," she said.

Coop grinned. She was starting to sound military. He did like a girl in uniform. And hoped he'd get a chance to—he stopped the thought. Just in case she was listening.

"We're closing on our bogeys," Tiger said. "I mean our friendlies."

The HUD popped up, giving Coop a readout on their birds' specs. Birds being a spot on description. The ships looked like birds. If he had to pick one, it would be the gannet. He'd seen some dive bombing in Newfoundland. Not something a guy forgot. The aerodynamic sweep of the body and the wings were in the dive position. He felt the itch to try one out. Strung between the six ships was what appeared to be a golden net. The HUD read it as energy, not an actual net. Still looked like a net.

"I'm gonna make a wild guess that I'm supposed to fly into that?"

"That's both cool and some serious pucker factor," Tiger said.

"Begin deceleration maneuver now," Arian said. "Half speed," she added before he could ask. "Counting down to quarter speed...cut engines."

Coop felt the loss of momentum and didn't like it as they tracked toward the net. Now he knew how a fish felt. The nose of the shuttle made contact with the energy field. At first, it felt like nothing, then there was a jerk. Before reverse momentum became a problem, the energy net appeared to wrap around the shuttle.

"Brace for the jump," Arian said.

"Home plate, we have contact with our escort and are preparing for assisted hyperjump."

"Roger that, Alpha Flight. Good luck."

A bright flash of light. A yank that felt like it came from his belly button. And they were along for the ride.

17

THEY COULDN'T HAVE actual eyes on anything during a jump. Without the protective panel, the screen would shatter from the stress of even a brief hypertransit. So the shuttle's system rendered their view as a series of elongated gold lines flowing past, a view that made Coop feel a bit queasy. He glanced at the camera, checking on his passengers. The two geeks looked a bit green, the Marines stoic. Arian looked calm, her attention on her station. The dragon shifted position in the seat as if he was nervous.

Would that be so surprising?

Well, you haven't done a whole lot of expressing since we met, Coop pointed out. He'd assumed the dragon couldn't feel nervous.

My hide is rather resistant to expression. That does not mean I do not get nervous.

Sorry. He'd never been good at PC. Which was probably why Pappy had told him not to flap his lips with the aliens.

And yet here you are...

Coop hid a grin. *Technically not flapping anything.*

The dragon angled his head as if acknowledging the hit.

"How are we doing?" Coop asked Tiger.

"Fine so far. Structural integrity is well into acceptable range. Radiation levels are low. Cloak is holding at one hundred percent."

"Cloak?" Derwent straightened. "But..."

"Not that kind of cloak, doc," Coop reassured him. "They can see us. Just keeping a little something back in case things don't go well."

Derwent glanced around. "That's why we are using the Garradian shuttle. But—"

Tiger cut in, "If things go well, they'll never know. If they don't, you'll be glad we have it."

Talk about flapping lips. Had Derwent missed the memo about the top secret classification of all things Garradian? Coop gave him a look, and Derwent subsided with a look of chagrin.

The systems started pinging. "We're coming out of the jump." He tensed because, well, who knew what would be on the other side. "Be ready," he told Tiger, his voice pitched only for him.

"Roger that."

The golden lines widened, tightened, and then faded as they dropped into normal space. Their escort did not fade away. They formed a tight escort around them as if testing his piloting abilities. Momentum carried them forward, but he fired his engines in preparation for entering the planet's atmosphere.

"Sending planet approach vectors to your station," Arian said.

The data popped up on his screen. He wasn't thrilled about entering atmosphere this cozy with six ships—then the spread widened—the lead ship dropping enough, so Coop didn't end up tasting their tail feathers when everyone started braking maneuvers.

"Roger that." He adjusted course. The alien birds on either

side were still close, but the shuttle didn't seem to mind. She almost flew herself. "Which planet is this?" Coop asked Tiger.

Tiger tapped some stuff and got a HUD for his station with the in system planets' data. "It was designated Primary A," he said. "The big one."

That was good. Maybe they'd have resources to share.

"Lots of smaller planets we didn't see before," Tiger murmured.

"Habitable?"

"According to preliminary scans, about fifty percent of them are inhabited."

Both the docs shifted restlessly in their seats, craning to see the updated HUD.

"They are scanning us again," Arian said.

This time there wasn't a green line. This one was pink. He tensed. What would they see? And how would they react? It seemed to take a long time to track through the ship, front to back, only fading when there was no more ship left. The wait felt long, but it wasn't more than thirty seconds before Arian's station signaled an incoming message.

"Final approach instructions." She looked up as if she knew he could see her. "I guess we passed their test."

He keyed in the coordinates, adjusting the course himself, watching the clock ticking down for when he needed to fire re-entry engines. They hit the atmosphere and didn't bounce off. Could feel the little ship fighting its way through. In a smaller ship, it all felt more personal. Every time he did it, he had greater respect for the early astronauts who flew knowing pretty much jack about all this stuff.

Once more the computer 'helped' them out with a visual representation of what it looked like outside the ship—a fireball. Sweat popped out on his skin. "How is she handling the heat?"

"Like a champ," Tiger said. "Atmosphere is not that different from Earth, a little thicker maybe."

The HUD scrolled a readout of the various elements. He ignored it. All that mattered right now was how bad did the atmosphere want to keep them out, and could they breathe in it when they got there. Suddenly the resistance eased. The protective screen rolled back automatically as they broke through a bank of clouds on a low orbit. It felt good to have eyes on...a desolate looking nothing. "Are you sure those coordinates are right?"

"Verifying." After a pause. "They are correct. Initiating a scan—"

The shuttle jolted or shuddered as if it had passed through an energy barrier of some kind and suddenly there was a whole lot of something to see.

"Hot damn," Tiger said.

Coop couldn't argue with that. He frowned. That had felt a lot like passing through the Garradian outpost cloaking shield.

"Is that..." Derwent craned forward but was jerked back by his restraints. His hand went to the release.

"Don't even think about it, doc," Coop warned.

"Remarkable," Gessner breathed out.

It was that. The city—if that's what it was—looked like something straight out of a sci-fi flick. Rising from a sea of brown, there were a series of spires in varying heights and colors. The brown bore a strong resemblance to mud from up here. But pretty mud, which made his eye twitch. Some of the spires were connected in clusters, others stood alone. The atmosphere had a green tint, which was on the eerie side—just in case being on an unknown planet in an unknown star system wasn't unsettling enough. There was a lot to see, too much while he was driving, but he did catch a glimpse of a pink river winding through a canyon that he'd have liked to buzz. Still on the course he'd been told to fly, he started looking for a place to land. Everything looked rough or pointy. Didn't need a lot but they did need a solid stretch of flat. With each decrease in altitude, the ground looked less and less stable, almost like it was all swamp.

Skimming along just above the tallest of the towers, the only signs of life were patches of what could be plants in areas that might be bodies of water or at least low lying patches of water.

"Sending you the final approach coordinates," Arian said. "You should see a platform circled in green lights. We are requested to land there."

Or what? Like he didn't know that. Zapped out of the sky by an alien laser...beak.

"I see it." Coop lined them up and throttled back, bringing the shuttle in careful and slow. Didn't want his flying to piss them off before the talking—or chirping—started. Apparently, they liked green. And pink, don't forget the pink. The Gadi had liked pink, too, but they'd gotten over it when they bumped heads with the earth expedition a few times.

The shuttle passed through another protective shield of some kind—apparently, they'd been cleared to land or he had a feeling it would have fried them. He throttled back, making a perfect four-point landing in the circle, before cutting his engines. Take that, aliens. "What's it like outside, Tiger?"

"Looks good. Don't think hay fever is going to be a problem unless the flowers are out of sight. As long as we don't catch an alien bug, we should be golden."

"Our hosts say we won't need respirators," Arian said. "The air is particularly clean inside the enclosure."

"But shouldn't we protect them from us?" Derwent asked.

"They don't seem too worried," Coop pointed out. The last scan had been different. It could have decontaminated them. He just hoped it hadn't done anything else while they were passing through it. He did want to have kids some day.

Their front screen gave them a nice, almost unobstructed view of the city, or region. He studied the apparently lifeless scene. He'd kind of expected birds to be, well, flying around. Nothing out there or on this platform. He did a quick scan with the various exterior cameras. Nope. No welcoming—or unwelcoming—committee.

He glanced sideways at Tiger.

"Maybe E.T. is shy," Tiger suggested.

Lights flowed from the outer edge of the circle, making a path from their ship to a shadowy hatch opening in a wall where a spire reached toward the sky. Coop didn't like it. Could feel his shirt turning from camo to red. Unfortunately, the only other option was to leave. Or try to leave. They were here to talk, to hopefully get some help, and he had a feeling that now that they were here, inside this hidden city, leaving wasn't going to be that easy. The fly was well and truly in the web. Would the birds object to being compared to spiders? He didn't know, but he hoped these birds—if they ever showed their beaks—were vegetarians.

He unstrapped and got up, turning to face his team. No one looked too thrilled, except the Marines who just looked like Marines. And the dragon who couldn't emote.

Tiger opened his mouth, probably to object, but closed it again. "Watch your back, Banshee," he finally said.

"And you." Wasn't sure who had it the worst, those going to meet the aliens or those who had to wait and wonder. Coop activated the rear hatch. Thick, warm air rushed in. It didn't smell bad, but the hairs on the back of his neck rose. It was so alien. *D'oh.* "You're in charge, Tiger. Monitor events and if you suspect a Charlie Foxtrot, well, you know what to do." Tiger had been briefed by Pappy. Coop glanced at the two scientists. "Neither of you has to go if you don't want to. The aliens said we couldn't have more than five leave the ship. Didn't say five of us had to go." Pappy had told him to give them the out. And they looked like they could use it.

Both men visibly hesitated. This was not the "boldly going" they'd signed up for.

"If you'd like to make some observations from here, we'd all understand." He didn't say, if the aliens got nasty, they were probably all red shirts. The pucker factor was high on this op, no question.

"I..." Gessner teetered on the edge, then his mouth thinned to a straight line. "I'm coming." He almost managed to smile. "It is what I signed up for." He swallowed and fumbled his way upright.

Derwent got up without a yay or nay.

Coop turned to Arian and the dragon, wishing he could offer her—them—an out. Arian rose, her gaze calm, but not like the blank calm when they'd met the first time. This was different. Because he was a guy, he didn't know what made it different, but it made the hair on the back of his neck rise for a variety reasons. She settled into her version of the military stance. Dang, he'd like to plant one on her. For luck. And in case...

We are ready.

With some heat in his face from this reminder the dragon could hear him, Coop stalked toward the rear of the shuttle. He felt naked without something that could point and shoot. Not even a hidden knife tucked in his sock, in case the aliens could see down to his bones—why did that make him think about drumsticks?

"I'll go out first. Wait for, oh, a ten-count before you follow me."

Arian, who had followed him, now looked up at him, blinking slowly. "Why?"

He didn't know how to answer without freaking her and the docs out. "Because I asked?"

The smile was quick, the sly look from under half mast lashes stabbed him right in the heart.

"All right."

He looked at the docs but didn't say it. If the shooting started, they probably knew not to come out.

With a final nod to Tiger, he took a breath, reached for the P-90 that wasn't there, sighed and dropped his hands to his side. *Walk casual, but confident,* he told himself. Easier said than done. A fine line between the two, too fine for a flyboy. Not to mention, he'd always had trouble with thin lines. He gave his shoulders a shake, then started down. His footsteps sounded loud against the ramp in the eerie silence of the alien planet. Didn't feel natural on a planet that looked, well, natural instead of high tech.

At the bottom, he hesitated about stepping down onto alien soil, well, alien some kind of surface. Felt like he ought to say something profound, but the best line had been used. And what if he was stepping into a human sucking trap? He'd feel really stupid for turning a red shirt moment into something profound. Not to mention, he sucked at profound. And he'd seen way too many alien abduction movies.

One step for mankind, or dinner. What the hell. He jumped lightly onto the surface, landing with both feet. Didn't suck him into anything. It was solid, a little rough—kinda looked like that teapot his ex girlfriend had picked up in New Mexico, only flat. Because it was a platform and not a pot.

Maybe he should think of something else since he had a dragon in his thoughts.

The path of lights stretched toward the opening in a straight line from their rear hatch—which was kind of weird because he could have sworn it had appeared in front of the ship. He moved forward until he was clear of the shuttle and could draw fire if the aliens planned to shoot them.

Okay, didn't seem to be the plan. He looked around. View hadn't changed much, but he could see the four, well, they weren't corners, because the platform was round, but four positions, like guard stations. He couldn't see any guards or weapons, but he felt the cross-hairs of at least one alien ray gun on his chest.

He looked back at the shuttle, wondering now that it was too late, if Arian knew what a ten count was. Felt lame just standing here. He resisted the urge to kick something—since there wasn't anything to kick. Just platform and lines. He looked down. The temptation to step outside was almost overwhelming. Too bad Pappy knew Coop that well. His orders had been meticulously precise. Don't step out of line and don't screw this up by talking too much. He sighed and shoved his hands in his pockets, resisted the urge to whistle. The silence was really silent.

If it hadn't been for the tingle on the back of his neck, he might have enjoyed the view. This was what he'd thought it would be like standing on Mars, except for the structures. And the lighting. Okay, so maybe not that much like Mars but this was beyond Mars. Way beyond it.

There was the scrabble of claws against metal as Arian and her dragon came down the ramp. He turned and watched them approach, both of them rubber-necking.

"It is very..." her voice trailed off, she cleared her throat. "It's very high."

"You didn't do high on your planet?" She shook her head. "Then when you went down the shaft..."

"It was my first time at that as well," she confessed.

"If I'd known you were afraid of heights—" he rubbed the back of his neck.

"How could you know what I did not?"

A reasonable woman. Wow. He glanced back. Had Derwent and Gessner bailed on them? There was no reason for them to do a ten count. Just then Derwent peered out, then came down the ramp in a nervous stumble. After a brief pause, Gessner followed him.

"Point of no return."

Gessner stared past him, his jaw on the slack side, and finally shook his head. "I...no."

The whites of his eyes made him look a bit bug-eyed. If they really were meeting some birds, he might want to work on that. Coop cocked a brow at Derwent. He gave an uncertain nod. Then a more determined one.

"Let's do this then." Coop turned and led his motley crew toward the opening at the end of the green trail. The surface, whatever it was, muted most of the sound of their footsteps, except the click of the dragon claws. Coop's heart rate might have kicked up a bit. There was a faint hum coming from somewhere. Could swear he could hear all five of them breathing. Someone smacked their lips together. Could one hear their adrenaline rising? Felt like all of him was on high alert, for all the good that did him. He knew some hand-to-hand, but he was a flyboy, not an ass kicker.

The opening loomed larger the closer they got. It was big. And shadowy, or something more than shadowy. He couldn't see past the opening. A bit like looking into the fog. Another reminder of the Garradian outpost. The portals were kind of like this. The hairs on his arms rose.

Don't hesitate, Banshee. Just keep going. Yeah, the chips were gonna fall where they were gonna fall. Nothing was gonna change that now. His life didn't exactly flash before his eyes, but he was aware of a few things he wished he'd done. Needed to stop thinking about kissing, sooner rather than later, though what good it did to be on high alert when he didn't have a weapon...

The opening loomed and then he was in it. For a minute, he felt like he'd shifted sideways. When he shifted the other way, he staggered, then steadied. Realized he was on his feet and in a room. His gaze narrowed. Oh yeah, that was a lot like Garradian portal transport. Was gonna take a wild guess that they weren't anywhere near that arrival platform anymore. And possibly well out of radio signal range with Tiger.

His wingman wasn't going to like that.

Coop didn't like it.

Was it good that this place didn't look like the outposts? Looked and felt like his dentist's office. All that was missing were the chairs. And the elevator music. And Doc Payne in his surgical scrubs.

His other companions arrived in varying states of confusion. Arian had an expression he hadn't seen on her face before.

"I think we were transported to another place," he said.

She placed a hand on her stomach. "It was a bit unsettling."

"What do you mean, transported?" Derwent asked, showing the whites of his eyes now, too.

Coop opened his mouth to explain, then closed it. How to explain without saying Garradian? Had these two needed to know about portals? Before he could figure how to explain without explaining, a panel in the wall directly in front of them slid open.

18

THE TENSION ARIAN felt reminded her of waiting for an Enforcer examination, but this was not Bosakli. An Enforcer was not coming through the opening. An alien was. Which, for now, still seemed preferable to an Enforcer.

There was a stir in the shadows, a sort of flutter of wings. Did she think this because they believed these aliens were birds, or because wings had fluttered in there? She heard a scrape of something against the floor, and the first alien entered the room.

She felt her jaw slacken, tried to close it, and could not. She had thought it a mental adjustment to meet the non-human Rhubreak but this...

The alien was broad across the chest, perhaps two of her widths and taller even than Coop, who was the tallest of their group. Its body was clearly avian, with an aerodynamic curve from front to back. It was hard to be sure of its exact shape because it wore protective coverings on its head, chest, and legs. Protection also seemed to extend along its back and sides, but that protection—if that is what it was—had a different appearance, somewhat translucent, she decided, since it exposed the pattern of feathers. But it could be an illusion.

The long legs bent backward as it walked *toward* them. She stared. The way it walked made the gait an unusual mix of ungainly and graceful. Its neck made a long, gentle curve from head to body.

The head was also...very avian in shape but disconcerting to one who had never seen a bird of that size. Where it connected to the neck, it almost seemed an extension of that neck, but then it flowed into a narrow beak that made a substantial curve downward on the end, like a hook. This beak was pink where it connected to the head, but had a slash of dark dead center. Its eyes were dark beads in a circle of white.

Its head rose high as the arch of the neck lessened, and it looked down on them with an imperiousness that reminded her of...something. It did not look anything like the birds on Bosakli —in so many ways, she lacked time to list them. One difference she could not help but notice, was it's webbed feet splayed on the white stone floor.

Its feathers appeared to be white, but she could not be certain because of the protective elements. The chest and head protective gear glowed a faint green, but when the big bird moved, the color shifted to a pale gold. There was a seal affixed to the breastplate, that was too small to see, but she had a sense of knowing what it looked like—no, she could not go there. Not now. *Focus.*

The alien lifted its head even higher and studied each of them. If it blinked, she missed it.

"Fla..." Gessner coughed once and then tried again. "Flamingos?"

"I thought flamingoes were pink," Coop objected.

"Their color is determined by their diet," Gessner said, softly, but with much awe. He rolled forward on his feet as if he wanted to get a closer look. Coop grabbed his arm.

"Nope."

"Oh, right."

The...flamingo repositioned itself to one side of the opening, making way for another one to enter, one that appeared to be almost identical in appearance. This one took the position on the other side of the opening.

"Marines," Coop murmured.

The doctors gave him an odd look, but Arian understood the reference and almost smiled. They did indeed have the manner of an advance guard. More entered until three guards stood on each side in a line facing them, their aspect ceremonial, but also protective. There was a moment of silence, then the line of flamingoes let out chanting croaks, their wings flapping. Under the wings the feathers were white, but the tops flickered with little flashes of gold. If there was something protective on the wings, it was highly flexible in nature.

The flapping created a wind in the space, one that tugged at her cap, almost lifting it from her head. She grabbed the brim, holding it—and her ground, as the heavily scented air rushed past her face.

The sound was so loud, it hurt her ears, but to her relief, it stopped as abruptly as it had begun. In perfect synch, each bird lowered their necks until their beaks were aligned with the center of their chests. They all lifted the same leg off the floor, the angle of the bend the same height.

There was a long, not comfortable pause, then another stir in the opening and two more flamingoes entered.

These two were different in coloring, size, and gear. Their beaks were all black and their black, beady eyes were surrounded by crimson red. Blood red. Somewhat smaller than the guards, one was vibrantly pink along the back and wings, the other a softer pink with more gold and white mingling in its feathers. Both wore protective gear similar to the guards, but much more ornate. The pink flamingo's gear was predominantly black and gold, the other's red and gold. The seals on their breastplates were bigger but looked to be similar to the guards, though Arian could not be certain. Once again she felt that flash of a forgotten memory. It made no sense, but not much had since she lifted off from Bosakli, she thought a bit wryly.

These two new birds stopped just before becoming even with their guards, their heads lifting high for a long time, then slowing sinking in a move that had an element of ceremony to it. It could be a form of greeting, she supposed. She had been briefed by Derwent before this mission, so she knew it was unwise to assume these aliens actions meant the same as they would to a human. Unfortunately humanity was her only frame of reference.

She was not certain, but it seemed that the black and gold bird studied each of them more intently than the other one. None of their eyes tracked the way a human's would, so she was not sure. She felt herself sway slightly. She softened her knees, and it helped, but it also appeared to attract the attention of the red and gold bird.

Did this ceremony or whatever it was, require stillness? Were they being measured in some way, judged by what they did or did not do?

Finally, the apparently dominant flamingo turned its head to its companion, ruffling its wings as if impatient. Don't assume, she reminded herself. When the silence stretched to the point of screaming, the black and gold bird emitted a series of raucous honks. It was not as painful as the guards had sounded, but went on for a very long time. Perhaps their language required many... sounds. She hoped it was not too long for Rhubreak to translate. She sensed unease from her dragon, sensed the effort it took him to process this communication.

Coop glanced down at him. *Well?*

It is not enough to translate what I believe are the words. I need to understand their intent.

What troubles you? Arian halfway expected him to respond with *everything*, but he did not.

The first part was a greeting, but then...it changed. Our coming has disturbed them in some way. I think they called it an omen or harbinger. I am not certain.

An omen? Coop sounded puzzled. *Did they say about what?*

The closest I am able to translate is 'the munshi.'

What's a munchie? Coop asked, before Arian could.

Munshi. If my translation is correct. I have only found two languages with a similar word. In Garradian it means "one who knows." Or "one who comes." On Earth it seems to be a clerk, at least that is one of the meanings. I could do better if I had access to our ship's database

I thought you said it wasn't Google? Coop protested.

It is designed to assist in situations such as this one.

That did not seem to fit with the ship's mission of collection, but perhaps the mission sometimes required first contact situations—only if this were first contact, then there would be nothing in the database, would there? He hadn't said first contact. He'd said "situations such as this."

She looked up and found the red and gold bird looking at her. *One who comes or one who knows.* Which was it? For some reason she did not understand, she felt certain the word meant both. *Who do they think is the omen?* But she knew before Rhubreak answered her.

You.

Arian didn't flinch. *She knew,* oh, not what they thought she knew, but she felt their belief that she was this *munshi* or whatever. That was strange enough but at some level...she believed it, too.

The black and gold bird honked and flapped its wings.

What was that about? Arian resisted the urge to retreat a step. Or flee.

They desire an answer.

To what?

The question.

What's the question? Coop asked.

Arian would very much like to know that, too.

————

Questions. Again.

Answers can be interesting, Rhubreak had told her. It felt like a lifetime ago. Now here she was on an alien planet being asked to answer a question that she did not know. What did they want? What did they think she knew?

Weariness almost made her stagger. She had not slept much since she left Bosakli. Her mind would not stop circling all the things she did not know, things that she felt she should know, that she felt she needed to know right now. Or yesterday. A clock ticked inside her head, but ticking down to what?

The two doctors stirred restively. They had been left out of the discussion if one could call it that. An answer. They needed, they wanted, an answer. She needed to provide one that wouldn't get them all killed. Or one that wouldn't cut them off from the assistance they needed so desperately. For some reason, this made her think of an Enforcer interview. There she had known the answers they wanted, but the questions always started with careful formality. It was a form that was also used on the rare occasions when they met with someone outside their tight community. Meetings with strangers were always danger-ous. For some reason remembering this steadied her.

She lifted her arm in the traditional greeting, the one she'd used on her first meeting with Coop's Colonel—for a few seconds she was distracted with wondering why hadn't she done this with Coop? But she pushed this thought away. She could not afford to be distracted.

"I thank you for allowing us entry into this place." She dipped her head and then lowered her arm, waiting for Rhubreak to translate this for her. *The truth shall make you free.* How did the truth work here? Rhubreak could be wrong, she told herself, without believing it. She might not be the omen.

You're doing fine, Coop's voice was distinctly different from Rhubreak's and a cool balm for her jangled nerves. *No one is shooting at us. Yet. See if you can get some give and take, get them talking or honking or whatever. Maybe they'll give you a clue to the question.*

All right. She inhaled slowly, exhaled even slower, seeking for her calm place. It felt seasons, not days since she'd needed that place.

Keep it simple. Very simple. It will provide less opportunity for misunderstanding, Rhubreak advised her.

Right.

Simple. "Our ship was attacked." She paused, waiting for some sign of a response. The two speaker flamingoes looked at one another, then returned their attention to her. "A wormhole opened. It pulled us here. It was an accident."

The silence turned tense, and her companions all turned to look at her. It was only then that she realized that the series of croaks and honks had emerged from her mouth. She stared at the speaker flamingo, her eyes so wide, they felt dry.

I wondered when you'd realize you are speaking, er, bird. Perhaps he felt her sudden panic, because he added, *as near as I can ascertain, you are better at bird than I am.*

The angle of the speaker flamingoes heads changed. It could have been a sign of interest. Or disbelief. She'd spoken the truth

—in their language, she hoped—but would they recognize truth? Could they read a human?

Let them ponder what you have shared, and we will see if they believe you or understand what you said.

How could they understand what she did not? For a second disorientation threatened as two...views opened for her. She swayed, and the red and gold bird gave the guard an order to activate...something. The guard on one end moved to one of the raised walls and did something that caused two wide blocks to rise from the floor behind them, stopping at the right position to be seating for people in their height range. It was angled so that the blocks formed a shallow "v." The red and gold flamingo waved its wings.

Please to sit.

"We thank you for this comfort." Arian turned to her companions, "We can sit down."

The presence of this type of seating would seem to indicate prior contact with humans, Rhubreak said.

Not our kind of humans, Coop objected, *it's foxtrot hard.*

With this warning, Arian sat with care. It was very hard. Was that what foxtrot meant?

It's an expletive wrapped up in a brown wrapper. Coop sounded apologetic and perhaps embarrassed.

This explanation did not supply clarity, but she had other concerns. Sitting on the block, her feet side by side, she was pulled into the not-so-distant past on Bosakli and the pre-pact bonding visits. It carried her back to being judged, not for who she was, but by a measure outside her control. At least Trajan Bester had not looked like a bird. Though she might have liked him better as a bird.

Despite the strangeness and discomfort, she still preferred this to what she'd faced back there. Though, she'd thought

Bosakli the ultimate in a closed off society. Compared to this species, her people were overly expressive.

What their side did not know could fill this system and beyond. If there were body clues from these avians, she could not read them.

Perspective, Rhubreak said, amused, *is everything.*

It's not everything if there's not a song about it.

This interjection from Coop made it hard for Arian not to chuckle.

Allowing them to seat themselves might indicate an easing of tension. Or they had noticed she was tired and needed to sit down.

"What are they saying?" Dr. Derwent asked in a low voice.

"Later, doc," Coop told him.

The two speaker birds nodded. They each folded one leg up and silence reigned for some time. She didn't know if they were thinking or communicating with someone else. It was interesting that they were able to mind talk like Rhubreak—and troubling. How much could they "hear?"

Finally, the black and gold bird ruffled ever so slightly. "You are lost."

Rhubreak must have given Coop the translation because he stirred restively.

"We're not—" He stopped. "Maybe we're a little lost."

"All who come here are lost," the black and gold bird said.

"We'd like to get found," Coop said, and then looked surprised. "Did I just speak..."

Almost smiling, Arian shook her head. "You spoke your language, not theirs."

"What's going on, Captain?" Dr. Gessner asked.

Coop waved Gessner to silence again, his gaze intent on the birds.

The bird turned its head to one side. "Many have come here through the anomaly."

"And how many of them leave?" Coop asked.

The silence that followed this question was troubling. Both birds ignored Coop, staring at Arian.

"Will you answer the question?"

Arian wanted to protest. She still didn't know the question, but she did know the correct answer. It welled up from some place deep inside. She stood in a desert, the ground parched and pale. In the distant were high, misty covered mountains with spouts of steam dotting the landscape. The dry wind lifted her hair and she tasted heat and metal on her tongue. She looked the other direction, and the sky was filled with a moving cloud —one moving against the wind. Not clouds. *Birds.* Fear rose in her throat. She turned back and now she stood on a rock above a lake, one that was red and white and pink and gold, shifting as if it were alive. *It was alive.* The sound of their agitation filled with air. And in danger from the...*Mycterians.* In that place, she also spoke to them in their language. Because she was the *munshi.* The omen.

She rose to her feet until she was eye-to-eye with this...*Phoenicopterian.* She'd helped them before. She could not see all that happened the last time, but she knew one thing for sure. She knew the pledge she'd made then, one she needed to make now. "Yes, I will help you."

19

"WHAT DID YOU JUST SAY?" hissed Derwent before Coop could ask.

Arian looked very pale, facing the line of birds, but her jaw was stubbornly set as if the birds had challenged her in some way. She ignored Derwent, her gaze steady on what appeared to be the main bird facing her, the black eye surrounded by bloody red watching her without—as near as he could tell—blinking. Okay, there might have been something kind of like a blink, but it was fast and seemed to come from up, or from top and bottom, rather than a lid. Wasn't sure why he wanted them to blink, well, okay, he did know that. Whoever blinked first was in coyote position. A sign of giving a little ground. No sign of that here. He'd been almost nose-to-nose with some scary people, but this was his first time facing down birds. All the usual ways he figured out who was friend or foe didn't work here. If there was an expression in those eyes, he couldn't find it.

"Come." The black and gold bird turned, followed by the other one, then three of the guards followed them, the other three formed a line that seemed to be a rear guard.

"Did it just—" Gessner asked.

"Yes," Arian said.

Coop looked at her, sensing she'd changed again. She shifted her shoulders, much like he sometimes did before going into battle or a fight, then started after them. She didn't move like she had when he first met her, and not like her recent attempts to mimic military moves. This movement was different, purposeful, and confident. It might have been sexy, too. He glanced down at the dragon.

"Is she all right?" he asked him, forgetting to think it.

The dragon's beard flared black. *We must follow them or be left here.*

Coop hesitated, but then Arian paused in the opening and looked back at him, her brows lifted.

"The opening will close. You will not be able to follow."

Her tone was neutral, her gaze, too. She didn't ask, and he felt a gulf opening between them, one that had nothing to do with this mission. *He didn't want to lose her.* He didn't know what losing her meant, didn't want to think about it because he was a guy and he sucked at feelings and crap. So he didn't think. He shifted his shoulders and started toward her. Heard the scrape of claws as the dragon came, too.

"Captain?" Derwent sounded startled.

"Come or stay. The offer is time limited."

The last three guards were already moving forward, coming between him and the two docs. There was a long pause, then the scuffle of footsteps that meant both docs had decided to come. Coop glanced back in time to see the opening close behind both men, close enough they jumped forward. The guards paused, for the two docs to move ahead, then closed in behind them. Coop picked up his pace, pulling even with Arian.

"Are you okay?" He kept his voice low, his gaze darting to the line of guards just ahead of her.

She glanced at him, her lips curving up a bit, making her more like herself.

"I am well."

"So what just happened?"

She frowned. "I am not sure."

"You do realize you are not empowered to commit the Expedition to anything," Derwent said, his voice low but frustrated. Apparently, he'd picked up his pace, too and was now right behind them.

She glanced back. "I spoke only for myself, and they know this."

"What kind of help do they want from you?" Coop asked.

She half shook her head. "I do not know. It seemed urgent that I agree to help them." She looked rueful. "It was a strange sensation." She touched her heart with her hand.

"Do you think they did something to you?" If she was being influenced by them...

"What do you mean?" Now she looked puzzled.

"Well, mind control or something. You were speaking bird, then you weren't, then I—" he'd understood them at one point and thought they'd understood him.

She frowned, as she considered this. "They do not control me. Indeed, I feel more self-directed than I have for most of my life." Then she smiled ruefully. "But perhaps I would not know."

He had to chuckle. Her gaze looked...unfettered. Of course, his experience with mind control was from the movies. He changed the subject. "I thought I heard them say we are lost."

"We are not just lost," Arian said, "this place, this system is a sanctuary."

A bird sanctuary. Why was he not surprised? "So what does that mean for us?"

"At any other time, I think it would not mean good things for the *Boyington,*" she said, her brow creasing again, "but they seem exercised about the omen, the *munshi.* It is my hope that it is a..."

"Game changer?" he supplied.

She considered this and then nodded. He wanted to grab her arm, to stop her, and protest. He did put his hand on her arm, but there was a kind of hooting protest behind, so he slid his hand down her arm until he held her hand. "If you're doing this for us..."

Her hand gripped his back. "I wish to help you, but this...this leap is also for me." She touched her free hand to her heart again. "I feel it here and here." She touched her head. "There was a purpose in my collection—a purpose that was chosen for me by someone else. A purpose I can not see. The *Phoenicopterian* asked, but they did not require. I chose. I choose to aid them if I can. This feels correct to me."

Coop stared down at her. "And then..."

"And then I ask for their help for you."

"And if they can't or won't give it?"

Her lips thinned into a straight line. "We find another way."

He grinned, his hand tightening on hers. "I like the way you think."

Her lips bloomed in a smile that dang near took his breath away. "And I like you."

For the first time in his life, Coop was sorry a woman hadn't used the scary, other "l" word.

———

Was she in charge of her mind? Her will? Arian felt Coop's grip on her hand, the roughness of his palm against hers. She heard the soft scuffle of their steps against the alien surface, inhaled the old dry smell of this place. The strangeness of it felt as if it sharpened her clarity, her sense of where she was, of who she was.

And who she was becoming.

That thought almost stopped her forward steps. Becoming? She faltered but managed to keep going, and no one appeared to notice. Who was she becoming? The person she'd been meant to be? Or someone else? In her observations of Coop's people, she'd noticed they aligned themselves somewhat differently based on circumstances and who was with them. When they were off duty, for instance, they were more relaxed. Her life before had not allowed for variation in who she was. Perhaps it was variations of herself that were emerging, not some other personality trying to overtake her mind.

She considered the memories she could not remember having. Even factoring those in, she did not feel as if she were losing herself so much as becoming what she'd always felt she could be. As if restraints were falling away. That did not mean the memories did not trouble her, but so far they had helped her, not hurt her.

She felt oddly happy, considering they were heading into an unknown situation with considerable risk. She traced the line of emotion back to Coop and his grip on her hand, rather than any confidence in herself. She wished she could pucker up, but she sensed that kissing was something one did in private, or if not complete privacy, then not in this particular situation. However, if it looked like they were going down, she would like to go down kissing him.

She felt her lips curve up at that thought and how it would look to others. Slanting a discreet glance, she caught him looking at her. He grinned and squeezed her hand. She was unsure if he wished to convey that they could do this, or he wished to kiss her, too.

They'd been walking for what felt like a long time, traversing a series of hallways that seemed to be taking them higher. It was difficult to be sure, since there were no windows, but she felt a resistance, felt pull as they climbed, as if the core of this planet had a light grip on them.

It is called gravity, the force that holds a thing onto a planet's surface.

Gravity, she repeated to herself and was surprised when an equation appeared in her mind. It had both scientific and symbolic meaning she would have liked to consider at another time.

No dust arose from their passage. If she had to guess, she would say the walls and floors had been constructed of highly refined mud that had hardened over a considerable passage of time. The scent of old dirt mixed with the rather spicy, somewhat earthy smell of the *Phoenicopterians* that drifted back as they walked. She sensed air currents shifting this way and that, and sometimes it seemed she passed vents giving off the distant hum of machinery. She wished she could stop and touch these places, connect with what she sensed deep below.

Machines.

Coop lifted his free hand, rubbing his neck, then it drifted down, settling over his radio. He caught her look and said, "I hope Tiger and the others are okay. Long wait for them."

She heard a faint crackle she suspected was an answer. She hid a smile. "Do you think they are well?" she asked, her eyes wide and carefully innocent.

"Yeah," he said, giving her a quick, slashing grin.

It warmed her that Coop was here, that he'd chosen to take this leap with her. Perhaps he did trust her. It was both a comfort and terrifying. What was she leading them all into? What if his trust was misplaced? She did not wish anything to happen to him.

The corridor made a sudden, steeper climb and she smelled

fresh water from above where a bright light beckoned. Their path leveled out and they emerged into a large hall or cavern. Light fell down on the space from some source far above, casting strange shadows onto a floor that felt more spongy than the hard corridor they had been traversing. In the center of the cavern was a large basin filled with water that looked as if it were being filled from a structure in its center. This structure curved up, twisting in many lines that rose out from the water reaching toward that distant light. Water also flowed from lower places in the center structure, splashing into the basin. The play of water against water was almost as rhythmic as the music on the ship. She tipped her head. The shape felt familiar to her in some way.

Their guards gently herded them toward the basin, their hosts continuing down another passage without them. The guards blocked that and their retreat. Her companions shifted a bit, uncertainty written on their faces. Then finally they all turned toward the water.

"Nice fountain," Coop said, with a wary glance at their guards, he extended a hand into one of the streams. "Chilly." He withdrew his hand, shook it, and wiped the remaining moisture onto his pants.

"You probably shouldn't interact with substances on this planet," Gessner said, bending over the water as if he wished to touch it, too.

"I think we've moved past that, doc. If we're hosed, we're hosed," Coop said, though she noticed he looked at his hand, flexing it like he expected it to suddenly grow another digit.

Dr. Derwent moved close to her.

"You need to loop me into the negotiations." His voice was low but urgent.

"I will attempt to do so," she said absently. The falling light now revealed strange designs in the walls, not visible unless one stood in the center. She circled the fountain, her eyes on the walls, fighting the urge to touch, to connect—to interact—with this place. She completed her circle, stopping by Rhubreak. He'd scrambled up onto the lip of the basin and now regarded the center carving. *What do you think?*

That you have made great progress.

What do you mean?

You have learned to shield your thoughts.

How did he know this?

I was not supposed to notice the sudden silence?

He didn't feel hurt or offended, but perhaps he shielded that from her. *Am I doing the correct thing?*

It is a little too late to wonder that.

It felt right when I did it. Now...I am not as certain. I wish I knew what...

...we don't know? It will become clear in time. There was a pause. *This is a most curious place.*

Was it? The hall was wide but narrowed as it rose toward the light. Were they in one of the spired structures they'd observed as they arrived? The coloring of these walls was more colorful than the passages. The mud reflected the light in a variety of colors, some coming from the drawings, others from the play of the water and light. Did this mean something to these *Phoenicopterians?* Was it important or merely decorative?

Dr. Gessner stepped back, tipping his head so he could observe the carving in the middle of the fountain, a look of awe forming on his face. His hand traced the pattern in the air in front of him. "A double helix."

Coop exchanged a look with Arian. "What?"

"That statue in the fountain, it's a double helix. DNA, the helix represents DNA strands." He shook his head. "I wish the colonel had let me bring my camera."

Dr. Derwent tipped his head to one side. "DNA? Theirs?"

"Well, I would assume so. If I were going to go to the trouble of making a statue, I wouldn't put someone else's DNA there."

"DNA?" Arian asked. A statue. She filed both words away for further consideration. It must have taken great effort to shape the mud. She felt a stirring of something, a sense that she had seen something like this before.

"Deoxyribonucleic acid," Dr. Gessner said, without removing his attention from the statue. "The building blocks of life. You like machines? This is where living machines, where everything that lives and grows, comes from. DNA is the greatest computer in the universe. It can make skin cell or a whole human from the same genome."

"It is very large..." she said.

"This is just a representation of DNA. The real thing?" He pushed his hands into his hair. "You can't see the cells this creates with your eyes."

Arian looked at her hand. Turned it over. Felt on the edge of knowing something...

"Skin cells, organ cells, every part of you is made of billions of cells. And they all have genomes, DNA inside them, telling the cells what to do, what to be."

"What would it want them to do or be?" Still, she stared at her own palm.

"Well, they know when it is time to make more skin or fight a sickness. In theory, with a strand of DNA you could grow..." he stopped.

"Grow what?" Arian asked, a chill creeping over her that was not atmospheric. It was quite warm in this chamber.

"Well, anything that grows. We have cloned plants for years, even cloned some animals."

"Cloned?"

Dr. Gessner nodded. "A genetically identical organism. In

theory, it's a way to save an endangered species or bring back an extinct one."

Coop looked up, studying the statue. "There are days I wish I could clone myself," he admitted.

Dr. Gessner chuckled. "We all have days like that."

Arian stared at him. "Why would you desire an identical you?" She found it difficult enough to understand a single Coop.

"Well, so we could get more done," Coop said, "but my clone would probably not want to do the same things I don't want to do."

"Technically that's not possible," Dr. Gessner said. "A clone does not acquire the memories of the original."

"Does...it...not?" Arian asked, surprised her voice sounded merely curious. It felt as if a sound reverberated through her mind. Like the bell that called them to the town square for judging after the season of the harvest.

"In theory, the clone would need to go through the learning process, like a baby, even if its body were full grown," Dr. Gessner said, his tone still absent, his gaze locked on the statue. "And even then it wouldn't be exactly the same as the original, because it would have different experiences."

It. He'd called the clone an it, even though it was an almost exact copy of a human.

What am I? She looked down at Rhubreak, careful to direct this question only to him. *Am I an it?*

I do not have the answers you seek. But you do not look like an it to me.

Her lips twitched, easing, but not erasing the sudden tension, her sense that she'd learned something important. Or not learned it? That seemed a better description. She studied her surroundings once more. If this DNA was so important, why would they place it here?

It could be a place of worship. I have only been in human religious spaces, but this has some of the sense of that.

She started to ask him the meaning of this new word, when, like a flower opening in her mind, she knew. *No, it does not feel like a place of worship.* It felt more like a memorial, a place of remembrance, to her. Were the other drawings for their honored dead? She turned, studying them more closely. Some of the drawings were more faded than others. And there were empty spaces. A work in progress?

A stir, in the corridor where the *Phoenicopterians* had gone, called her from her thoughts. She turned as the guards fell back from the corridor ahead. It was indicated they should proceed that way now. After a short traverse, they reached two massive doors, so tall they appeared to reach upwards—and narrow—as they disappeared into the shadows of the circular cavern above their heads. These doors had many shapes carved into their surface. Flamingoes and other birds flying together and fighting other birds. One bird was so hideous of aspect that she shuddered. Its beak was sharp and long, his head grizzled and it appeared to hunch its black feathered shoulders, the splay of its webbed feet as sort of dark mockery of the flamingoes more graceful feet. She knew, she did not know how, that this was a *Mycterian*. The enemies of the *Phoenicopterians*. If these truly were their enemies, then she could see the need for a sanctuary.

The great doors opened onto an even greater hall, one with a soaring ceiling and filled with light, though a light with a green cast to it. A table—though this did not feel like an accurate word for it—ran down the center of the room. On one half of the table, was a basin or long trough, cut into sections. This side was much higher than the flat side. Chairs ran along the flat, more table-like side, but not along the trough side. At the head of this table, the basin made a right turn, to service the bird standing there, the flamingo from the reception area, the one wearing black and white gear.

Their guards directed them toward the side with the chairs. Arian did not desire the seat closest to the head of the table but somehow ended up there. Next to her was a seat with another platform on it, for her dragon, she assumed. Coop was encouraged to stand behind the seat next to Rhubreak's. Neither of the two doctors seemed happy to be relegated to the lower seats, but not enough to protest with more than looks.

Arian rested her hands lightly on the seat back, but did not pull it out, sensing it was not yet time. At four of the five places there were plates and utensils, cups, and a bracelet of beautiful and curious design. Rhubreak's place had a sort of basin, with two sections, but no bracelet. From his spot on the floor, Arian sensed a mix of rueful and resigned at his limited view. At least the chairs and service seemed to indicate they were guests, not the meal. She glanced at Coop and saw his lips twitch, as if he'd come to the same conclusion.

The guards moved away from them, forming a line along the wall at their backs, their heads lifting in what felt like coming to attention. Behind the guards, Arian noticed that these walls also had images of the double helix, though there were differences from the one in the main chamber. Many differences, she realized. Each of the strands had unique features. Above the head of the table was a large clock, at least, that was the closest name she could find for it. It had distinct differences from other clocks of her experience. This one had seven arms and many symbols carved at regular intervals around the central circle. Each of the arms were on a symbol, in intervals of seven, she realized. *The tangram.* She did not know why she had this thought, other than she knew it also meant seven in some way. *Seven,* she thought, then, *I am the third.*

The *Phoenicopterian* at the head of the table appeared to

signal and the guards honked in unison, this call less strident than back in the other chamber, then all fell silent. Through the door they'd entered, a line of *Phoenicopterians* entered, led by the other flamingo they'd met. The ones that followed wore different colors and had unique coloring, and other elements unique to them, such as beak shape and the color of their eyes. She sensed that each was a representative of their sub-species.

"If your companions will don the circlets, it will aid communication," directed the bird at the table's head.

Arian picked up hers, studied it briefly, and slid it on. She held her arm up so her companions could see it "If you wish to communicate with them more easily, you need to wear one of these." She assumed Rhubreak didn't need one because he'd already managed to talk to them.

The two doctors exchanged uneasy glances with each other. Coop's look was different. He caught her look. "It's kind of pretty for a dude."

Arian had to fight back a chuckle. In the end, they all slid them on.

"The Draze may be seated."

Arian helped Rhubreak up into his seat. He rested his paws on the table and looked around, his beard flaring, then subsiding. Finally, he turned his snout back to the head of the table.

As if it had been waiting for this, it spoke. "I am Hoteimai." It moved a wing, indicating the others. "This is Juriojnai, Fukurokai, Bishamontai, Benzaitai, Daikokutai, and Ebusuai." As each name was spoken, one of the flamingos across from them lowered their heads in greeting, then raised them again. When Hoteimai finished the introductions, they all lifted their beaks and honked, then fell silent.

"We are pleased to be in your presence. I am called Arian Teraz," Arian touched her hand to her chest. "The Draze Dragon is called Rhubreak. Captain Jackson Cooper, Dr. Adam Derwent,

and Dr. Kevin Gessner." As their names were called, they each
gave a nod. "We thank you for your hospitality."

Hoteimai nodded its head. "You may sit."

Arian tugged her chair out and eased down a bit warily. This
time the seat had padding, which was nice. It also seemed
more...welcoming, though that was an assumption, she
reminded herself. Now she became aware of being hungry and
weary, felt the strain of staying alert. In some ways, it felt as if
she'd worked most of a day in the fields, instead of taking a short
ride in a ship, followed by a longish walk.

There was another honking sound and slots opened in each
section of the trough. A thick fluid flowed into each of the
troughs, a different color for each bird. There was a feeling of an
energy charge in the air, then blocks of green appeared on the
plates in front of them. By each plate a small pitcher also
appeared. Rhubreak's basin filled with something she did not
care to examine too closely when she realized it was moving. It
appeared he also got water to drink.

"You may consume your sustenance, and then we will
converse," Hoteimai said.

The *Phoenicopterians* dipped their beaks in, the shape
making sense to her now, as they scooped the sludge up. Arian
studied the green block. It was sadly similar to what they ate
every day on Bosakli. She picked up her fork and separated a
chunk, lifting it to her mouth. Oh yes, it was very similar. Not
unpleasant, but not that pleasant. They'd farmed many things,
beautiful things, that were then reduced to taste-less, nutritional
blocks. She'd always known it could be better, because she'd
sampled the things they grew on the farm. Not even the
Enforcers could count every piece of produce. Despite the
blandness of it, she felt her energy returning, though it could
not assist with the tiredness. She stole a look at her companions
and noticed Coop ate with resignation, the two doctors with

reluctance. Hopefully their hosts would not be familiar enough with humans for this to be a breach of etiquette.

The liquid in the pitcher was faintly green when poured and did seem to help ease tiredness. It also tasted better than the block. She ate swiftly, it was better that way, and set down her utensil, folding her hands in her lap. After a time, the *Phoenicopterians* also settled back from their consumption. Out of the corner of her eye, she noted her side had also learned the lesson of eating quickly. Their plates were clean, well, aside from a few crumbs.

There was a general ruffling of feathers and Arian had the sense that the talking was about to begin.

20

Coop glanced down at the communication device and wondered if he should have put it on. He was not confident of his ability to contribute to this confab. Also not confident of his ability to keep his mouth shut. This was one weird set up, no question. The head bird turned its weird gaze toward them. Actually, kind of reminded him of Pappy, the way it looked at each one of them. That kind of helped. At least it was something he recognized in a whole lot of holy crap.

Arian sat very straight, her feet planted, her hands lightly clasped in her lap. He felt an urge to grab her hand again but resisted it. Not when it felt like Pappy was watching.

The main bird lifted its wings some, then settled down. "You may speak."

Arian lifted a hand, gesturing down the row. "Dr. Derwent is the appointed spokesperson for his people. May he address you on their behalf?"

The great bird appeared to nod.

Derwent cleared his throat, glancing at them before shifting to directly address the Pappy bird. "Like Ms. Teraz, I thank you for your hospitality. We arrived in this system unexpectedly, and, while we work on leaving, we're hoping we can negotiate with you for supplies," his voice faltered for a moment when his gaze strayed down to the few crumbs on his plate, "and information."

"This system, as you call it, is a sanctuary, a place of safety. Why would you desire to leave?"

He considered his response carefully, Coop was pleased to note, his respect for the diplomat rising. Guy hadn't exactly shone during first contact with Arian.

"With respect and admiration for what you have achieved here, our homes and our families are out there. They hope for our return. We hope for our reunion with them."

The birds all shifted in place as if this startled them.

"You traveled forth without your flock? That is not our way."

"We did not wish to risk our families when we did not know what was out here. We are explorers, not settlers. We left our homes to learn, to meet other species, to learn about them, and from them."

Once more there was the impression that this startled, or perhaps interested them, was the better assessment.

"Learning is important," Hoteimai agreed. His head appeared to turn toward Arian. "Sometimes one leaves because one must, not because it is what one desires."

"Your home was invaded," Arian spoke suddenly, then looked startled by her words.

"The *Mycterians* sought to destroy us. With the assistance of the *Munshi*, this sanctuary was established for us, and for other lost ones. Leaving is...it was impossible."

"Was impossible?" Coop couldn't help but ask. He got a look from Derwent and waved a hand. "Sorry."

Again, it seemed as if the bird looked at Arian.

"The arrival of the *munshi* is a drop of water in a deep pool. It spreads and in the end, all will be touched. Even the those who do not wish to be found."

Coop blinked. He'd heard some non-answers in his life, but this was probably the most non-answer answer ever.

Arian leaned forward. "The beginning of finding, of feeling less lost, is knowledge. It would comfort these people to know where they are. I am certain such a great species as yours has this information. Would it be possible to see star charts of this system and beyond?"

Hoteimai tipped its head to one side, studying, or possibly considering her request. It glanced down the table, causing a ruffling of feathers that didn't look like an answer, but ended up being one when it said, "This feels reasonable. It will be arranged."

Coop had a feeling this didn't bother them because they didn't believe they would be leaving.

"Good job," he muttered out of the side of his mouth. Her lips twitched, but her tone was sober as she offered thanks for this additional kindness.

Though the birds couldn't push back from the table, nevertheless, Coop had that feeling they had.

"We would learn more of your exploring. We will adjourn to the pool."

Coop might have been happy about that. He loved a pool, but was pretty sure it wasn't going to be their kind of pool.

———

Tiger was clearly relieved to see them return to the shuttle. Coop was not sorry to return. It had been a strange day. He'd been right to not expect much from the pool. It was more like a muddy lake full of birds. Thankfully, wading had not been required and in fact, had been discouraged. It sure as hotel didn't smell great. And the noise. Coop wasn't sure how Hoteimai expected to continue a conversation in that racket.

Though he had learned one thing. They had some seriously fine technology, because this had been the view he'd expected to see from the air. Birds. Birds wading. Birds flying. Birds dancing and getting it on. A vast sea of birds being birds in every direction.

If anyone had gotten face time with the Pappy bird, Coop hadn't seen it. The seating got a little better and he might have checked out, took a little nap. He wasn't sure. He'd had no sensation of waking, just the feeling he'd missed something and everyone was on their feet but him. He'd scrambled up, but hadn't realized they were returning to the shuttle until they landed back on the platform and he had eyes on it.

It was the closest thing to home in a whole lot of weird, and he sank with relief in his seat, though he swiveled it around to face the back of the shuttle.

"Do you think it's safe to transmit a report to home plate?"

"We've been in touch," Tiger said. "Pappy was plenty worried, but I was able to tell him you were all still breathing. Your power nap was interesting." Tiger grinned. "You should get your snoring checked, bubba."

So he had been asleep. He wondered why he still felt tired.

Tiger sobered. "You were gone almost twenty-four ship hours, sir."

Coop dropped his hands. "What?"

"And you started speaking bird, all of you. At least, that's what it sounded like."

The bracelets. He covered his wrist, but this was gone. Looked like all of them were. "Any idea how far away we got?"

"After you entered the doorway, you transported several hundred miles. After that, well, you seemed to jump around quite a bit." He hesitated. "For a while, you were on one of the nearby planets."

"Their technology is similar to that used on this shuttle," Arian spoke suddenly. She'd sat in her former position, but had not touched the controls or said anything, not during their return or since boarding the shuttle.

Gessner's gaze shot to Coop's, his eyebrows jumping almost to his hairline. He cleared his throat. "This shuttle?"

Arian looked at him. "It is Garradian, is it not?"

Coop swept the group with a "who talked" look. No one confessed. "How..." he stopped, not sure what to ask.

She rubbed her forehead like it hurt, giving him a wry smile. "Hoteimai told me the Garradians are the ones who set up this sanctuary. It is because you have Garradian technology that they were willing to speak with you."

"And if we hadn't?" Coop almost wished he hadn't asked. What hadn't happened wasn't strictly need-to-know.

"When ships enter this sanctuary, they are scanned, then a suitable habitat is terra formed." She frowned. "I believe that is the word they used. Contents are transferred to their haven and..." She stopped.

Contents? Coop didn't like the detachment of the word.

"And then what?" Tiger asked.

"Their ships are destroyed." She pressed her thumbs into either side of the bridge of her nose, not trying, or not able to hide her exhaustion. "Anyone leaving is considered a breach of security. It used to not be an issue. No one could enter and no one—none of their people— wanted to leave. Then the anomaly appeared. I had the impression the—contents—of those ships desired to leave."

Coop opened his mouth to ask why, other than possessing Garradian tech, they weren't being fitted for a habitat, but Arian gave a slight, very slight shake of her head.

"Did they say how long that has been happening?" Gessner asked. "The wormhole, I mean?"

She seemed about to say something else, but changed her mind. "They mark time differently than you or I. My sense is that for them it is recent, but perhaps not for us. Some of the habitats are generational by now."

Coop felt cold run down his back at that thought. The crew was family, but he did not want to live out his life with only them.

She hesitated. "They believe the anomaly is caused by an attempt to breach the sanctuary."

They believe? What did she believe? For the first time he realized she never called it a wormhole. "That would be why the heavy military presence?" How was this system protected? And what did that mean for them?

Gessner cleared his throat. "Did they say anything about the DNA art all over the place?"

"They told me that the room with the fountain is a memorial, a genealogy, and the other paintings are a record of the species who have come to the sanctuary."

"A...they track species by DNA?" This question came from Derwent.

Arian nodded. Her gaze slanted to Coop's. "They do. There are many species represented throughout the...I believe they called it the cathedral."

"It would be a more accurate way to keep track of things," Gessner said thoughtfully, "but their technology must be very advanced. We've still got a ways to go to crack the DNA code."

"Whether you stay or not, yours will be added," Arian said. "Your DNA is similar to humans who have come here through the anomaly, but also contains new markers. They would take more time to get to know your people, and how you came into possession of Garradian technology, but they have other urgencies."

You, she'd said. Were they calling in her promise? His gut tensed.

"Sir, we've been cleared to return to the *Boyington*," Tiger said, spinning to his station and verifying the data.

"We have?"

"I need to brief your Colonel. They have not said they won't help you." She glanced at Coop. "They have a request."

The other urgency? Her gaze contained warnings, but he asked anyway. "What is their other urgency?"

Her brows arched, as if this were obvious. "They are preparing for an invasion."

"What happened to the sanctuary part of sanctuary?" Other than the wormhole—anomaly.

"It seems that during the millennia since they fled their world the *Mycterians* have become space capable, too." She paused then added, "They believe it is the *Mycterians* who are causing the anomalies."

How did they know that, he wondered, and why did it sound like she didn't agree? But of more pressing concern to him, "And what is your part in all this?"

Arian hesitated, then smiled wryly. "They wish me to do what the *munshi* did for them before."

"And what was that?"

"They want me to prevent the invasion of the *Mycterians*."

"Oh, is that all?" No pressure. And wouldn't Pappy be thrilled about that?

PART III

PART III

21

ARIAN HAD ALMOST LAUGHED at Coop's expression when she passed on the *Phoenicopterians* request. She was not laughing now. There was something about Coop's Colonel that killed any impulse to humor. She knew he did not trust her or Rhubreak, but something had changed since they'd returned to the *Boyington*.

You did give them access to the ship.

Yes, she had. Actions had consequences. Even on Bosakli, this was truth. So she waited for the consequences, knowing that she could stave them off because they needed her, but she could not escape them.

Back in the ready room, Doctors Derwent and Gessner gave their reports and left. Now Coop was speaking, but she noticed the Colonel's gaze kept straying toward her, with storm clouds in their depths. She retreated inside, but could not help it, not even to build rapport could she bring herself to leave the safe place. And she did not believe it would work this time if the problem were what she suspected.

When the colonel turned toward her, she braced, forcing

herself to meet his gaze calmly and without guilt. Indeed, it was not her fault, but would he believe that?

"The Captain says they have asked for your help?"

She nodded warily.

"What does this help entail?"

Arian took a steadying breath. He was circling in, but not ready to pounce. He would gather information first. So be it.

"May I access your system? It will be easier to show you the problem."

He hesitated, then nodded sharply. With a wary glance between them, Coop pushed the control device within her reach. Arian accessed the system data, searched for what she required, and sent it to the screen.

"This system is relatively small," she heard herself say as if she were some other person, perhaps the one she sensed trying to emerge. "I believe your people postulated that there could have been planets in the sector where we arrived, but they were destroyed, thus contributing to the massive debris field."

She noted the colonel exchanging a look with Coop, one she could not parse.

"I remember hearing something like that," the Colonel said.

"They were correct, though the destroyed planets were not inhabited. They had been explored for their potential for future settlements and resource exploitation, but were abandoned as unsafe when the anomaly began appearing." She glanced at Coop. "They speak of it as recent, but for us, this has been a long process of destruction in the sector. They measure time differently, as well, so it is difficult to match to yours enough to create an accurate timeline."

Coop nodded. "You mentioned that."

"What does this have to do with their request?" the Colonel asked.

"They believe the anomalies are caused by the *Mycterians* trying to breach this system," Arian told him.

"They think technology is causing the wormhole?" His frown deepened.

She wondered why they persisted in calling it a wormhole. It's formation was distinctly different from a wormhole. Its properties were more like a tunnel than a wormhole.

"So how are you supposed to assist them with that?"

"I am not." Arian hesitated, wondering if she should mention that she did not believe the anomalies were as random as they had first believed. Then decided it would cloud the issue at this time. "This is where they need help." She changed the display to the outer rim of the system. She noted that both men straightened and their gazes narrowed sharply. The computer rendered it as if the whole system were enclosed in a net, not unlike the one the aliens had used to carry them to their planet. The technology was not dissimilar. "When this sanctuary was created, it was protected, hidden actually, by the use of what you'd call satellites. Cloaked devices, only visible from this side." She zoomed in on a section of the net. "They aren't sure why, but this section of the system has gone offline."

There was a long pause, then both men looked at her.

"Wanted, one machine whisperer," Coop said.

She shrugged with a wry smile.

The Colonel's fingertips tapped the top of the table. "They think you can fix it."

"It is possible that I can if there is anything there to fix. It has been in place for a very long time. But that is not why I hope you will let me try." Arian glanced at Coop. "From what I can tell, the satellites also keep everything contained. Much like the net they used to carry us to their planet. Because they need my help to repair it, I believe that is why we aren't already in one of those havens." And because they believed she was this *munshi*.

"You think it is a route out of this system." The Colonel stared at the display. "But they want you to fix it. If you do, we're stuck, if you don't..."

"They transport us to a haven and blow up your ship," Arian said.

"Which they might do anyway, even if you fix it," Coop pointed out. "Sanctuary rules."

"It is a possibility," Arian admitted. "They have not agreed to let you leave."

The Colonel leaned back in his chair. "I assume you have a third option?"

"The technology is Garradian—"

He stiffened his mouth opening, then snapping shut.

"So is your shuttle. That's another reason why we aren't already in a haven." She did not know why it distressed him that she knew this. "If I could use this shuttle—" The Colonel stiffened so alarmingly she stopped and glanced at Coop.

"Why can't you take your ship out there?" the Colonel cut into her words.

"It is not Garradian. And the ship does not serve me or answer to me."

"You're the pilot—"

"But not its master."

"The dragon, is it the master?"

She shook her head.

"So our shuttle is the only way?" He did not sound as if he believed her.

"It is Garradian," she repeated. "The programming is compatible. It is my only chance of effecting the repairs. If I can get into the system, there is a chance I can make a...door for the *Boyington*. Additionally, by fixing their devices, it would give you negotiating leverage," she felt compelled to point out, though she felt this was blindingly obvious.

"You think," the Colonel pointed out. "You don't know if any of this is possible."

If there was something there to repair, she could do it, but saying this would cause more explanations since she could not explain how she knew this. And she seemed to have plenty on her plate already.

"They have compatible technologies. I have...high confidence that I can do this." She hesitated. "The *Phoenicopterians* are willing to share star charts with your scientists—"

"They already have," the colonel said unwillingly. "Even with the charts..."

"Your home might be out of reach." She bit her lip. "I understand—"

"Do you?" He huffed out a frustrated breath.

She looked at him. "No, I do not. The last thing I want to do is go home." She glanced at the screen. "I expect the *Phoenicopterians* would give me sanctuary, if I can fix what is wrong and preserve their home." Coop may have shifted. She was not sure. Her lips twisted. "I do not think this is where I belong."

"Where do you belong, young lady?"

Arian didn't know how to answer this question. She wanted to belong with Coop, wanted to belong here. But this lack of a place to belong—it was not a machine she could fix. What she felt, what she desired, it was complicated, confused by the knowledge that kept surfacing inside her head. Attempting to explicate it for him was not possible for her without more rest or more data. And even then, it might not be possible.

The Colonel slid the control device from in front of her until it was in front of him, and did something that changed the view on the screen. It was a view of the cold sleep pods. And their contents.

"What about here?"

———

Coop stared at the screen, trying to process what his eyes saw, stuff his brain said wasn't possible. Of course, cold sleep, cryo-stasis involved frozen bodies. He got that part. It was...what was frozen in the pods. He looked at Arian. Then at the screen. Then at Arian.

"Are those...clones?" The two figures weren't exact matches to Arian, but that could be because they were frozen.

"I do not know. I had not heard that word until..." Arian's lashes dropped over her eyes, then lifted, so much sorrow in there that his chest hurt. "I assume that is what they are." She looked at the Colonel. "You are repulsed." She gave a laugh without mirth. "How do you think I feel? I am not certain if I am...the copy or...the original." She looked at the screen and flinched. "It seems likely that I am the *it*, since I have no memory of creating these things. Isn't that what Dr. Gessner said of clones? That they are an it?" She shifted to face the Pappy. "Does it matter if I am an original or a clone? The knowledge that is emerging in my brain might be your only chance to get home. Unless your scientists have come up with a plan while we were on the planet?"

"Why would you help us?" Pappy's voice hadn't softened at all.

Not that Coop expected him to. Soft wasn't his go-to place.

She sat very straight in her chair, her gaze not flinching away from Pappy's.

"Perhaps I have learned something from my time with you. Perhaps it is in my...cloned DNA. All I know is that if there is a chance that I can help you, that I can help these *Phoenicopterians*, then I must try." She shrugged. Her tone said believe me or not.

"You said you are not the master of your ship, so you don't know why it is...collecting...versions of you?"

Coop wasn't sure versions was a better choice than clones. She glanced at the dragon, though.

She shook her head. Pappy's hard gaze shifted to the dragon. "Do you know?"

Coop didn't get an answer in his head. The dragon did shake his head from side to side.

"To some extent, we are both at the...mercy of the true master, the owner of the ship." She took a breath, shooting one more look at the dragon before back to face Pappy. "I do not wish to be controlled by something or someone who hides their motives. I will choose for myself now." She was quiet for a minute, her gaze pointed away from both of them, then smiled wryly. "As much as I can. If you wish me to depart, I will make the ship fly again. You have many problems of your own."

"Do you think it can get out of this system?" Pappy asked.

"I do not know. Perhaps its master can call it through the force field. Or it may call the master to it."

Pappy's brows shot up. "So another player might be incoming right now?"

"It is possible." She frowned as if considering this. Then she nodded with a sigh. "It is most possible. It's...cargo must have value, or why go to so much trouble?" She glanced at the dragon once again. "I—believe—it is not the only ship traveling with a Companion."

Pappy looked at the dragon again. He seemed to want to ask it something but instead, he sighed. "Like you, I am curious about the motives of the owner of your ship, but..."

"You have more pressing concerns."

"Unless he shows up for his ship," Coop pointed out.

Now Pappy did look at the dragon. "Can you tell us anything about the ship's owner?"

Coop sensed a hesitation from the dragon.

I am only given information to assist in collecting, but my species does not willingly assist...evil.

Coop passed this on, deepening the old man's frown.

"So you're not sure either."

It wasn't a question.

"Why is Ms. Teraz the only...person not in a pod?"

The hesitation was long enough to make Arian twitch.

The others were in pods when collected.

That was interesting, though Coop wasn't exactly sure why.

And no, I do not know why. It was not...need-to-know.

"Do you believe the owner will reclaim the ship?"

Coop wasn't sure who this question was directed to, but it was Arian who answered it.

"I would assume that someone who has invested so much would not allow the ship to disappear."

Pappy considered this. "There are empty pods on your ship."

"Yes," Arian said evenly. Now she glanced uneasily at the dragon. "And time is..." She stopped, her gaze distant.

"Time is what?" Pappy asked.

"There is a clock," Arian said, slowly. "An Urclock." She shook her head as if to clear it.

The Urclock *waits.*

"Urclock?" Now Pappy looked puzzled.

"What does it wait for?" Coop asked, shooting Pappy a warning look. Pappy did not look happy. Coop could almost hear him wondering if they were being played. But if this was being played, well, she wasn't doing it very well. She was stuck here with them. Even she'd offered to help to get out...

Do you know what the Urclock *is?*

Yes. And no.

The dragon felt as troubled as Arian and the old man looked.

I don't understand.

*An Urclock is an ancient clock, but **the** Urclock is different...and when the countdown begins...*

Yes?

The tangram will begin to come together.

Tangram. That was something to do with number seven...his thoughts jerked. Were there other ships? *Seven ships? What happens when the tangram forms?*

I do not know.

The dragon may not know, but it bothered him. Coop felt his unease. Did that make the ship's owner a good guy? A bad guy?

Not everything or everyone is black and white.

Coop's gaze narrowed. Collection? Collector? Just curious? Expensive hobby, he decided. He realized Pappy was looking at him and wondered if he'd missed something. Pappy arched a brow and Coop realized he wanted in on the off the record convo with the dragon. He gave a slight shake, let his eyes say, "Later."

There was no sign Arian had been in on the conversation, but he sensed trouble from her, too. Not a place he usually found himself. Emotions were messy, no question.

Pappy looked at Coop. "Remind you of anything?"

"You mean the usual, sir?"

"Yeah, the usual."

Arian looked uncertainly from Pappy to Coop. He gave her a crooked grin. "We call it FUBAR, which translated means if something can go wrong, it will."

Pappy straightened in his chair. "Okay, we take this one problem at a time." He tapped the table top. "First up is their protective...array, we'll call it that for want of a better word."

"Array does seem applicable, Colonel," Arian agreed.

"I'm not turning the shuttle over to you—"

Arian stiffened, her mouth open to protest.

"—without a team of my people. Captain, you put together a team for both shuttles."

"Both shuttles, sir?"

"If something happens, it will take time to get to you. This may be a small system, but it's not that small." He turned back to Arian. "What other help do you need?"

Her mouth twisted wryly. "I was going to say another me, but we have that."

"You want to defrost...yourself?"

She shook her head. "But you might want to post a guard or two."

"Why?"

"It is not my ship," she pointed out.

"You sure you're up for this, young lady?" Pappy asked, worry in his gaze.

Arian did look young and white.

Her slight smile trembled around the edges. "I will do what I must." Her gaze met his. "I give you my word that I will do my best, for what it is worth."

Pappy's lips twisted. "We'll call this your second lesson in trust." He held her gaze. "Don't let me down."

Her chin lifted. Her fist pressed against her heart. "Only death will stop me."

"If you let us down, you'll wish you had died." After a long pause, Pappy gave a sharp nod. "Let's do this then. Captain, put your teams together. Pick another pilot and a couple of teams of Marines, ten per ship?"

Coop nodded. Ten Marines went a long way in a fight—but not a fight in space. He tried not to think about a scenario where he'd need them.

"You'll go in cloaked until we find out what we're dealing with."

"You think there's more than a broken array, sir?"

"They're worried about an invasion," Pappy pointed out. Something in Coop's expression made Pappy give him a grim smile. "An opportunity to excel, Captain."

————

"What did your Colonel mean?" Arian asked when they were in the corridor and heading back to her ship.

"About?"

"An opportunity? Doesn't he realize how dangerous—" Coop's quick grin cut off her question. Of course, he knew. The Colonel was a man who saw further than they did, which was why he commanded this vessel.

"It's a thing, a saying. It means a mission with the odds stacked against you. An opportunity to..."

"...excel." Arian found she could chuckle and it lightened the worry that had weighed so heavily on her since pledging her life to this mission. She'd given the only vow she'd known in her life, the one required once a year by the Consortium. Only when she'd given them her word, she had not meant it. They were words with no meaning because she'd had no choice. This time she'd chosen. It felt good and terrifying. She'd made choices since leaving Bosakli, but this felt like her most serious act of free will. It had felt larger than the moment as if had been recorded by a power she'd not been allowed to believe existed.

"Tiger will pilot the other shuttle. He loves to excel, too, but what about the geek?"

"The geek?" she frowned.

"A scientist for the other shuttle? You've met most of them now? Who could back you up if, well, who could do it?"

She was not sure anyone could, but he was correct. If something happened, they needed to have their supplies not limited to one container. Still... "It is very dangerous..."

"Maybe your top three? We'll take the one who will go." He smiled. "No pressure applied. I promise."

"Dr. Janeck? Dr. Davis." Not as brilliant as Janeck, but very good with code. She considered the last name. It was a sobering responsibility, even if they ultimately got to choose. "Dr. Trent?"

"I'll start with Janeck." He shot her a sideways look. "You sure you're okay with this?"

She did not answer right away because she knew what he really wished to know. Finally, she nodded. "I am very...okay."

What about me?

They both looked down at Rhubreak.

"I don't think the Colonel is going to let you go, dude," Coop said.

Dude? Arian blinked, then half smiled at the relief she felt from the Companion.

I did not sign on to face an invasion.

They both sobered, their gazes meeting over Rhubreak.

She did not regret her promise. She did regret the lack of opportunity to tell Coop, well, she was not sure what she would have told him. The feelings were a stone in her chest, but she did not know the words that would free them. Or if those words would be welcome if she did.

22

So, he might have kissed a clone. Hadn't felt like kissing a clone when he kissed Arian. Not that he knew what kissing one felt like. Unless he did. Because if she were one, then he'd kissed her, and now he knew what it felt like to kiss a clone. But, if she didn't know, then how was he supposed to know—

He stopped that thought. It was getting too complicated for a flyboy. What he knew about clones could be summed up in a couple of movies. But what he knew of Arian, of holding her in his arms, of tasting her lips, she was real and human. All the way through, well, as much as he could tell from the hugging and kissing. She made him feel...stuff.

Never before had he wished he could buy flowers and chocolate and do something, well, romantic. There'd been a song playing in the lounge, about doing romantic crap and he would have, if the *Boyington* had anything romantic a guy could buy. Which it didn't. If he couldn't buy her flowers, then he wanted to protect her. His mind had flinched when he heard her saying she didn't know if she was the copy, and he didn't like thinking about the look in her eyes. How would he feel if he found out he might be a copy of himself, and not the real deal?

Crappy as hell, is how he'd feel.

What was it Gessner had said? That life experience would make them not exact copies? That made her unique, with a couple of twins in the freezer. Like her, but not her. Not Arian. If someone lined them up, he'd pick her. Wouldn't he? A voice on the radio called him back to his pre-flight check.

It helped steady his mind. It always had. He realized whatever she was, he was more invested in a relationship—there, he'd thought it—than ever before. He was involved with her as she was right now. Who she was right now.

So when Arian settled into the co-pilot's seat next to him, he was able to look at her without all the clone questions in his eyes. Seeing her steadied him even more. She was who she was, like anyone, like any of them—a mix of all the stuff that made them who they were. He didn't know why the sight of her clean jawline, or the resolution in her eyes, made his heart jump in his chest. The little bit of color that liked to creep into her face and the way her mouth tried not to smile when she wanted to be business-like lit heat in his middle like no one had before. Whatever it was that made guys attracted to girls? Well, he had it for her.

He grinned, a bit wry about his own, unfamiliar thoughts, and her wariness faded, replaced with the smile that made him want to forget where he was and just kiss the girl until she wanted him as much as he wanted her.

He sighed. Kissing girls had been a theme in his life—when he wasn't obsessing over flying. Guys were, well, guys. They pretty much thought about kissing every girl that even slightly attracted them. He didn't plant one on random gals because he was a grownup and he'd been too shy when he wasn't. He had self-control, and there were consequences for kissing girls. Expectations raised. When you knew you might be gone for months, years, or forever, it was better not to raise them. But with Arian, he not only wanted to raise them, he also wanted her to expect things from him. And here was the plus with having a relationship with an alien, she was already out here. She might not know the score yet, but she was a faster learner. He could see her in his life, could see a future together, like he never had before.

He saw color run up under her skin, her expression softening.

"It's going to be okay," he told her.

Her lips curved up, her gaze meeting his briefly. He was not sure she believed him. He couldn't say he blamed her. She didn't know him well enough. Yet. Her life had taught her not to expect much. Well, he could help with that, too. He knew all about expectations.

Her color deepened. She faced forward, her tone careful bland. "I do not understand how Marines can help during flight?"

Coop nodded. Pappy had seen the movies, too. "He wants to give us a fighting chance if trouble pops up." Though the kind of trouble the marines could help with, well, he hoped they wouldn't have that kind. There'd been some objections from the geeks about them using stealth mode. They thought the *Phoenicopterians* should know they were trying to help. That would let Derwent start negotiating right away, but he hadn't heard the word "invasion," like he and Pappy had. No, it was better to go in dark, then de-cloak if everything was clear at the border.

She glanced back at the Marines. "They appear to be fierce warriors."

No argument from him on that, though, "I'm a fierce warrior, too, but flying my bird."

She laughed softly. "Yes."

But in her gaze he saw shy agreement. He'd take it as a good sign. "Have you been able to link to Dr. Janeck?"

Coop had probably met Janeck at some point, but he hadn't realized how young he was. Hadn't been thrilled by the non-geek look of interest he gave Arian. Wasn't sorry the guy would be on the other shuttle with Tiger.

"I am initiating the sequence now," she murmured, her hands settling on the controls like they'd been there before.

Coop felt a twinge of unease—reminded himself it was good for her to know what she was doing. He'd seen her do stranger things. A HUD—a heads up display—popped up, but it kept changing so fast it made him dizzy, so he focused on his pre-flight, checking his comm with Tiger.

"All present and accounted for, Banshee." Tiger's voice in his ear was familiar and comforting.

He'd been Coop's wingman since their first flight school. For whatever reason, no one had wanted to break up the band. Or maybe no one else wanted the job, he thought with a grin. One of the images on the HUD caught his attention. It was the array.

"That's sure pretty," he murmured. It looked like a smooth net. The connections were bright points of light except along a ragged tear. "That's a nasty break."

"It is much more extensive than it appeared from my first scan," she said, looking worried.

From here it looked big enough to drive a ship through. "Can we scan for threats that might be present outside the array?"

"When we are closer. The array, even damaged, resists scans outside its perimeter."

Always try to see what's coming was his motto, one these birds needed to learn. Of course, it might just be them having trouble getting eyes on what was outside this system. No one had said the birds couldn't see outside their net.

"Do we have a course to send to Tiger?"

"Let me acquire it for you." She tapped things on her panel

and the HUD changed, a new course forming at the base of the array.

He frowned as he did some math, helped by his controls. "Let's hope we can get there before anyone uses that hole." With the shuttle's fastest propulsion, it was going to take them the better part of twenty-four hours.

"To be of use, we must use the comet drive—"

"The what?" Coop frowned.

"The comet drive?"Arian looked at him. "It is much more efficient and faster than the standard propulsion, though it uses more power. We won't be able to use our shields until we drop out of comet drive, but the cloak should still be effective, particularly if I can link the drives between the two ships. With linked propulsion, our transit should be almost instantaneous." She frowned at the HUD. "We will need to move a safe distance from the *Boyington* before we initiate the drive. It creates unstable space in all directions, and that would not be good for your ship to experience."

Coop opened his mouth. Closed it. Finally asked, "What is a safe distance and are there any side effects or anything I should warn our passengers about?"

She gave him the distance. "They should strap in and so should we," she said. "It is very fast."

"Flyboys like fast," he said, hoping he liked the comet drive's "very fast." Instantaneous? He opened a channel to Tiger. "We're going to link the two shuttles, so we can make the transit, um, jump together to the array. Oh, and strap in. Once we get a go, we'll proceed to the coordinates I'm transmitting, then link and...um, jump."

Coop edited out the part about the comet drive. He was pretty sure Pappy would cancel the mission if he found out about that before they left. Forgiveness was more likely to get than permission to use the tech, especially if it worked as advertised. And of course, they needed to accomplish their mission without losing the new tech. On the downside of the upside, if they lost the tech, they probably wouldn't be alive to face Pappy anyway.

"Kicking some tires and lighting some fires," Tiger said with his usual good humor. "And strapping in, sir."

He wondered how happy his wing man would be once they *kicked* the tires into comet speed. He shrugged. Tiger liked fast, too. He called the *Boyington*. "Are we go, no-go on Operation Array?"

The pause felt over long, and he felt his gut tightening. To say Pappy was not thrilled at the moment was a massive understatement. Like the king and queen of understatements. This wasn't just a rock and a hard place. This was all that, and a FUBAR place.

"You have a go, Banshee. Repeat Operation Array is a go." A pause. "God speed."

"Strap down, guys," Coop told his passengers. He activated pre-launch procedures, shutting the air tight doors of all sections, and lowered the armor protections for all view screens. They had some pretty big viewing ports up top, a section he figured had been for bigwigs. It wasn't standard procedure for normal flight, but he didn't know how old these shuttles were and he was pretty sure no one had used this comet drive for a very long time. If a breach was inclined to happen, he figured it would be inclined now. Good old Murphy's Law.

He took the lead in exiting the bay, felt Tiger's hot breath on his six. The shuttle should have felt clunky after his *Dauntless*, but he was finding it a pretty sweet little ship to drive this time. Which felt odd. Same ship as he'd flown for the bird meet. But it felt different. Maybe because this mission was about stopping an invasion. And he knew it had a comet drive. He took it easy after they exited the bay, though, no fancy flying. No reason to tick off Pappy before he had to.

Arian kept her attention divided between her controls and the HUD. "I'm initiating the pairing sequence between the comet drives, and bringing them both online. We will jump in thirty seconds."

The countdown felt both slow and fast. If the drive operated as advertised, it was sure to cause unique stress factors for the shuttles.

"Brace for jump," he said, including their ship and Tiger's in the warning, only wondering when it was too late if they should be wearing speed jeans to help with the incoming G-force...

"Initiating comet drive now." Her voice was so flat, it reminded him of the sim computer's voice.

The yank came between blinks. Pressure on his chest was bad, like a gorilla sat down to eat a banana there. Followed by the jolt as the speed-brakes came on. The distant sound of Tiger cursing. A babble of questions from the *Boyington* that needed to catch up with his ears.

And then everything was back where it should be. He hoped.

Arian's brows arched. "They sound very upset."

"They'll get over it," Coop said. Maybe. "Why don't you start doing what you're going to do and I'll try to explain what just happened to home plate." And Tiger.

23

Up close, the damage was impressive. Some of the satellites were gone, others damaged though still tenuously connected. There were gaps in the coverage, resulting in a critical weakening in the array's ability to hide itself and the system. Arian scanned the satellites around the damage, frowning as she initiated a connection request between this ship and the array. While she waited for this "handshake," she considered what was visible to their eyes and scanners.

The *Phoenicopterians* seemed sure an invasion was imminent. Was it based on the fact that the breach existed, or did they have the capability to see outside their sanctuary? It was not something they would want known by outsiders, if they hoped to secure them in a haven, but the idea of it made sense to Arian. Surely they would need to see beyond their borders from time to time? And if they could not? Then how current were the star charts they had provided to the *Boyington*? It must be possible, she concluded. That they had not informed her of this...

All of it came back to trust. She could understand why both sides were troubled. The *Phoenicopterians* feared for their sanctuary, and Coop's people wanted to go home. Competing interests could complicate trust. Could she find a way through this tangle that would satisfy both? And if she couldn't, who did she sacrifice? Her insides flinched at the thought of this choice. It seemed inconceivable for her to betray either. She had to find a way to help both. If she failed...

She did not know what would happen, but she knew she could not let either side down. She must succeed at both or die.

Because she did not wish to dwell on dying, she glanced at Coop. He seemed to be explaining about the comet drive. How could they not know about this drive? That seemed most odd to her. How long had they possessed these shuttles? And why did they only have two of them? She felt that quiver of knowledge just out of reach, of knowing without actually knowing, but it was not relevant to their current circumstances. She was here to do a job, and that must be her only focus.

The array was quite remarkable, even without all the expectations swirling around it. And not just because she'd lived most of her life on a farm and this was even more complex than anything she'd ever seen.

It looked like a net—she frowned—what did she know of fisherman's nets? Whatever, the design was quite similar, with strands of energy linking them together. The satellites were the joining points that both hid and protected the sanctuary. It traced the edges of this small galaxy of a star system. The satellites themselves were circular, with spikes sticking out in every direction. Some of those spikes were antennas to communicate with the others, but others were...just spikes. She sat back. That was interesting. Why spikes when the devices had both cloaking, shielding, and deflective capabilities?

She turned her attention back to the breach. The energy lines were thinner, but still there, the devices appearing to cling together as if they knew the importance of their mission.

Almost, she had a sense of being there when they were devised, of standing in front of one with tool in hand...

Her hands flexed, then closed around a tool not there—

Coop retracted the shielding on the front view screen, so they could see the array in real time. This view of the actual devices startled her for some reason. They looked so much... older than—she shook off the past, though it left reluctantly.

"Is that weapons damage?" Coop asked.

She shot him a look, noting his frown.

He tapped his radio. "Sorry, sir, we are attempting to assess the situation. It's complicated. Yes, I did say weapons fire, sir. Could you please hold while we figure this out?"

It was a very polite way to tell his colonel to back off, though he was only able to do it because they were out of reach, Arian surmised, with a slight smile. If he were here, the Colonel would be pacing. Almost she wished she could move around, as the shuttle computer argued with the array's systems. No handshake yet—there was a discreet trill.

"I'm into the first layer of programming," she said. It was not the level she needed to access, but it was a start, this maintenance level. "The devices have cloaking capability. When they are functioning correctly, this sanctuary is virtually invisible."

"Virtually?" Coop queried.

"Well, if someone flew into it, perhaps they would know something was there." She tapped deeper into the maintenance program. "No, it has quite sophisticated deflective ability, so if a ship flew straight into it, it would be deflected without damage." She frowned.

"It would just bounce off?" Coop shook his head.

"It is designed to divert objects prior to impact. They would miss the array, possibly without realizing they'd changed course."

"But wouldn't that make it impossible for someone to shoot at it?"

"It should." Arian explored the data some more. "According to the maintenance data, some of the satellites began to experience programming failure, which weakened the deflective capabilities in this section."

"Why?" Coop asked.

She looked at him. He believed her able to know more than was possible. His confidence in her made her want to try. "It could be a factor of aging. It is very old." A notation caught her eye. "Once it began to fail, it also became vulnerable to meteor strikes."

"Which compounded the problem?"

"That would be my guess." She scrolled through the data after the strikes. "Because it wasn't repaired, over time the breach widened. The master program tried to adjust for the failures, but eventually, the cloak began to fail, as well."

"So, not weapons fire?"

She dug deeper. "There is data that suggests the array has experienced weapons fire."

"Suggests?"

She nodded. "The array does not know the difference between a meteor and directed fire, but there are energy spikes that would not be consistent with meteors." He arched a brow. "Whatever caused the impacts, the protective capability is compromised."

"So it's probably visible on the other side?" Coop asked.

"I would postulate that at least this damaged section is visible."

"Which would be why the birds are afraid of an invasion."

"It's such a small area," Arian protested, "in an immense galaxy. If someone saw it..."

"It's kind of typical to try to get past a wall. Curiosity and all that."

She nodded slowly. She knew all too well about wanting to breach barriers. "The presence of protection would be perceived as evidence that something valuable was inside."

"Pirates, most likely." He grinned. "They do get around."

"If there were attacks, early data indicates they were weak and ineffective. The intensity of the impacts has increased recently."

"Recently?"

"Well, recently for the *Phoenicopterians*. It has probably been many hundreds of your years. The impacts commence and stop many times." She sorted the data, pulling out what she believed would interest Coop. "The type of energy signature varies when those impacts begin to occur, but for some time the energy signature has not varied as much, except in intensity."

His frown deepened. "Someone, or something, has stepped up the attacks."

It was a logical conclusion. She pressed the programing, trying to access the next level. They needed to see outside the array.

"Can you fix this thing?" His worry was evident.

She shared it. Fixing the array was essential to negotiating their exit from the sanctuary and to protecting the *Phoenicopterians*. Though, even if fixed, something or someone appeared to know this system existed. Would a persistent enemy just leave?

"I can not fix destroyed devices." She had this sense that, with enough time, she could have built replacements. And resources, she reminded herself with an inner scoff. She had neither. "The programming has been trying to link the healthy satellites together. Perhaps I can help it. But if the attacks continue, it is only a..."

"Bandaid? A temporary fix," he added, assuming—rightly—

that she would not understand the other reference. "Can we see what is on the other side yet?"

"I am attempting to access the next level of programming." It did not want to let her in.

"I wonder..." Coop changed course so that they were sitting in front of one of the larger holes in the array coverage. He leaned forward as if he could see through the array.

"That is interesting. It still blocks our view out, at least..." She sighed. She needed that access and then the next one after that. She supposed it made sense, but it was most frustrating when she was trying to help. "I am not sure I would keep the ship here, however—incoming!"

Coop veered the ship as sharply away from the gap as he could in space. Luckily the incoming was bound by the same laws of physics as they were. The shuttle's shields took a glancing blow before they reached a position behind a stronger section of the array.

"Did they see us?"

"I am not certain," Arian said. The energy pulses had not followed them, however. "We need to see more."

"What's the problem?"

"The array's programming has many levels. Each one is harder to access than the last one."

"Can the geek doc help you with that?"

"Tell the Captain I'm trying."

The geek doc's voice sounded amused in her comm.

"Bastards are undoing my work almost as fast as I can do it."

Arian suddenly found herself in the next level of programming. It was not the highest level yet, but now she could see the other side of the array. She stiffened. "I see why the *Phoenicopterians* are concerned."

"—holy—"

Arian did not recognize the word Dr. Janeck used. She suspected it was more exclamation than technical term.

"That's not good," Coop said.

"No," Arian agreed. If this is what the *Phoenicopterians* had seen, it was no wonder they lived in fear.

———

The enemy fleet consisted of thirty large ships, with about one hundred smaller ships in various sizes. The larger ships were thinner toward the nose, thicker in the middle, and then they narrowed again. Ships of war were designed to look intimidating. The *Boyington,* for instance, was a ship made for war, even if its primary purpose was exploration. But these—these were war birds. They'd been crafted to inspire fear before the shooting began. The lines and angles were predatory. They reminded him of flying dinosaurs, birds of prey like the Klingons had, only these weren't digital or special effects. And the size of the fleet told Coop they did not intend to go home empty-handed this time.

A hundred-plus against their two ships.

The array's protection felt minimal.

If they were forced to bump heads with these bogeys, they weren't going to last long. They needed a different strategy, one that took advantage of the one advantage they had. Their cloaking technology. Stealth...

"This remind you of anything, Tiger?" Coop asked his wingman.

"Which FUBAR should I remember?"

Tiger sounded pretty amused considering.

"Those old World War Two movies we used to watch."

"Okay, I might need one more clue."

"The Silent Service." The wolf pack subs weren't cloaked,

but they might as well have been until the allies improved their radar.

Coop could almost see Tiger straighten.

"I'm starting to follow you, Banshee."

"We're not exactly a wolf pack," Coop admitted, "but we have one thing those early subs didn't have."

"Cloaking tech." Tiger's tone said his wheels were turning, too. "We need to let the old man see this."

"Already sent," Coop said. Would the birds help? They had cloaking tech, but home plate didn't. If they came—and he was sure Pappy would come if at all possible—it would have a big, old target painted on it. He looked at Arian. "You two have to fix that hole. If that many ships get through—"

Her face was pale, tense. She nodded. "What is a sub?"

"If we survive, I'll show you," he promised. He considered the problem. He'd like to go through that hole and do some damage, but he wasn't stupid. "We have to assume at least some of them will get through..."

"I estimate they will breach the array in two of your hours." A thread of strain ran through her voice. "Or less."

"Keep working on fixing it, both of you. If some ships get through, we'll deal with them, but let's keep as many out as we can." Divide and conquer. This wasn't dogfighting. This wasn't like anything he'd trained for, but in an opportunity to excel, that was pretty much SOP. It wasn't going to be enough to think outside the box. It was time to kick it to the curb. "What kind of weapons does this crate have?"

24

THERE WAS SOME GOOD NEWS. Reinforcements were coming.

There was some bad news. None of them had a comet drive.

The birds could fly faster than the *Boyington,* and they had those sling things. If they could rig the *Boyington,* then they'd arrive in twelve hours—give or take a lot of uncertainty because the birds didn't count time in the same way they did. And if they couldn't get the sling rigged? The *Boyington* wouldn't like being last to the fight, but Coop would be happy if the bird fleet arrived before they got blown out of space.

That was, if they knew how to fight. They'd been a sanctuary for a long time, near as he could tell. And they hadn't exactly talked about fighting at the last meet up.

"I wish we had some mines," Coop said, then had a sudden thought and turned to Arian. "What about the array devices? Could they be rigged to explode on contact? If we could detach some and scatter them around?" He frowned. "But only if they could remain cloaked." Otherwise, the aliens could just shoot themselves a path through.

Arian looked interested, then thoughtful. "At this level of programming, I think I can move them. I'd need to disable their deflection programming while keeping the cloak online..." Her voice trailed off as she leaned into her station, her hands a blur on the keys. "Where do you want them? To cover entry?"

"No, if the first ship hits something, they'll fire a concentrated spread to clear their path. We want to lure a few of them in, then close the door behind them," Coop muttered, studying the tactical HUD and mentally playing out scenarios. They'd have to enter one at a time, but then they'd need to spread out into some kind of defensive formation. But once they hit the mine field—

If they put the minefield there, then the ships behind would be forced to veer in these directions. If he and Tiger each took a side—he frowned. He was used to having Tiger on his wing, used to them covering each other. With this plan, they'd be far apart if one of them got in trouble. He kept trying scenarios, running them from beginning to end. There wasn't any other option that he could see. Maybe Tiger could see something he couldn't. He put together the plan and shot it over to his wingman. "Take a look at this, Tiger. Tell me what you think."

He knew his tone told Tiger that he wasn't happy with it either. He turned back to the plan. If they did take up positions on either side of the breach, Tiger low, their ship high...

Of course, there was no high or low in space. It was all relative, but flyboys needed to at least pretend there were some fixed points so they wouldn't accidentally shoot each other. "Be a bummer if one of us shot the other accidentally..." he muttered.

"These shuttles have programs in place that allows them to avoid friendly fire," Arian murmured.

That could be good, but also unpredictable. "Can I turn it off if I need to?"

Arian looked startled, considered it, then nodded, even as she used her HUD to pluck devices out of the array and set them tracking toward the trap coordinates. "When we go into combat mode, the option will appear on your screen."

"I'm a control freak," he said. Short answer was all he had time for. In battle he needed to control all the shuttle's movement. Didn't want, or need, it jinking on its own just as he took aim at something. Her lips twitched, but she did not comment. They were both busy. He turned back to his battle plan. His comm pinged.

"Go ahead, Tiger."

"This has some pretty sweet weapons systems for a passenger shuttle."

"Perhaps," Arian said, without looking up, "the passengers lived in dangerous times?"

"The lady has a point," Tiger conceded. "Or the passengers were high value."

"Well, I put a high value on us. Let's try to stay alive and fighting fit until the reinforcements arrive." He hesitated, not sure how to ask.

"It's the only way, Banshee."

No surprise Tiger knew what was bothering him. "Yeah," he agreed. It was the only way.

Time seemed to slow and speed up. It was like that before battle. Nerves tightened to shatter point and then smoothed out when the action started. In the heat of battle, it was all reflex, split second decisions, and surviving because you were a little better, a little quicker, or boom you were gone because the other guy got the drop on you. He'd lost men in battle. Knew the feel of this, felt the change in the air as he briefed his contingent of Marines. Must be crap to be strapped down, your life in some other guy's hands. He'd have left them back at home plate, but Pappy always had his reasons. If they were boarded—well, he'd be glad they were here.

"We've got incoming." The voice was Janeck's.

Arian looked from her HUD to Coop's. Janeck had been monitoring the breach and working on how to shut the door at the right time, while Arian worked on her minefield.

"They are sending in scout ships." Coop cursed under his breath. He should have thought of that. If one of the smaller ships hit their mines before the bigger ships came through—

As the small group entered sanctuary space, it almost looked like the array devices were riding on a current. When a ship came too close to the devices, they bobbed away. Then drifted back into place behind the scouts as they began to move into positions well clear of the breach.

"Nice job." Coop relaxed about a millimeter. Had to tense again when the scouts put their feelers out, scanning for threats. They shouldn't find anything, not when everything was cloaked, but they wouldn't know for sure until the shooting started. And they lost their advantage. After a tense period, while the ships settled into place, in a staggered line of high and low, he let his breath out. They were looking the wrong way for trouble. Well, the wrong way to see the shuttles. The *Boyington* on the other hand...

"How far can they see?" Coop asked, not expecting an answer.

"They are smaller, with less sophisticated technology," Arian said. "I doubt they can see that far into the sanctuary. Most of their interior is given over to weapons."

"What kind?"

"Energy based, but they do have a couple of devices that are similar to your missiles."

"Can we update home plate?"

Arian hesitated. "It would be a risk."

"I'm surprised the array doesn't have something that will shoot," Coop murmured, making a small adjustment to position mostly for something to do. "Hold fire until the first mine strike," he told Tiger, even though he didn't have to.

"Roger that." Tiger didn't sound offended. His focus had intensified, too. Coop would hear it in his voice.

It felt like forever for anything to happen outside the breach. Then the first of the big ships started to move.

"Why so slow?" Not that he was in a hurry—okay, so he was ready to get this done.

"They can not be certain it will get through." Arian checked something.

They watched it make small course adjustments as it drew closer to the array.

"It's gonna be close," Coop muttered.

"Very," Arian agreed.

If it didn't get through, they'd probably start shooting again. And if a stray shot came through the gap and hit one of the devices—felt weird to be hoping the bad boy would fit. He tensed as the HUD showed the ship intersecting with the array. Almost felt like he heard the scrape of metal against the hull as its thickest part reached the point of critical contact. Did the alien ship hang there? Time slowed—and then the fat part was through. Coop released a breath he hadn't realized he was holding.

"How many do we let through?" Janeck asked.

Coop assessed the ships. "No more than four." That would be pushing it, but he also wanted the bogeys to feel some pain. He glanced at Arian. "Can you arrange a mine strike at the same time we shut the door?"

Arian shot him a look. Gave a tiny shrug. "I wonder why they don't widen the gap? They could send more ships in a faster rate?"

"If it were me in charge over there, I'd worry about how closely the array is being monitored. Maybe they are hoping the breach will appear small enough to keep the birds from reacting in time." Is that what would have happened? He couldn't read the birds well enough to know their tactics. No surprised, the birds hoped the array would get fixed before there was a battle, but they'd known it was coming. What kind of defenses had they built up as they watched this happening? Did they have enough ships to take on an armada of this size if they did break through? Had they failed to act because they couldn't fix the array? Or were the birds sacrificing them to buy time? His two-ship wolf pack should be able to cause them some problems, but if too many ships got through, all they could hope for was to last long enough to distract and annoy them as they moved deeper into the system.

And if, by some miracle, they stopped this incursion? Even if they got it all fixed, the aliens knew something was here. They wouldn't stop trying. Deal with the problem in front of you, he reminded himself.

Tiger spoke through the comm. "Those formations kind of look like battle groups. One big ship and two smaller ones."

That they did. Hadn't planned on the addition of the smaller ships. If he'd been a sea dog instead of a flyboy...

Would their modified wolf pack strategy translate successfully into a three-dimensional battle? He ran the plan through the systems again, but couldn't think how to change it. And it was too late now.

"Well, the subs took those on, too, Tiger."

"That they did, Banshee."

"We got two battle groups on this side. Janeck, stand by to shut the door."

There was a grunt Coop took to be an affirmative. Okay, he hoped it was an affirmative. The formation's resemblance to Naval battle groups increased as the smaller ships moved into position on either side of the larger ships, once they'd cleared the breach. On the HUD, Coop could see Arian's devices bobbing around the approaching ships like buoy's in an ocean. She'd have to time their movement just right. Which might not be possible.

The first ship continued to move forward, with its escort matching the forward momentum. As the second and third groups cleared the array, one of the groups adjusted into a course for the high element position, the other moving toward the lower element of the standard combat box. That left the first ship in the lead element. Did that make it the big boss alien element or the sacrificial lamb?

"Combat box." Coop spoke out loud for Tiger's benefit.

"Does kind of look like it," Tiger said.

Even if the best case happened, the rear guard ships wouldn't interact with the mines. Hopefully, they could make life difficult for them anyway. He tracked movement, looking for which direction he thought the bogeys on his side would break when the mines blew. He started adjusting course, saw Tiger doing the same.

Who were these guys? Were these just universal tactics or did they read history, too? In WW2, the B-17 bombers had used a combat box to concentrate fire and for self-defense, but they'd been defending against diving Stukas and barrages from ground defenses. Were they prepared for the two shuttles' surprisingly interesting defenses? He hoped not. And he hoped he'd picked the right placement for the battle. He was putting ships—and their crews—pretty far out on a limb.

"The fourth battle group has cleared the breach," Arian said. "Dr. Janeck, close the gap now. Firing reverse rockets on the devices."

Coop's heart started to thump a hard countdown when the gap didn't close. "What's the holdup, doc?"

The doc ignored him. Maybe he was busy. Another battle

group passed through the gap.

"That's five."

"I can count," Janeck snapped.

Coop didn't speak when the sixth group cleared the breach. He did start sweating.

Number seven was approaching, the two smaller ships in the lead. On his HUD he saw thin lines begin to track across the breach, like flashes of lightning that stayed connected and grew thicker instead of flashing out of sight. Bogey number seven must have seen it, too. It began decelerating and went into a ponderous turn. The two smaller ships were too close. The last lines knit into place. Light flared, and the two ships disappeared from tracking.

"Any damage to the array?" Coop asked. Six big bogeys and twelve little ones—relatively speaking. All twelve ships were significantly larger than their shuttles.

Arian studied the readings. "The repair fluctuated, but it is holding."

He ran a hand across the top of his head, then settled deeper into his seat. He activated the internal comms. "Everyone strapped in? We're gonna start bumping heads."

Arian checked her strap. "Ten minutes until multiple device impact with the lead ships."

In the three dimensional HUD, Arian's minefield looked like a net bending to enclose the first three battle groups. On the HUD, it looked like a knockout punch. In reality, they could have used more devices in play. She'd had to pluck them out carefully, and there'd only been time to pull from around the damaged area.

"Do we know how powerful those things are?"

"They should destroy any smaller ships that take a direct hit. Damage to the larger ones will depend on their shields."

"So, that's a no." He itched to launch the battle drones. They were small and deadly, which would make them hard to target, but they had a limited power source. Without the data from the first strike, their deployment wouldn't be as effective. The goal was maximum confusion for as long as possible. Yeah, they were cloaked, but as soon as they started doing crap, even a stupid and confused enemy should be able to figure out their general position. They had the maneuverability advantage over what they could see. But if those ships had small fighter craft—which he would expect—then they'd lose that edge.

The last two battle groups added to the combat box, settling into staggered position—low and high—relative to the rear element. He'd guess that the distances gave an indication of their standard firing spread. They wouldn't want to shoot each other either.

So, best case scenario, their minefield took out the lead ship in the front high position, and the front low ships. That would leave three groups to bump heads with. Of course, best case was a dream. A faint hope. It was going to be a knife fight in a phone booth kind of battle, a real fur ball.

It felt like a slow-mo shot as he waited for the group on his side to enter his tactical box. He activated his comm to the Marines. In the camera view, they were all fully rigged out, including oxygen masks in case of a hull breach. Locked and loaded. Even if they couldn't help him that much, it was a reassuring sight.

"We engage the enemy in three minutes..."

25

Lights flared, one or two at first, but it quickly spread into what appeared to be a charge running in a moving line, from ship to ship. Secondary explosions flared in the wake of the running charge. The flares grew bigger, spreading, so many that the sensors were overloaded, the field of battle a concentrated white light. Arian felt Coop's tension as they waited for the sensors to catch up, for the HUD to update.

White faded slowly, then out of the white shapes images emerged, beginning to resolve into real data once more.

The lead element was completely gone, both the large ship and its accompanying smaller ships.

The ships in what she'd call the center of the formation were not damaged, though they had received debris impacts from when the larger ship blew up, she noted. The outer groupings had sustained damage. One of the larger ships on Tiger's side of the formation was drifting out of position, it's propulsion offline. The smaller support ships were both gone.

On their side of the formation, the two smaller ships were gone. The larger ship had slowed, but still had some propulsion.

There were signs of confusion, the bogeys' orderly formation dissolving as the following ships altered course to avoid mines.

She drilled deeper into the data, pulling out the ships with weakened shields and sending the data to Coop. "You should target these with the battle drones."

She heard Coop's long sigh of satisfaction. His eyes were alight and a small smile played around his mouth.

"Launching." The shuttle shuddered as the first wave of drones left their tubes.

On the other side of the field of battle, Tiger's drones moved in a swarm toward targets. Both shuttles were already altering position as fast as was possible in the vacuum of space. The swarms flowed among the ships, most going for the weakened ships, but also for other targets. The smaller ships had no chance. Four more exploded, the force of it rocking the larger ships, pelting them with chunks of debris. More of the drones punched into the larger ships, a few getting through their shields and piercing armor.

"Three large ships and two small ships operational," Arian said. "One large ship has lost propulsion, another is at half propulsion."

"Any data on their weapons systems?" Coop asked. His hands on the controls made light adjustments, just enough to keep them in motion.

"All remaining ships have weapons capability—fighter craft is launching from remaining large ships." Her lips thinned. Luckily this ship could count because there were too many targets for her to count visually. "Thirty from each of five ships."

"That's a lot of little ships," Coop agreed, his smile widening.

"Yes," Arian agreed. One hundred and fifty—their drones turned to target this new threat, taking out several, but leaving many targets behind.

"Firing the second wave of battle drones," Coop said.

He'd called it the second wave, but it was also the last of the drones. And the fighter ships were going after them. Because they were the only visible target for them, she reminded herself. They wanted this outcome.

Coop flashed her a quick grin. "Don't look so worried. This bus still has a few surprises left. " The shuttle veered right, shuddering from a glancing blow from one of the randomly fired enemy blasts. He used the blow to change course again.

Arian worked on rebuilding the shuttle's shields and cloak.

"That was close," Coop said.

It was as if he'd become one with this ship. It responded to his lightest touch. Had she, in memory, felt possessive of this ship? It was yet another puzzle she lacked time to tease out. Time...something about that thought, that word caused her hands to tremble briefly before she got them under control.

"They have damaged many drones," Arian said, surprised her voice sound calm when it felt as if her insides shuddered like that large ship taking fire.

"They're drawing fire for us," Coop said, an odd resolution in his tone.

———

"How far out are our reinforcements?" Coop asked, his mind comparing options as his battle drones winked out like stars at daybreak. If he dropped the cloak now, it would be a figurative unzipping of his fly. He didn't want to do it until he had to. And he hoped "had to" would be never. They wouldn't last long if the enemy could see them.

"I do not know. This shuttle can not see the *Phoenicopterian* ships when they are cloaked."

They could sit tight until the drones were all destroyed, but that was crap tactics. If the enemy eliminated the drones, then

the remaining ships would be able to concentrate all their attention on looking for them. With weapons. Right now they weren't
sure who and what was doing this or where they were. As if
Tiger heard him thinking, or was thinking the same thoughts,
his comm activated.

"Time for round two, Banshee?"

Round two was just short of unzipping their flies. But they
did need to take advantage of those weakened shields while they
could. They needed every advantage they could squeeze out.

"Time for round two," he agreed. "I'll go in first." This was
going to be worse than a knife fight in a phone booth. There was
more room in the phone booth. "If I make it, then give it a go."

"And if you don't?"

"You're in command. You get to decide." Coop grinned, but
when he glanced at Arian the grin faded. "I'm sorry."

She held his gaze for a long moment. "You believe we are
going to die."

He shrugged. "High probability." He didn't have to look at
the HUD to know he'd be navigating through a randomly
swarming anthill—that couldn't see him and dodge.

"So be it." Her lips pursed together, her eyes closed.

He glanced left, then right. "Arian? What are you doing?"

Her eyes opened. "I am puckering up." Coop shook his head,
bewildered. "For the good-bye kiss."

His grin came back. "You don't know how much...sweetheart
if I kiss you now, I'll lose the plot. But you just gave me a good
reason not to die today."

The pucker faded into a smile that lit every part of her face.
Almost, he gave in—he turned resolutely back to the HUD.
Their very small window of opportunity was closing. He wasn't
ashamed to admit he said a little prayer. There were no atheists
in fox holes or cockpits. He studied the darting fighter craft,
noted how they moved. "The drones will veer away from us?"

"Yes." She'd gone back to her keyboard.

That was both good and bad. If the enemy were watching—and he had to assume they were—the drones movement gave them clues to the shuttle's course. If they were lucky, this enemy would figure it out after. He banked the shuttle and started into the anthill, heading for the closest of the remaining big bad boys. He'd have preferred to start with a ship that had more damage, but he might only get one run at this. Tiger would have a better chance if all the ships had some damage.

As he wove through the swarm of enemy fighters and drones, the shuttle screamed multiple warnings—they cut off abruptly. "Thanks."

"It is not as if you do not know." Arian sounded calmly amused. "The first energy pulse weapon is ready for you to fire."

"Optimum range?" he asked.

"To reduce the chances of interception—"

"Close. Got it." He should be scared. He'd done hopeless and survived. This was worse than hopeless. He fought the urge to bank hard when an enemy fighter cut across his path. There was no room for hard banking. He came close enough to the fighter that their shields bumped, sending it spinning out of control. It crashed into one of the scout ships, and they both exploded. He'd call that a win, though the enemy was probably looking at the data to see why. If they could add...

He cut in close, this time forcing a drone off course, and drew a bead on his target. It had been the last ship through the breach, had the least damage, except to the shields from drone attacks. Time to change that. His thumb was light on the trigger as he made small course adjustments for his approach.

"Warn me when we're three hundred meters from the target," he asked.

"Roger that."

He found he could still grin, even as he narrowly avoided a

collision with two enemy fighters. Did their collision alarms go off? Were they tracking him now? There was an itch between his shoulders as he steadied course for the final part of his firing run.

"Three hundred meters in five seconds."

He angled so they'd skim just outside the target's shields.

The collision alarm blared, even though it was supposed to be off.

He didn't blame the shuttle. He didn't like it either—one more meter.

He thumbed the trigger, felt the small jolt as the missile left the tube. He changed course as fast as the laws of physics allowed. This weapon was not cloaked. So they could guess where he was unless he could stop being there fast. Enemy fire filled the space around them.

The missile flew straight and deadly, too fast for the enemy to destroy it and not hit their own ship. It passed through the weakened shields and impacted solidly.

Beams of fire filled the space around them. The shuttle rocked as it took some glancing blows. If he'd fired any further out, the enemy fighters would have got it. Whoever this was, they could shoot. And track.

"Shields at ninety percent, cloak at ninety-two percent."

The enemy fighters tried to peel away from the concentrated fire. Coop tucked himself in behind a couple of them. No reason to linger where the shooting was.

Light flashed in irregular patterns across the surface of the ship he'd targeted, then it went dark. Dead in space. Gotta love those energy pulse weapons. As soon as the big ship lost shields most of the remaining drones closed on it, making it marginally easier for Coop to continue to exit the area.

Multiple fire patterns continued to criss-cross through where they'd been and where the shooters hoped they were going.

Depending on how sensitive their sensors were, flying almost up their six was working for him for right now.

There was a change in the pattern of the fighters. They were trying to box him in. Where he wasn't.

Don't get cocky, he reminded himself, and shifted to the six of a couple of different ships, riding their tails and moving closer to his next target.

"That's how it's done," he told Tiger.

"Didn't look that hard."

"A walk in the park," Coop agreed, hitting his speedbrakes when the fighter in front of him slowed suddenly. Did it see him? If you knew what you were looking for, a good pilot could "see" trouble on their six. He found someone new to shadow and checked the HUDs. Only two fully functional big ships remained. Only two, he mocked himself. They'd be watching for the next run, and now the fighters were doubling down on the drones. And moving to screen the remaining ships. They'd seen the danger of having their shields reduced. They knew Coop was out there, but they didn't know about Tiger. Almost, he wanted to hold him back

He started a new run, this time directed at the ship with reduced propulsion. They'd be expecting an attack on the undamaged ships. If he could distract them, Tiger might be able to take out one of them before their drones were all gone.

"Something is changing," Arian said.

He only had time for brief glances at his HUD. He'd followed the last fighter into a swarm of them. If he wasn't careful, he was gonna end up in the middle instead of on something's six. He frowned as he processed what he could see. She was right. The swarms of fighters were reforming, gradually settling into smaller versions of the combat box. Maybe they were trying to link up their systems to catch him. And if he wasn't careful, it was gonna work. He throttled back, finding a spot between two boxes while he studied the situation.

Combat boxes were being deployed to protect the last two ships. Lots of movement so that the moving boxes could cover the larger ship. Then the formations began to tighten, closing the gaps between to try and force him into the "safe" areas in the center of the boxes.

If it smelled like a trap, even if he couldn't see the trap yet, then it was a trap. Not that he couldn't see some of the trap, just couldn't see what they gained with this yet. So far, he could still thread the needle. Just how ballsy was this enemy? How far would they go?

"They are attacking the array again," Arian said. "We are staying stay ahead for now."

"Good job," he said absently.

"What are they up to?" Tiger asked, his tone almost absent.

The combat boxes appeared to dissolve and reform, their dance not pretty, but yeah, it was designed to flush him out. Tiger was still outside the dance, since he hadn't started his run when they initiated the change. But Coop was getting squeezed from all directions. And he'd have to work his way through several of the moving boxes to get clear.

And lose his shot at the big ships.

"You keep clear, Tiger. They don't know you're here. You're my ace in the hole."

"That's—yes, sir." His voice was tight, not happy, the "sir" a clear indication he knew it was an order.

Instead of fighting the dance, Coop tried to use it to get closer to his target, pushing back what would happen once he fired on something. They'd have all their sensor eyes on those big ships watching for that move. He slipped between two fighters without bumping shields this time, watching for external threats in this complicated dance, and trying to figure out where the trap would close.

He keyed a channel to his Marines, in lock-down in the rear. "It's gonna get bumpy, guys. Hang on."

This shuttle had the best inertial dampeners the Garradians could devise, but even they weren't up to what he was making the ship do. He had to fight to keep clear of the spaces opening up as the boxes dissolved and reformed. The drones didn't know to not get sucked into clear space that was widening in each combat box. They darted into it, then launched at the fighters again.

The moving box at the outer edge ejected multiple objects into the center, then pulled back as the space lit up with brilliant, sensor blinding light.

When his sensors got their eyes back, the box had collapsed, forming a screen around the next box. Multiple exploding objects again.

"They're clearing the field," Tiger said, his voice grim.

The drones were disappearing faster, and they were forcing him closer to the big ships in his efforts to keep out of the center of the boxes.

Something on his HUD caught his eye. Weird the scout ships weren't doing anything.

"Do you have time to scan those scout ships?" he asked. "Why are they just sitting there?"

They were almost dormant, he realized. None of the drones had targeted them.

"All their resources are directed into scanning. I can launch counter measures."

Coop would have blinked if he'd dared. "Counter measures?"

"They are different versions of the combat drones. Fewer of

them, but they will create false energy signatures in a variety of places. It should confuse them."

"Confused is good." They needed lots of confusion right now, but at the right moment for maximum impact. His gaze darted around the busy HUD. He gave her a quick glancing grin. "I'll tell you when to launch." His hand light on the stick, he began the complicated moves that would bring the shuttle closer to his target.

26

FOR THE FIRST time since she boarded this ship, Arian was glad she was not its pilot. Coop's hand appeared relaxed on the controls, a slight smile edging his mouth, his gaze laser-focused on finding openings in the morass of ships to slide theirs through.

"Their shields are rebuilding," Arian told him. "There is a weakness remaining on the rear portside." She shot him the coordinates, then resumed her efforts to keep the array closed against the rest of the alien fleet, using her left hand, so that the right was always on the counter measures fire button.

Each time she breached a security level, she shot a packet of information to Dr. Janeck, so he could continue her work if they did not make it, then she attacked the next level.

As Coop was maneuvering between two formations of ships, the formations dissolved, leaving them in a clearing space. Coop muttered something and began the turn toward the relative safety of a cluster of ships.

"They are firing," she said, the clench of her stomach a contrast to a tone that surprised her by its calmness. She had lived in death's shadow for so long, perhaps that is why she felt little fear now.

The alien barrage began to detonate. The shuttle rocked.

"Hull breach," she said. On the upper deck. With her free hand, she closed the hatches, then worked to restore pressure to the rear compartment. She checked the camera. The Marines were strapped in and geared up. With their oxygen masks in place, it was not possible to see their expressions, though based on her last experience with them, there would not be expressions to see. "Shields down to sixty percent. The cloak is holding at eighty percent."

"Not sure which would be worse to lose," Coop muttered.

They did need both. He had not given the order to launch counter measures, so she waited. She did wish she had more hands. As if the aliens knew, they stepped up their attacks on the array while she focused on the shuttle.

"They've figured out something," Coop muttered, "just not sure what."

"You believe they can see us?" That was not possible.

"Not see us, exactly." He frowned. "They know that we have two options. We are either heading for their ships or trying to escape..." His gaze moved around the HUD.

Arian tried to discover what he saw while still working on the array. She was distantly aware her head hurt and pain tracked along both hands into her arms.

"So they are covering their big ships and escape routes..."

To Arian, it appeared he relaxed even more.

"I wonder what would happen if I blew up those escorts screening that big bad boy?" His free hand indicated one of the two remaining ships.

It made Arian's eyes hurt to look at the swarms of ships, the formations appearing, then dissolving and reforming. The explosions blanked their sensors again and again. This was a most determined enemy. Determined...

Was it possible to use that against them? They would require precision to maintain the correct safe distance for their ships as they deployed their weapons. Might that distance function as a buffer for them? Were the weapons controlled or attracted to each other? If the devices were designed to draw together, would it be possible to draw them in another direction? She needed more data. She wished to rub her eyes, but she dared not. Instead, she blinked. There.

"The devices they are launching, they are designed to come together and then detonate."

"How are they controlled? Can you crack it?"

"I am searching for signs of transmissions to the devices..." She found something that looked promising and raced to trace it back to the source before they detonated and she had to start over. She left the array to Dr. Janeck—he seemed to be catching up with her—and even took her hand off the fire control for the counter measures. If they could turn their weapon back on them —her system found something and began tracing it back, like lightning tracks on her screen. Suddenly a view opened onto the bridge of a ship. She could not stop a sharply inhaled breath, pulling Coop's attention her way.

"What the—"

———

"Can," Coop's gaze darted from the view forward to that of the enemy bridge, "they tell we're in their systems?"

"I do not believe so," Arian said, a quiver breaking the calm tone for the first time.

Now, when it was too late, he realized he hadn't asked what a

Mycterian looked like. That should have been his first question. Seriously need-to-know. Closest thing he could come to in his experience was a stork, but not the cute kind that delivered babies. This bunch was the real mean looking deal, the kind that ate other birds' babies. The bridge crew all had blood-red beaks that were long, straight and a honed-to-a-knife-edge sharp. The ring around its eyes was red, too. Its tuft of gray hair should have been a comic element since it looked like it had stuck a claw in an electric outlet. Only there was nothing funny about the way its creepy head seemed to sink onto broad shoulders, giving it the look of an evil banker, the kind that foreclosed houses and tied gals to the railroad tracks. And invaded systems not its own.

It appeared to be wearing a uniform, one that upped the creep factor by quite a bit. All spikes and red and black. Coop was willing to go out on a limb and guess that even their babies weren't cute.

A shift in the enemy fighters grabbed his attention. They were doing a new dance, an intense series of maneuvers. In the swarms of hostile signals, he felt a lot of alone.

"Let me help, Banshee," Tiger said in his ear, his voice tight with worry.

Coop wasn't sure Tiger could get through their fighter screen now. However, "If you see an opportunity, don't pass it up, but let's see if we can take down the ship controlling those...depth charges, first." That's what they reminded him of. Depth charges. They even appeared to leave the ships on a rising and falling arc.

"Roger that, Banshee."

Coop could tell it bothered Tiger not being on Coop's six. He frowned, literally one eye on the big picture trying to figure out what was making his gut twitch while he dodged the shuttle through the little picture. His gut twitched harder. Something about they way were forming bothered him, but it was moving so fast...

"I have a targeting solution for you," Arian said.

It popped up on his HUD. "Good job." He keyed Tiger. "When I unzip my fly, all kinds of bad things are gonna happen, but you'll have your best chance to join the party."

"Roger that."

Lots more enthusiasm in his tone this time.

Coop eased in, watching his targeting for optimum firing.

"I'm gonna hit the speedbrakes as soon as we fire." It was their best chance for not getting blown up. They'd expect them to dodge or flee. So they wouldn't. "Still gonna be ugly."

His gut twitched harder.

Targeting flashed. He pressed the fire button and felt the jolt as it left them and then the jerk as he hit the brakes as hard as he could.

Two things happened simultaneously.

The *Mycterian* bridge image shivered and then vanished as the ship went dark. The depth charges the ship had launched exploded prematurely, sending a good bunch of the enemy fighters into the next world, or into uncontrolled spins. There were multiple impacts, but he didn't have time to enjoy it.

Two reasons for that. Being stopped only helped them with the shots fired, not with the random spin of out-of-control fighter craft. Or the debris from the escort ship when it exploded. He had some momentum left for small movements, but not for big ones. Mostly he watched and prayed. While his gut upped the twitch to bitch level.

"I got a bad feeling—"

The other smaller escort launched weapons. Something new.

Before he could ask, Arian said, "I am scanning the objects."

She inhaled sharply. "They are similar to the weapons the pirates launched before our anomaly transit."

"The ones designed to take down our defensive systems?"

"I believe so."

Always trust the gut.

"They might not be completely effective," she said. "They will not be familiar with your systems."

"Launch those counter measures," he said. "Tiger, hold position."

————

Arian fired the counter measures, two packages of them from the rear of the shuttle. It seemed as if they moved away from the ship in opposites directions too slowly to help.

The enemy devices had been fired in a spread, but enough were on a trajectory to intersect their ship. If the counter measures did not draw some of them off...

"How much longer—" Coop's question cut off when the devices activated.

Like seed pods, they exploded in multiple directions. Her HUD lit up with hundreds of targets. She would imagine the same was happening to the enemy.

"Hotel sierra!" Coop and Tiger spoke almost together.

Attracted to the targets, many of the devices changed course. That was, as Coop would say, the good news. The bad news? The remaining ships began to fire on these suddenly inviting targets. Energy blasts crisscrossed everywhere, including where they were. The shuttle rocked and shuddered.

"Multiple hits to our shields," Arian said. "We are down below fifty percent on shields. Cloak is at forty-five percent." And this before the other devices reached them.

There was nowhere for Coop to go. The shuttle continued to

take hits. Tiger was, she presumed, cursing. The string of words was not something she recognized.

"Three of the devices are still on track to impact with this ship," Arian said. "Perhaps I should have deployed one counter measure," she added apologetically.

"That was two? Holy—" Coop bit off whatever he'd planned to say. "How long to impact?"

"Ten seconds," Arian said.

The enemy was taking out many of their own devices in their efforts to target the counter measures. One of these shots reduced their incoming to two.

"Brace for impact." Even as she said the words, her fingers worked frantically on the keys, diverting power to their weakened shields. The cloak would have to fend for itself.

One device was somewhat ahead of the other. The shuttle shuddered violently once, then they took the second hit.

———

"Shield status?" Coop fought to get the shuttle back under control.

"Down to twenty percent," Arian said. A pause and then, "The enemy is firing more of the disabling devices."

"How many heading for us?"

"All of them."

"All—"

"Our cloak is at five percent. They can see us."

Coop heard the sound of keys. Didn't have time to look at her.

"I'm endeavoring to restore cloak, but—"

"Shields were more important," he finished for her. It was the right call. But it wasn't going to save them. The closer of the big ships launched two larger versions of what he guessed were shuttles. "They are going to try to board us."

Against his will, he heard Yoda in his head. Yeah, they weren't gonna try. He keyed his radio to the Marine Staff Sergeant in command in the rear compartment. "Prepare to be boarded."

———

Arian doubled down on her controls. Nothing she could do would be enough. The shuttle wasn't entirely visible, but the aliens didn't need to see all of it. She scanned the approaching enemy shuttles. Their configuration was different from this one. From what she could see, there was something that looked like an airlock on the front, one surrounded by shafts that could be weapons or securing devices.

"Can they punch through what's left of our shields?" Coop asked. His tone was icy cool.

"I believe so."

"They want us alive," he concluded. "They could blow us out of space right now."

"They wish to know who we are," Arian agreed.

"And collect intel from us." He gave a sharp nod, his hand slack on the stick. Any move Coop made now was pointless.

The enemy fire had stopped. The enemy fighters were moving to surround them. They were confident but wary. If he did anything, they would be blown them out of space. Tiger was still out there, but she could not see what he could accomplish on his own without ending up in the same predicament. She had more counter measures, but they would not fall for that again. At least, not easily. Her mind raced, inventorying their remaining weaponry and how it might be used. But her numbers kept coming up short. As good as their weapons were, the enemy had more of everything.

"Powering down," Coop said, unstrapping. He did not rise, however. He shifted so that he half faced her.

Arian met his gaze, noted the calm resolve in his eyes with, she hoped, the same in hers.

"I presume we have a self-destruct in their somewhere."

She felt a sudden chill, but she nodded. "When—"

"Is the rear compartment secure? Pressurized?"

She nodded once more. The breach had occurred in the upper deck. She'd sealed that section off from the rest of the shuttle and restored the oxygen and pressure back there.

"How much time do we have?"

She ran the numbers. "Fifteen minutes."

He nodded. "Okay, I'm gonna have a chat with Sergeant Major Wilkins back there." He hesitated. "I'm not going to say it. But when I say its Zulu time, you start it, okay?"

She nodded.

He started to rise but stopped. "Arian." He leaned toward her, his gaze so filled with regret her heart ached.

She released her strap so that she could turn more fully toward him. She could not stop her hand from lifting to touch his lean cheek. Words choked her, but none of them seemed right for the moment. His grin was crooked. He bent, his lips hard against hers. They wanted to cling. To savor. To dive deep but there was no time...

Time. She felt something twitch in her mind but, she half smiled, there was no time to think about time. All they could do was their best. And then...die.

He eased back, stroked one finger across lips that trembled at his touch. "Use the radio to keep me updated. And lock the door after me. No one gets in or out. Got it?"

She wanted to protest, and perhaps he saw it in her eyes.

Now he touched her cheek. "You saw them. Just...destroy the ship when I say it's Zulu time."

"Yes. I—" She did not know the words to express what was in her heart.

He looked at her as if trying to memorize something. "Me, too, sweetheart. Me, too."

He hit the control, and the panel slid back. Arian caught a glimpse of the marines, fully geared up and strapped down. Just before the panel slid back, she saw one of them start to rise.

She swallowed the lump in her throat, locked down the cockpit, dashed at her eyes, and attacked her keyboard again. She had to finish. If they did not make it, this must not be the end of her promise to the *Phoenicopterians*. She set up the HUD so she could see the approach of the enemy ships, then went back to her work on the array programming. But part of her mind was searched for a way out...

———

"The first enemy ship is on approach. They appear to be targeting the rear hatch." Arian's voice was as calm as an air traffic controller in Coop's comm.

He had used the time to huddle with Wilkins. They all wanted to fight. They were Marines. He owed them a chance to die fighting. And the truth was, it would provide them with intel. It wasn't enough to see the enemy ships. They needed to see the enemy, see what they were up against, or at least, what the birds were up against. He'd asked Arian to keep the cameras in this section recording as long as she could and to send the feed to Tiger.

At least they'd die for something.

He'd geared up and holstered his hand gun, and holding his P-90, he tried to blend in with the Marines.

"You're in charge of this knife fight, Master Sergeant Wilkins," he said, giving him a grin before pulling his oxygen mask into place. This was their specialty, their show. He'd gotten them into this, and all he could do now was fight at their side. "Your orders, sir?"

Before Wilkins could speak, Arian's calm voice came over the comms. "The second ship is changing course. I think they might be targeting the upper deck." A pause. "I have disabled the access controls from there to your compartment."

It was clear that Wilkins had been thinking while Coop geared up. "Sir—"

"Call me Coop."

"Coop, you and Franks at the rear. Provide back up and watch that access from the upper deck. We don't need them coming at us from front and back."

Coop might have protested inside his head, but his chin went up and down in a terse nod, and he followed Franks to the rear.

Wilkins deployed the rest of his team to take advantage of the cover provided by the rows of seats, ordering them all to hook in with carabiners, just in case the enemy depressurized the compartment.

There was no sound of approach—other than Arian's terse updates.

They felt a thump, then heard a kind of hiss.

"Kill the lights," Wilkins ordered.

The shuttle's interior went dark, blacker than night dark. Coop pulled down his night sight but didn't turn it on. The compartment would most likely get light when the aliens cracked the hatch. But you never knew, maybe the storks could see in the dark, so he had it ready.

Franks voice was quiet. "Any idea what kind of weapons we're up against, sir?"

"Coop," he corrected. "Not a clue."

"No one fires until I say so," Wilkins said, his voice now coming through the comms.

The hissing sound increased, then a thin red line began to track around the hatch, creating a circle slightly larger than a man.

Now there was a shriek of metal, and a thin beam of light appeared around the edges of the rear hatch.

Coop might have been praying. Bet he wasn't the only one.

The red light connected, then there was another teeth gritting metal shriek as the edge of the circle began to bend backward. They were trying to protect themselves as long as possible, he figured.

"They have breached the upper section, too," Arian said, also using the comms now. "The shuttles rear cameras are still operational. I count twenty combatants assembled to board the lower compartment, the same targeting the upper."

"So we outnumber them by a lot," one of the Marines said with satisfaction.

Marine math, Coop thought with an inward chuckle. And he knew he wasn't included in the twelve they were counting. Until he proved himself, he was a liability.

"Wish we could get a look," Wilkins said, and in a few seconds a HUD appeared in the air in front of them.

The storks were lined up in rows of two. They appeared heavily armored but carried no visible weapons. For what felt like a long time nothing moved on either side. Then a circle hatch retracted in the ceiling above the storks. Something began to lower—

"Is that a—"

"No talking," Wilkins ordered.

Not one word as the *human* in the cage descended, the cage clanking to the deck in front of the first two storks. Now he could see these two's uniforms were slightly different. But they were in front. In their world, that was the red shirt section. The sides of the cage hit the deck. The human—male—screamed and kept screaming as the storks stabbed him. And then ate him.

Wilkins didn't have to tell them to be quiet. It took all Coop's courage to hold his ground when the two storks looked up, blood and entrails dripping off their beaks, and looked their direction.

Coop could almost feel Wilkins thinking.

"They want to demoralize us. But they can't, can they?"

"No, sir!" The Marines' shout was soft but emphatic.

No, Coop thought, and the flyboy won't either, even if he wished...

"I have restored some measure of the shield power," Arian's voice had a distinct shake to it, "and I am retracting it to cover you."

The shield wouldn't protect them from a physical assault by the storks, but it helped to hear her voice. In the HUD they could see the storks readying for their assault.

The cut-out circle fell, hitting the decking with a loud clank. And multiple weapons fire hit the shield.

"They are firing stun weapons," Arian told them.

Stun. So the storks could eat them.

"If you see us go down, it's Zulu time," he told Arian.

———

The flare of weapons fire ceased. Seemed like a long bit of nothing, then the clicking started. Like thousands of annoying students tapping on their desks. Another pause while the tapping increased and then another sound joined the tapping.

The sound of claws on metal as the storks started forward.

Still no sign of weapons that he could see, but the storks

looked heavily armored. Were they trying to draw their fire so they could use their stun weapons again?

"Hold your fire." Wilkins voice was soft in the comm.

So he figured they were trying to get them to expose their positions, too. Once they were far enough into the shuttle, the storks would block their own fire. Only...their tactics had been solid up to now. Were they sacrificing...fighters or was there something he was missing? Did they have something up their—wing?

The tapping and click of claws on metal were as bad as chalk on chalkboard. Coop fought the urge to twitch his shoulders, something about the blood-red eyes made moving seem a bad idea.

The line of two widened into three as the first line stepped onto the shuttle, then widened into four.

"Steady—fire!" Wilkins ordered.

Their shots sparked off the bird's armor and began to ricochet around the interior of the shuttle.

"Aim for their legs and heads!" Wilkins shouted now.

Coop was too far back to see their legs, but there were a lot of heads to target.

The first line of birds went down. The tapping got louder, even competing with the sharp sound of their shots. The lines of birds began to blur as the storks adjusted to their tactics.

Smoke drifted in the air.

The tapping increased.

They couldn't use grenades in the confined space. Wouldn't need to self-destruct at that point.

"Stun," Wilkins ordered.

Against the light from the stork ship, Coop saw a figure rise and toss something. As the stun device clinked against metal, two of the storks charged that position. Shots pelted them. One stork went down but the other stabbed at the Marine with its beak.

It's beak.

The soldier's body armor deflected the attack, so the bird shifted, finding the connect point in the plates.

The beak lifted, red dripping from the point. The man shrieked as it stabbed again. Someone concentrated fire on the stork as it started to drag the screaming man away.

The stun device detonated.

The stork went down.

The screaming turned to moans.

"Cover!"

Two figures darted forward and dragged their comrade back.

On the shuttle, the storks appeared to be regrouping. They'd beat back the first wave, but how did they win this battle?

"More shuttles incoming," Arian intoned in their ears.

And then Coop heard a hissing sound at the top of the curved stairs that led to the upper deck.

———

Arian was aware Dr. Janeck was struggling to keep the array locked down but she could not help him if they died now. There had to be something on this ship she could use to tip the balance of the battle—

She stared at the list of weapons again, picking then discarding items as the *Mycterians* launched their second assault. On the upper deck, they were almost through that door.

Suddenly she stiffened. Perhaps she was looking at the wrong list. She pulled up the propulsion options and stared at the last one.

Comet drive.

She glanced at the video feed. The Marines were fighting desperately. Another one went down from a vicious stab from a cruel beak. His comrades fought them off. Again they used a stun weapon to drive them back. The chatter in her comm told her what she needed to know. If the *Mycterians* breached the upper hatch, when the third wave launched, Coop would say the words.

She would have to end all their lives.

She had seconds.

She flicked on her comm. "Secure for comet drive transit."

Coop gasped, might have started to protest, then snapped, "Brace for...impact."

Even as she spoke, her fingers input the jump data. They only needed to jump a short distance. Even so, it might tear the ship apart.

How did they wish to die?

She initiated the drive.

———

If she'd asked, Coop might have opted out of making a comet drive jump with two enemy shuttles suctioned to their shuttle. In the seconds before the storks started to come back, they had just enough time to use their carabiners to secure themselves and the injured.

He'd thought it was weird to make the jump from the cockpit, but apparently, the location just made the view more interesting.

A sort of ripple, like being under water. Ripples flowed out, passing first through the stork shuttle. It elongated, first one direction, then the other. He had a vague memory of Arian mentioning unstable space around a comet drive. This was why they'd moved away from the *Boyington* before the jump, he guessed. He might have closed his eyes, but he opened them immediately, and the view had changed.

The stork shuttle broke in half. Stuff not nailed down rushed past them as the compartment depressurized. There was no way to fix this, so he hung on. As near as he could tell, so did the Marines.

At least one of the storks had tried to hang on. Its claws were hooked into the decking, the legs bloody where a body had been.

He wanted to ask Arian about what hostiles were left from the larger battle, because he had a feeling they'd be super pissed, but his brain might still be bouncing around the inside of his skull. And then he realized it might be the shuttle bouncing...

———

Arian opened her eyes, shook her head and blinked. Where—?

She was in the shuttle, but when—her eyes jerked open. She looked right, then left.

Lights were flashing multiple silent warnings. Dazed, she looked around, trying to figure out—emergency power. Most systems were offline, including inertial dampeners. What data she had reported hull breaches in both the rear and upper chambers. The view screen had several fine cracks running from one side. She tried to close the cover and couldn't.

Comms were down—Coop. How long had she been out? How long would their portable oxygen systems last? Where was the enemy? She tried tapping her comm but heard only a buzz and a brief crackle. Videos were offline, too.

They were in a spin, she realized. Looking out made her dizzy, so she focused on her controls. Smoke drifted in the air, some of it coming from the control panel. She put her hand on her restraint clasp, hesitated, then shrugged. If the front screen blew, she was dead anyway. She crouched down and pulled open the panel. It was a mess. She made what adjustments she could, and then scrambled back into her seat and tried communications again.

If Coop was gone...Arian slumped for half a second, what did it matter who was out there?

And then she heard it. Tapping, someone was tapping on the door to the rear compartment. She flung herself at it, pounding, hoping to be heard. She had no tools, she looked around, found the panel cover and clanged it against the door.

She heard two sounds, then silence. She leaned against the door, her cheek pressing into the metal, tears running down her face and blood dripping from her hands where the panel edges had cut deep. Pain and hope warred for dominance.

Then the shuttle jerked, as if grabbed by a giant hand and the spin began to slow. She staggered over to the controls, but the self-destruct was offline, too.

———

Arian was still alive.

For now.

Coop leaned his head against the hatch and took a couple of deep breathes, until he remembered he would need every bit of oxygen he had left. Using hand signals—their comms were offline—the Marines tended to their injured and their dead, then everyone strapped into the seats.

He could tell, from the view out the rear, that they were in a slow spin. Now he knew how Apollo 13 felt. He kept trying to look, to see if he could tell if their transit had done any damage to the storks.

There was a sudden lurch, a definite jerk as if something had latched onto them. He looked at Wilkins, who looked back, but neither of them could do anything but look. Then they turned toward the rear, where a section of the stork ship was still attached.

A ship loomed up in his sightline, and his heart might have stopped. Or skipped a few beats.

Until he realized it was pink.

The good birds had arrived.

27

GHRYM WAS A GENIUS, which is why Bester paid him enough credits to keep his loyalty. His price would go up after this. Bester could still not quite believe what had happened. He tossed back the drink. That felt real enough.

What weapon had destroyed so many ships?

What was this place? What did the *Mycterians* know what no one else seemed to know? Bester did not know what to call this...hole...in space, the gap the *Mycterians* had been attempting to expand by firing on the areas around it.

"We have to get ahead of them, Ghrym," he told his captain. For the first time, he wondered if Ghrym would refuse an order. The crew was loyal to Ghrym, not Bester. But Ghrym was as loyal to credits as Bester. Their accounts grew together. In the end, the credits tipped the balance, though barely. "They can't see us. Surely that gives an advantage?"

When Ghrym had begun to thread the ship through the mass of *Mycterian* ships, Bester's courage had failed. To stop himself from rescinding his order, he started drinking. He'd been drunk enough to appreciate his captain's cleverness. He'd maneuvered the ship in to where it was almost resting on one of the big ships as they slipped through the opening.

On the other side was a hidden star system. If the *Mycterians* wanted in so badly, there must be much to plunder here.

And his artifact.

His artifact was here. The beacon was stronger on this side. Now he could also see a massive and intricate array. Elfel almost drooled at the sight of it. Ghrym had slipped the ship away from the battle formation as soon as he could, speeding up their flight when the opening closed behind them. Bester didn't ask how they would get out. His attention was completely on what was ahead.

They were barely clear of the *Mycterians* when the front line of the formation exploded, the intensity of it blinding their sensors. Ghrym pulled them back, and waited, not daring to move until their sensors came back on line—just in time to give them a front row seat for the battle.

When it was over all that remained was one damaged ship, a debris field of *Mycterian* ships, and many questions.

He'd been tempted to order the capture of the damaged ship that had done this, but who else might see them if they dropped their cloak now? The array must have eyes on both sides.

Caution had been rewarded when the unknown and mysterious fleet uncloaked to collect not just the damaged ship, but another smaller ship. And then it was gone. Leaving them stuck inside with an unknown number of cloaked ships.

Stuck. Inside.

That troubled him more than he cared to admit, despite the level of alcohol medicating his metabolism. Once they'd secured his artifact they had to leave. According to Elfel, this was the only weakened section of the array. He would be working on how to get out while they got their artifact.

Bester had his finger on the comm to call Ghrym and get them headed toward his artifact, when Elfel called him.

"Now what?" The euphoria of the drink, and the adrenalin from the battle were fading. He had a headache and a knot in his middle that he didn't like. It felt something like fear.

"Now that we are inside, I have been able to scan more precisely for the beacon." Elfel hesitated. "I am sending you the data."

Bester didn't want to see it. Not now. But he opened the file when it arrived. He studied the ship. Noted the beacon flashing from inside a larger ship. "They have my artifact?"

"It would seem so, sir."

The disposition of the big ship puzzled him. It was on an intercept course with this region, but even as he studied the data, an update alerted him to a course change. It was heading in system, toward a cluster of planets well away from this region. He altered the view. Huge debris field there. Cluster of planets in the bottom half of the system. There was almost a line that divided the debris from the planet section. "No one can see us, can they?"

"I don't think so," Elfel said, though he did not sound certain.

"Were you able to scan them?"

"Very limited data, sir." A hesitation from Elfel. "I needed to take care. The surface of their ships is—" he stopped.

"Is," prompted Bester impatiently.

"Do you remember those sea creatures we transported to—"

"I remember," he cut in. The memory of the creatures still bothered him. And put a price on his head in certain systems where the creatures were protected.

"Every part of the surface was a sensor. I believe these ships are the same."

Bester blinked. "Sea creatures?"

"Sensors, sir. Hypersensitive sensors. Able to detect almost imperceptible movement and sound."

Bester glanced around. Could they hear them talking?

"Have we ever seen anything like these ships?" he asked Elfel.

"No, sir." Elfel sounded regretful.

Bester felt regretful, too. Something that unique—he was here for another purpose. Once they'd delivered the artifact, they could return.

Perhaps.

He sobered enough to do some equations. Two small ships. All those *Mycterian* ships turned into drifting debris, the fleet outside the array in full retreat. They would need to tread carefully in this system. And focus on getting out with their prize. He touched the comm control. "Set a course for that beacon, Captain. And let's try not to leave an energy signature for them to find."

PART IV

28

IT STILL SURPRISED Coop that they weren't all dead. One casualty. Coop tried to rub that memory away. They'd more than avenged him. The comet burst drive's instability had destroyed the ships too close to them, setting off sympathetic detonations that had turned the stork fleet on this side of the array into a new debris field.

Wilkins had been injured in the battle. Coop had stopped in to give him an update on the other two injured men. Both should be all right, but it had been a near thing. Wilkins thanked him, but the news didn't lighten his expression much. He'd lost a man.

As he made his way back to the bay containing the two shuttles, Coop faced the fact that they'd lived but that wasn't necessarily the good news. The shuttle was a wreck, and they weren't dead, so he'd be making explanations to Pappy at some point. At least they hadn't lost both shuttles, though Tiger wasn't happy at missing the fight. His shuttle had been tossed around some by the multiple explosions, so he wasn't surprised when he found Arian working on repairs there.

The wreck of their blood splattered shuttle was a sobering

reminder of what they had survived. And just why the *Phoeni-copterians* feared the *Mycterians*.

He would have liked to know what the birds thought about their near invasion miss, but it wasn't his job to ask questions. He propped a shoulder against the side of the shuttle and watched Arian wrestle with some wiring.

"At least we didn't lose this one," he muttered, as the sight of her started to mess with his thinking. She had streaks of what could be oil on her forehead and cheek, both bandages, and scratches in a variety of places. She'd stripped off the jacket of her ABU's, which left her arms bare, the tee shirt hugging her curves—she winced, stopping to massage her ribs. "You hurt?"

She looked up, managing a smile despite the strain in her eyes. "I am well."

She wasn't. Exhaustion pulled at her eyes and mouth. He held out a hand. "Take a break. That's an order." He even used his order voice, but he was careful how he helped her up when she took his hand. She stumbled and he let her bump into him, then wrapped his arms around her, not as tight as he'd like, but for now, it was enough to hold her. It surprised him when the hand he lifted to smooth down the back of her head shook slightly.

After a slight stiffening, she relaxed into him, resting her head on his shoulder.

She didn't smell great. Neither did he. He didn't care. If he could have, he'd have found out just how alive they were. If he could have. Even if they'd had the privacy for that, he could tell her ribs bothered her more than she let on.

"I am sorry," she murmured against his chest.

"For what?"

"That I did not think of it sooner. That soldier…" She shuddered against him.

Coop's lips thinned. How long had the cameras kept working? "I'm sorry you saw that." He hesitated. Never had he been more aware that words weren't his thing. And he probably hadn't needed them more. "I could have told you to initiate the self-destruct sooner. I didn't because I still had hope that something could or would change." He gently tipped her chin up so he could see her eyes. "It was risky, right?"

"Very," she agreed, but her lips trembled.

"You did the right thing, waiting until there was no other option." He smoothed a hand along the side of her face, fighting not to pull her hard against him and erasing the haunted look in her eyes. "Okay?"

She nodded, then hesitated, biting her lip. He wished—he cut that thought off. "What?"

"Where I came from, I realize now, was...violent...but they had...smoothed the rough edges of it, kept it mostly out of sight. People just vanished. Or came back different. changed."

"First time in battle is hard for everyone. It digs down to the core of you, finds out how bad you want to live." He didn't tell her it was his first hand-to-hand, that his battles had been—not sanitized but less personal. It would be a long time before he forgot.

Maybe she saw it. He didn't know. She lifted a hand, resting the palm against his cheek.

"I do not know the words I feel inside." He opened his mouth, but she moved her fingers to stop his words. "I have changed. You changed me. When I left my world, all I wanted was away."

"And now?" As he spoke, his lips brushed her fingers, like a kiss.

"Now, I only want you."

Did she know what that meant? Looking into her eyes, he didn't think so. There was still so much innocence in her gaze.

"I...want...you, too." He knew what he meant, but he also

knew that this time it meant more than just sweaty time in the sheets. He cupped her face with both hands and pressed his mouth to hers, taking it easy because he felt like he could go up in flames. Didn't even need a match. He eased back, knowing they weren't alone, though they were alone inside the shuttle at the moment. So he whispered the words against her mouth. "I love you. I've never said those words to a woman before. I know you don't know—yet—what that means, but for me, it means forever. For always."

He was surprised to feel the warm tears slide into his fingers. He smoothed the tear away. "Please don't cry—" he stopped as his gaze connected with hers. The horror wasn't completely gone, but dawn was breaking in there, too. And hope. It was the first time he'd seen her show it, he realized.

"In my world, when we say those words to someone, that means you want to marry them. It's an...official way to tell the world you are a couple. Will you marry me?"

Her lips curved up, and the light in her eyes grew. "I would like that very much."

He opened his mouth, thinking he owed her more, but maybe one of then nurses could explain it to her.

"I...love you, too," she added. "Yes, that feels right to say." She touched her chest as if something had eased in there. "I love you, and I would like very much to marry you."

He started to close the small gap between their mouths when someone—Tiger—cleared his throat just outside.

"Got some incoming birds, Banshee," he said, his tone carefully neutral.

Well, warning was what a wing man did. And Coop was too happy to care what he'd overheard. He gave her a crooked grin. "Think they'll give us the dollar tour of this rust bucket?"

Her smile widened, though there was some color in her cheeks. Her understanding of slang had expanded a lot in not very long. She glanced outside. "I think they wish to speak with us."

He sighed. "I hope lunch isn't included this time. I'd rather have an MRE."

———

Arian and Coop followed their escort to a place that she did not believe was a dining room. For one thing, it lacked the table for eating. It was round, the walls much like those on the planet they'd visited, but without the DNA artwork. A block waited in the center—she presumed it was seating since—it was the correct height. The only other fixture was similar to the console she'd observed in the arrival room.

On the seating block were two of the communication bracelets. With a shrug, Coop slid his on, tucking it out of sight under his flight jacket.

"It's too pretty," he muttered when Arian lifted a brow in his direction.

Arian smiled, feeling both shy and more confident in his presence. *He loves me.* The way he said the words told her they mattered. She slid her bracelet in place, then sat down, feeling the hum of the ship's engines faintly through the unyielding block. It sometimes felt as if the palms of her hands were tuned to this hum, able to split the sounds into the engines themselves. She glanced around, but there was little to see in this place. Her hands rested on the block, but her mind remembered the feel of his skin against hers when she touched his face. She'd felt the thump of his heart, like an engine, through her palms, and felt the fire licking along his veins, sparking heat in her. *I want you.* These words had a heightened meaning, she sensed, something to do with how bodies came together in the act of coupling. She edged her fingers over, until they just touched Coop's where they rested on the block. Immediately his head turned her way, and he grinned, covering her hand and squeezing it. She licked her lips and saw flames flicker in his eyes.

"I do...understand...more than you think I do," she murmured.

His grin was hot and rueful. "Then we'd better hurry and tie the knot."

Her brows creased. "Tie..."

"Get married."

He did not appear worried, but Arian was not as optimistic. Would his Colonel let them get married? As if he heard her worry, he squeezed her hand again. "I'll handle it."

His confidence was infectious. "Sooner would be," she bit her lip and looked at him through her lashes, "better."

"We should probably change the subject or—" He massaged the back of his neck with his free hand, the wink of the bracelet catching the light.

"Yes," she agreed, trying not to grin. She glanced around, but there was nothing to distract except her usual. "This ship has fine engines."

"Yeah?" Coop looked around, too, giving a small start as another voice joined their discussion.

"Thank you, *munshi*."

Arian twisted to look at the bird standing in the hatch opening. She rose, pulling free of Coop's hold, and faced this bird, noting that its uniform appeared to have signs of what could be rank.

"You are the Captain."

The bird inclined its head. "Are you also a pilot, *munshi?*"

Arian gestured toward Coop. "Captain Cooper flew our ship during the recent battle." At least, until he had to turn the ship over to her. It was not exactly an answer, but their answers had been light on detail so far, so she did not feel guilty.

Again the bird inclined its head. "We thank you for your fierce defense of our border, Captain." Its head angled to one side. "We offer our sympathies for the warrior you lost."

Arian did not have to be touching Coop to know he stiffened at this, but he nodded. "Thank you." As if he wanted to change the topic of conversation he added, "And thank you for the lift."

"The...lift?" The Captain angled its head the other direction.

"The ride back to our ship?"

"It is our honor to convey you to your ship." There was a pause. "Please to be seated. Our Prime Minister is initiating contact momentarily."

The bird walked up, taking a position next to the bench, the long expanse of its neck bending in a wide loop so that it appeared that its head rested on its back. The wall ahead of them, actually a view screen, she realized, flickered once, twice, and then resolved into a video of Hoteimai, the bird from the feast.

"We thank you, *munshi,* and Captain Cooper, for your assistance during the breach of the sanctuary."

Arian inclined her head, but it fell far short of what these birds could do. "I kept my word, as far as I was able." She had not wholly solved their problem. She was certain Hoteimai knew this as well.

"Yes."

Did it seem as if Hoteimai relaxed?

"We have not battled the *Mycterians* for many..."

Arian was not able to translate this word for time that the Captain used. Marking time's passage felt like one of the larger barriers to understanding between them.

"We are reviewing the data you collected, but we wish to hear your assessment of the battle."

Coop's shoulders twitched as if he were tense, but he

sounded calm as he gave his report. This was his field of expertise, of course.

"They are fierce fighters," he summed up, "able to adapt quickly to changes in tactics. And they are damn scary up close."

Hoteimai's head moved in what could be agreement. "Will they return?"

Coop did not hesitate. "They will."

"The border is repaired," the Captain pointed out.

"The array has been patched but they know this system is here." Arian glanced at Coop as she said this. "They believe you are here."

"If they believe that, they would not have sent so few ships through the breach."

Coop nodded as if acknowledging this point. "It looked like a probing run to me, a test to see how closely the border is being monitored."

"You pushed them back." The Captain watched Coop intently.

"Yes, and they will go home and take what they learned and adapt, at least, that's what we do when an enemy smacks us down." He looked at Arian now. "Say, they rammed the array at that weak point? Could it hold?"

"No." She did not hesitate. She added, "Ramming it would be dangerous for them. They would lose or damage ships in the process. But it is the fastest way to get in."

"I don't think they care. They've been trying to get in for a long time," Coop pointed out. "They are what we'd call highly motivated."

"So they are coming." Hoteimai was silent. It seemed to sigh. "We have known, we have prepared, but it has been many..." Again that word that would not translate. "...preparing for invasion, but..."

"You didn't have the advance intelligence you needed," Coop

guessed. "Neither did they," he added when Hoteimai ruffled its wings. "Well, you've both had a look. What do you think of your chances, Captain?" He twisted to look directly at the ship's captain.

The captain hesitated. "Our people are brave, but they lack... the instinct to destroy. That is why this sanctuary was created for us. So that we could remain who we were, who we are."

Arian sensed more behind the story, sensed more that she knew this story if only she could remember.

"The *munshi* knew this. That is why they aided us," Hoteimai said, sadness in its voice. "But you are only one, not seven, and the Urclock is silent. This time, I fear, there will be no retreat for our species."

"The...Urclock?" Arian murmured the words as a question, but it was directed at herself, or rather that place in her head where knowledge—and answers—still hid.

"Seven?" Coop jerked, his gaze darting to her.

She gave a slight shake of her head. "I am...*meta*. The third."

"You can not form a tangram alone," Hoteimai said.

"No," Arian agreed, "but if I could start the clock..."

"Start an Urclock?" Coop sounded most dubious. "Are you sure you should?"

She half smiled. "Why not?"

"Well, Urclock sounds...dangerous." He stopped and rubbed his face, wincing when he got too close to a swelling bruise.

Arian looked at him. She smiled faintly. "Like love, it is a leap."

He stared at her, shaking his head slowly. "That's..."

"You can do this. You can start the clock?" Hoteimai asked.

"I believe so," she said, "but...you have to let them go. You have to let the *Boyington* leave when it wishes to."

Coop shifted sharply next to her. She did not look at him. She could not look at him. Not now.

Hoteimai did not speak for a long time. Finally, it nodded. "So be it." It made a movement that could be considered wry. "We could not require any people to stay when the sanctuary is no longer safe."

———

"What the hell was that??" Coop hissed at Arian as they were led back through the corridor's of the bird ship.

She didn't pretend to misunderstand. "I gave your colonel my word."

He wanted to stop her, make her look him in the eye, but they couldn't stop. "You remember what's out there? And the storks might not be the worst thing." And she'd promised to marry him. To go—she hadn't promised to go with him, he recalled now. Just to marry him. She didn't understand.

"I believe that leaving through the array is not the only way for your ship to get home, but..." She stopped just shy of the ramp. "I gave my word. He will decide your best path home, Coop."

"Arian," he looked around, then shifted around, dropping his voice, "I..." he hesitated, but if he didn't say the words, he might lose her. "We're getting married. We're staying together forever. Remember?"

She stopped and turned to face him. "I will never forget. I want to be with you forever, but I must help these people."

"Why?"

"Why do you fight for your people?"

"These are not your people," he pointed out. There might have been a hint of desperation in his voice.

"No, without you I have no one, but there is something that binds me to them, to their protection. If I fail..." her voice trailed off.

They turned and started walking again.

"Is this about that tangram thing?" he asked, finally.

"Yes. But more is at stake than the tangram." She rubbed her temples in frustration. "If only I could remember!" She looked at him then, the haunted look back in her eyes. "Coop, what if I am a...a clone?"

His heart jerked. The doc had said memories couldn't pass through DNA, but they'd seen some weird crap since leaving Earth. He took her hand, gripping it. He had to hang on tight for long enough.

"You're you. How you started—" He shook his head in frustration, and then lifted her hand to his mouth. They were just shy of the bay now. He glanced around. "It doesn't matter. Losing you? That matters. You're the one person—" Even as he tried, he knew why she would stay and help them. She may not know what to call it, but he recognized it. A sense of duty that made no sense to anyone on the outside or who didn't feel it.

"I spoke the truth when I said I felt I must save these," her head tipped toward their guards, "them. There is a storm inside. For you. For them. To take my joy in opposition to—" She paused in frustration.

"Duty. To your duty."

She looked at him, frustration fading. "Yes, if I do not do my *duty* I would break, it would break what we have. I have to try. It is a matter of trust."

"Then we'll just have to persuade Pappy not to leave because I'm not leaving without you. We're in this together from now on." She did not look convinced. "My word on it." Doubt lingered in her eyes. "My word on it. Trust *me*."

She smiled, but there was still sadness in it. "I do. Believe me, Coop, but the storm is not just inside. It is out there. I feel it here." She placed a hand on her chest.

He took her hand, clasped it to his chest. "I feel it, too." He lifted her hand to his mouth. He didn't care anymore who saw it. "Any chance we can get them moving back toward the *Boyington*?"

"We are moving. Can you not feel it?"

He looked down. He tapped the deck with a boot, but could not feel the change. "Really?"

Her smile was real this time. "Truly."

29

THE RETURN to the *Boyington* felt anticlimactic. In her heart, she had Coop's words, his love, and confidence in their future together. They'd somewhat accomplished their mission, but one shuttle was scrap, one shuttle damaged, one warrior was dead, three injured, and now they knew the risks of leaving this sanctuary through the array. It felt as if all her actions led either back to her ship or to this ready room where the unhappy Colonel waited for their report.

He looked weary, and as if he'd aged more than the few days they'd been gone from the ship. Lines cut deep into his face and around his eyes.

"It's not that I don't appreciate—" the colonel stopped speaking and scrubbed at his face as if his head pained him. He looked at Coop now. "Our guys have been able to get a fix on Earth, on how far we are from home."

His expression told her it was not the good news they'd hoped to get.

"How far, sir?" Coop asked.

"Best case? A couple of hundred years. Worst case..." he

stopped and leaned back in his chair, his mien that of a man who wanted to be moving, not sitting.

Coop's shoulders rose and then fell in a sigh. He glanced at Arian. "Plan B?"

Arian did not know what this meant.

"You said there might be another way home?" he prompted.

The dots connected inside her head. Leaving the long way home was Plan A. Her other option was Plan B. She nodded, aware the colonel was not going to like much about Plan B. He did not seem to like much of anything she said. She tried to order her thoughts, not easy since there were gaps still in what she knew, or thought she knew. Inside her head, she followed a faint trail that beckoned her to a distant light.

The colonel's brows arched interrogatively. "Let's hear it." His face, his tone, were not encouraging.

Arian thought for a moment, then asked, "Do you recall the anomaly that brought us here?" She heard the words and was angry with herself. How could they forget the event that had made them lost?

"The wormhole?" The colonel did try not to look more annoyed as he nodded.

"It is not a wormhole, at least, not in the way I believe your scientists would classify a wormhole."

"How is it different?"

"A wormhole is a connected point between two places in space that allows transit in one direction."

The colonel blinked. He looked like he wished to speak, but did not know what to ask.

"What we experienced was different. It was unnatural."

He straightened. "You mean someone made it?"

"I believe so."

"Who?"

"I am not certain." She suspected...but the knowledge

danced just out of reach, taunting her. Was it the *munshi*? A *munshi*? Yes, they had made it, she decided, but was some other entity trying to use the machinery of the *munshi*? Was the tangram forming? Or was it relic of a past when the tangram had formed the first time? But if that was the case, why was the Urclock still silent?

"I'm not sure I understand. Are you saying this isn't connected to two points?"

Both men did look confused.

Arian called up a HUD for them, noticed they both started at the sight. Had she done something wrong? The colonel looked at Coop, then looked at her.

"How did you do that?" Coop asked.

She blinked. She was not entirely sure. There was no control device for her. She'd just...thought it. Her eyes wide, she looked at him. "I am not sure..."

The colonel cleared his throat. "What am I looking at?"

"This is the anomaly," Arian said.

"It looks like a wormhole."

"That is how we perceived the section we could see," Arian agreed. She expanded their view. "But I believe it is more like a continuous tunnel. We entered it in one system, and then exited in this system, so we experienced it as something random, not a continuous event that caught us up briefly, then ejected us here."

The colonel frowned. "Are you saying, we can ride this back to where we came from?"

Arian shook her head. "It does not have..." She frowned, not able to find an analogy between the anomaly and anything in her previous life.

"An on ramp," Coop suggested.

She considered this and then nodded. "How and where it opens is determined elsewhere. If we controlled the machine..." She frowned at her diagram. Was the machine at the center of the tangram? She sensed the colonel shifting impatiently. "There is a device that the *Phoenicopterians* have in their cathedral that might open a way back to your system."

"The Urclock?" Coop asked.

She could tell this affected Coop's colonel in much the same way it had affected Coop, which was not well. She nodded, watching the colonel for his reaction.

"Might?" the Colonel asked, instead of the words she thought he'd use.

He kept surprising her.

"The *Phoenicopterians* believe it will save them from the *Mycterians* once more." This was not exactly the answer to the question he was really asking. He wanted to get his people home. He wanted "might" to change to "would."

"Why should I believe this clock can get us home or save the birds?"

Arian considered how to answer this, but there was no answer he would like. "The anomaly that brought us here was, I believe, a smaller version of what is possible if we could access the machine. It..." somehow she knew that she did not know this science, but she did know the machine and how to use it. She knew she had once used the machine... "...folds space together, making it possible to move..." she almost faltered at the look in the colonel's eyes "...even a whole system from one place to another almost instantly. A larger version of the comet drive on the shuttle craft."

The Colonel looked stunned speechless.

"It is how the *munshi*—though that is not the name they called themselves—" She frowned. "I am not sure how that name came about—but they moved them to this sanctuary and built the array that hid them. The *Phoenicopterians* know this. Their memory is long and time is...different for them. I sense that the clock did not just change their location, it changed how they mark time."

The Colonel opened his mouth, closed it, did this twice before he managed to ask with impressive calm, "How does this help us get home? It sounds like we just move to another sanctuary." *If it even works*, his tone said.

"You have the coordinates of home," she pointed out. For an instant, she saw the machine, saw how to enter the coordinates. "To help either of you or the *Phoenicopterians*, the clock must start." *Were the other six still out there to answer?* She did not know this either, not without the clock.

"Why is the clock important?" he persisted.

"It, I think it might be an alarm or a call to arms. Or simply a way to keep in touch." She made a gesture to her head. "Inside here, knowledge is stirring. It is there, but I do not have complete access yet."

"That's a big *yet*." His tone was flat, chilly.

She looked at him, waited until he met her gaze. "It is...a matter of trust, is it not?"

There was a long silence, so much silence she thought she could hear their separate heartbeats thumping like the ticking of separate clocks. Finally, he sighed.

"Those are two not-great options, young lady."

"Both are filled with risk and danger," she admitted, "but only one offers the hope of getting home before..." She stopped, because they knew better than she what they would lose.

"You," the Colonel pointed at Arian, "wait here and you," this time he indicated Coop, "come with me."

The look Coop gave her as they left tried to be reassuring.

———

Pappy led Coop to his ready room. When the door slid shut,

cutting them off from the bridge, Coop tugged at the collar of his uniform shirt and didn't sit when Pappy sat in the chair behind his desk. Instead, he stood at attention. For what felt like a long time, Pappy stared at the wall as if he'd forgotten Coop was there. Coop didn't make the mistake of doing anything to break the silence, even when a bead of sweat formed between his shoulders and rolled down his back. Might have got a few drops on his upper lip, too. Reminding himself that he was in love and that it wasn't a crime didn't help as much as he'd hoped it would.

Finally, Pappy shifted and said, without looking at Coop, "How deep are you in?"

Coop didn't ask him what he meant. "I love her, sir. I asked her to marry me." He hesitated. "She said yes."

Now Pappy swung the chair around to face Coop. "Does she know what any of that means?"

Coop's chin lifted. He came to attention. "Sir, yes sir, she does." He hoped.

Pappy's gaze bored into him, even harder than when he'd been interviewed for this expedition. He didn't flinch or look away. Dimly he knew that more was on the line this time, more than his life, more than dying far from home, or never seeing home again. He'd made fun of love, teased his mates who fell for it because he hadn't understood. *He hadn't understood.* A guy laid down his life for his country, but if he was any kind of man? He fought for love if he was lucky enough to find it. He didn't die for it. He lived for it.

"Sir, neither of us knows what's going to happen next. I'd like to have what time we can together."

Pappy suddenly looked tired instead of fierce. Had there been someone he'd left behind, Coop wondered. A love sacrificed to duty? It wasn't a question he could ask, but he wondered when Pappy nodded.

"All right, Banshee."

The use of his call sign was an indication that he was, for now, out of the doghouse. His gaze slammed into Coop again. "I hope you know what you're doing."

Coop grinned. "Does anyone when they are in love, sir?"

That surprised a laugh out of the old man. Then he signed. "We don't have time for anything fancy."

"We don't want fancy. Fancy takes too long, sir."

He nodded as if conceding that. "Get her in here then."

Coop's heart jerked. His brain might have, too. Then he straightened again. "Sir, yes sir!"

"Better get your wingman in here, too. You'll probably need him."

————

"I'm sorry it wasn't a fancy wedding," Coop said, as they left his colonel's ready room.

Arian lifted her hand, studying the small, sticky bandage that Coop had put there to symbolize what had happened. Not much of it had made sense to her, but she did not need sense. She was happy. A new sensation, but one she liked.

"How could I miss what I do not know?" she asked, slanting him a shy look. Around them, no one paid them any attention. She was dressed like them still, so perhaps that helped, but how could they not see the change? She felt as if every part of her had changed, even more than the changes she'd felt emerging from inside her head since leaving Bosakli. This...wedding— he'd called it—had left her feeling as if she were new. Not a clone. Not Arian of Bosakli, but someone else. Not a wife yet. But even that did not encompass the sense of wonder she felt. It was as if she turned over a leaf and discovered a new plant instead of the one that had been planted. Not *munshi* or *meta* or Arian. Not Mrs Cooper or Ms Teraz as they'd called her in the ready room. What or who she was had no name yet, but that was all right.

Partners. Couple. Two halves of a new whole.

You are becoming.

Thank you for coming to my wedding, but get out of my head.

There was humor in his fading words. *Congratulations...*

Coop tugged at her hand, drawing her into his side to murmur, "Nervous?"

She looked up at him and shook her head. "No." Trust. Was this what it felt like? If it was, she liked it, too.

He punched a panel, and a door slid back. The room was small and serviceable. Not unlike her room back on Bosakli and yet it felt entirely different. She eyed the bed.

All right, so maybe she was a little nervous. She didn't realize she'd stepped back until her back reached the closed door. A hand came to rest on one side of her head, then another hand—no, Coop's hand—came to rest on the other side of her head, trapping her in—no, not a trap or a cage. It was an embrace. A safe spot. It was a place she wanted to be.

He leaned in, feathering kisses from her temple, spent a little time nibbling behind her ear and then moved on to her neck and along her chin. It was very...pleasant.

Her heart rate increased. Her breathing shallowed. A warm languor stole through her, nudging out nervous and replacing it with something else. *Falling.* She was falling...

Her lashes lowered, and her head tipped back and to one side as he sought more access to the under side of her neck. She sighed deeply.

Trust.

She lifted her lashes because she needed to see him. His eyes burned with intent. She traced a lean cheek, then pushed her fingers into his crisp hair, releasing his scent into the air. She fell faster, but there was no fear now, just anticipation. His head lifted, his hot gaze meeting hers.

"Teach me," she said.

He grinned. "That's the plan, sweetheart..."

———

Coop walked next to Arian, her hand firmly clasped in his, their shoulders brushing together as they walked back to the hangar bay. Heat rose again as he recalled how nice it had been to wake with Arian next to him in the admittedly narrow bed. She'd been so sweet, so trusting, then so scorching hot as they learned how to please each other. As he'd noted when he kissed her the first time, she learned fast.

"We're headed in the wrong direction," he muttered.

She stopped glancing around, a puzzled frown twisting her mouth into the perfect shape for kissing. He noted they were already a bit puffy from his attentions. He resisted an urge to smooth a thumb across them because he was pretty sure that would lead to activities that would make them more puffy.

"Are we?" she asked, looking at him, then her lips curved up into a slow smile as awareness sparked in her eyes.

"Now, why are we going to fix your ship?" No, not her ship. She was one of them now. He lifted her hand to his mouth. He knew it, knew all of her so much better. Seemed a shame not to take what he'd learned and expand on it.

"Because your Colonel, um, suggested very strongly that we finish? I believe he is hoping we will find more information in its databases."

"Oh yeah. The old man sure knows how to kill a honeymoon," he muttered, tightening his hold on her hand so they walked as close as they could and still manage forward movement. He saw her mouth open to ask the question and added hastily, "What we did last night, that's a honeymoon."

She looked alarmed. "It is not over forever, is it?"

"We can take up where we left off tonight," he promised. She looked so relieved he to had think about Pappy at his most frustrated to keep from turning back. Old man could have given them more time, especially it if was going to take them a century to get home again. Damn nice of Tiger to make sure food arrived at regular intervals, so they didn't have to go anywhere.

They paused at the hatch door and she looked up at him. The reserve gone from her gaze. Now there was only love and desire. For him. For a moment he felt shaken by it all. She trusted him. He couldn't let her down. Because he didn't know the words to tell her this, he said instead, "I love you."

Her lips curved more. "And I love you." She sighed deeply. "I did not know happiness was possible. I did not know what it felt like until now. I feel...new and..." she shook her head and laughed. "I do not have the words."

"You don't need words," Coop said. "You can show me later." He hit the hatch control realizing he felt different, too. New. Older. Who had the totally appropriate hots for *his* girl, he might add. He gestured through the open doorway. "After you, sweetheart."

The dragon was waiting at the top of the ramp, his tail flicking slowly from one side to the other. His beard flared black for a long moment.

I did not expect to see either of you this day.

"I didn't either," Coop said. "Sure wasn't my idea."

"Coop's colonel wishes us to complete the repairs to this ship," Arian said, slanting Coop a smile that held a promise.

"So the sooner we get it done, the sooner we can—" Coop paused when color tinted her cheeks, "do something else. That's not fixing a ship."

The dragon turned away, his nails making a clicking sound as it headed toward the bridge.

"Sir?"

Coop glanced back. The ensign on guard there stood at the bottom of the ramp. He arched a brow.

"Someone called Tiger wants a word, sir."

Coop's fingers tightened on Arian's for a long minute. What did Tiger want now? He frowned. Okay, a lot of things. He sighed.

"I will get started on the engines," she said, returning his squeeze before easing her hand free of his.

"Don't get lost," he admonished.

"I will try not to."

Her chuckle was warm, and he hesitated for a minute, struck by how much she'd changed from their first meeting, what, two weeks ago? More or less. For a second he felt a flicker of doubt. How could anyone change that much? And then he realized how much he'd changed. He mouthed the words he couldn't say because of the Ensign. Her smile widened, then she turned and started down the corridor.

He didn't want to leave. He tested his gut. It was uneasy, but not twitching. He headed slowly down the ramp, turning at the bottom to look back, but Arian was out of sight. He stepped down and started toward the bay control console and pushed the button.

"Tiger?" He released the button so he could hear Tiger. Nothing. Had the dude called him and then left? "Tiger—"

The ramp of Arian's ship began to rise. He heard someone shout, someone that sounded like him yelling something about closing the bay doors. He ran toward it, would have thrown himself in the gap if the ensign hadn't grabbed him and pulled him back.

"Engines are firing, sir!"

Still struggling against the ensign's hold, Coop stumbled back, and finally let himself be pulled through the hatch. It closed just in time, but he could hear. He could hear the ship leaving, taking Arian with it. Could still hear her screaming for him from inside that ship. He sagged against the wall, his hands over his face, trying to think—

"Get to your *Dauntless*, Captain." The curt order from Pappy yanked him back. He didn't know when he went from walking to running. With the words from the dragon echoing inside his head.

She did not do this. I did not do this. I am sorry...

30

ARIAN TRIED to access the engine compartment and was thrown backward by a force field. Dazed, she scrambled to her feet, felt the engines begin to fire under her feet and raced toward the hatch. She slammed her hand against the hatch release, but it did not move. She threw herself against the metal, screaming Coop's name.

She could not lose it all. Not now when she knew what it was she'd lose.

The ship launched. She staggered, fell again, rolling over once before her head struck a wall. She slid sideways as the ship banked and began to accelerate. She rolled onto her stomach and managed to get to her feet. She staggered her way to the bridge, brushing the wetness from her eyes with an angry movement.

From his seat, Rhubreak looked at her as she sat down. She couldn't strap in. She hadn't fixed them yet.

"Did you—?"

I did not. I am sorry. I did not realize it was capable of launching.

She tried the controls, but without hope. The master of the ship had called. It obeyed its master now. She felt this, even as she fought it. She sank back, defeated for the moment, but steel formed in her spine. "I will never forgive this. I will not do what you want. I will not obey your master."

There was no response, though she had the sense the ship heard her.

She had a thought. "If you think I will help you breach the array—" She stopped. This had to be why the ship had kidnapped her. She had done the calculations in the Garradian ship, not this one. Did it seem as if the forward thrust slowed? "If you return me to the *Boyington,* I will give you the programming to leave this system. If you don't, I will not help you. I will die first." She felt Rhubreak looking at her and said, without looking at him, "Coop is my husband. His people are my people now. I am grateful for my rescue from Bosakli," now she looked at him, "but I did not ask for this. And you did ask me to do this." Neither the ship nor its master, could hold her to a bargain she had not agreed to.

The ship was not accelerating anymore, but it had not turned back.

"You have two copies in cold storage. You will have to be content with those." She looked at Rhubreak again. "Tell it that I mean what I say. Tell it!"

He blinked. *It knows.*

"I've changed. I'm not like them, or her, whoever I was copied to be like. I'm—"

You are becoming.

That wasn't Rhubreak. She knew his voice.

"I am becoming *me.*" She looked around her. It could keep her out of some of the systems, but she could still damage this ship. She saw her small bag of tools and grabbed it, yanking out one with a long, thin point. She held it over the control panel. "You will have to release me or kill me."

There is fighter craft launching from the Boyington.

"My husband is coming after me. His people are coming after you." She did not know until this moment that she'd wondered if the Colonel would let Coop come after her. "I am one of them now."

She felt the sensation of slowing as the engines began to power down, saw on the screen as the ship prepared to make the turn back to the *Boyington*. Her shoulders slumped with relief. She lowered the tool to her side.

Give me the code to access the array.

"Not until I'm on the *Boyington* and off this ship." She didn't know how, but she knew it hesitated. "I will keep my word." To Coop and to the *Phoenicopterians*. Her voice softened. "I am sorry I drove you into a ditch. I wanted to be free. I will be free—"

The ship jerked as if some great hand had grabbed it.

Tractor beam.

She staggered and almost fell. The engines whined, trying to break free. As if it knew it needed help, the ship released the controls. She dropped into her seat, her hands flying across the controls, initiating a scan of the ship that had suddenly appeared out of nowhere and grabbed them. When it appeared on the screen, her blood turned as cold as the clones in cold storage.

Pirates. It was a pirate ship.

Coop was deep in battle mode by the time his squadron launched. Part of him was amazed that Pappy hadn't hesitated to send them after her. But he knew why. Pappy had committed to her protection, too, when he gave Coop permission to marry her. He'd given his men an out, but they were all forming up around him. His men, his flyboys would help him get his girl back or die. Damn, he was proud of them.

At first it had seemed as if the ship would outpace them. When it stopped accelerating, he knew Arian was fighting back. If the dragon hadn't done it, who had initiated the launch? All of their people were accounted for. The *Phoenicopterians*? But why would they steer the ship on a course for the array?

I am not the ship's master.

She'd said that once. The dragon claimed he wasn't the boss either. The ship? Had the ship snatched her?

"Alpha Sierra is slowing and possibly changing course," came the voice of radar control on the *Boyington*.

Alpha Sierra. Alien ship. But Arian wasn't alien anymore—

All hell broke loose as a bogey popped up on tracking. His ship screamed multiple warnings. There were more from the *Boyington*.

"Unknown bogey!"

"Unknown bogey has deployed a tractor beam against Alpha Sierra."

Distantly he was aware of the *Boyington* demanding the bogey identify itself.

"Scan it! With everything you got while it's visible," Coop ordered tersely. "Eyeballs on it guys. It's going to cloak as soon as it can."

"Beacon is still active on Alpha Sierra," Badger pointed out.

"Can we pick it up from inside a cloaked ship?" Tiger wondered.

No one had an answer until the ship cloaked once more.

Coop's thoughts were racing. If that ship went ghost—when it went ghost—on them, it would be almost a reverse of the battle by the array. The storks had learned a few things from them, well, he'd learned a few things from the storks.

"Here's what we're gonna do, Bravo Flight…"

———

The ship scraped roughly against metal, before sliding to a stop.

She was not happy. The ship was not happy. That she could feel its unhappy was unsettling, but at least they finally had one thing in common.

"You should not have tried to kidnap me," she muttered, but they were past that now.

She and the ship had fought hard, but these pirates knew what they were doing. They had reeled them in like a fish on a line. She paused to wonder where that thought had come from and what it meant, then pushed it impatiently away as the grind of hangar bay doors closing came to her ears through the hull of this ship. *Trapped.* She hugged her body as shudders shook her. *Coop is out there.* He was coming. He would think of something— if he could see them. This ship had arrived cloaked. It would cloak again. Her chin lifted, and her arms fell away.

The beacon.

"Can we boost the beacon's signal?" Even as she asked the ship this question, she dropped to her knees and pulled off a panel, tossing it aside. She found the controls, looked around for her tools, found Rhubreak beside her, the bag suspended on his snoot. "Thank you."

His beard fluttered a bit, and he might have nodded. She found the beacon's power core. It still broadcast, but it could take more power. She diverted power from other systems, bringing it up to its max signal. She sank back, sweeping a forearm across her brow. It was something, but she could, she needed to do more. *Think.* She pounded her forehead. She scrambled up and flung herself into her seat.

"This ship must have weapons."

It is not a ship of war.

"Protections, then."

Mostly we run away.

"Surely you can't run away every time." When neither

dragon nor ship answered, she added impatiently, "They'll try to board us."

She didn't like the darkness that welled up, hated being trapped and feeling helpless. It carried her back to Bosakli, to every moment of her life there, up to and including, the pact bonding visits the day before the ship rescued her. Okay, so she might owe it something, but not her whole life.

"You should have asked for my help," she grumbled and felt something that might have been an apology from it.

Dread knotted her insides, put a sheen of sweat on her skin that made her fingers slip on the controls and clogged her thoughts. Against her desire, her brain pulled up images of the *Mycterian* boarding parties. Would pirates be better or worse?

She was not sure she wanted to see, but she needed to know, so she pulled up the video views of the outside. No birds of any kind, but the line of men—though they looked more like fierce animals—pointed various lethal-looking weapons at the ship. At least they did not have razor sharp beaks. But that was only positive. They appeared both wary and excited as they circled the ship like it was their prey.

Because it was their prey. She was their prey.

With her new knowledge of men and women, and how they could interact, she feared she knew what they would do to her if they breached the hull. Suddenly getting stabbed and eaten by the *Mycterians* felt preferable.

Her blood chilled enough to qualify her for cold sleep, but she squared her shoulders. From Coop, from his people, she'd learned that waiting on the enemy was a swift path to defeat. What as it Coop had said after the battle? That one fights until there is no hope left in the hope that something would change, or the enemy made a mistake. Though, from what she'd observed, Coop had forced that change.

As had she, when she activated the comet drive. This ship

did not have comet drive—did it? And if it did? From inside this ship, it was a fast flight to destruction. And it could take out Coop's squadron.

She noted a change in the circling men. They did a caricature of coming to attention, their heads turning toward something out of her sight. For no reason she could define, the hair on her arms rose and a knot coiled in her midsection. The men fell back in two directions, allowing someone to stride into her view. He looked right at the video feed as if he knew it was there. As if he knew she were there.

Trajan Bester.

She flinched back, her breathing turning to panicked gasps.

No...

There was no sign of the careful pact bond seeker now. She'd known, hadn't she? She'd sensed what he was. To avoid facing him, she'd walked onto a space ship to anywhere, with only a dragon as a companion.

Her communications buzzed.

"You will lower your ramp and surrender yourself and your ship." His lips had twisted up in a grotesque smile. "If you don't cause us too much trouble, we won't hurt you very much." He licked his fat lips, and a gleam of anticipation made her stomach lurch. "Who knows, you might enjoy it. You can't have had much fun on that backwater planet."

She fought to slow her breathing and unclenched her hands before she looked at Rhubreak. "What does he know that I do not?" Her companion's reluctance to answer was so strong, she almost reached out a hand to push it away. "Tell me."

He is known as a collector of rare artifacts.

Artifacts. "I'm an artifact." A thing. An it. A commodity to be traded. She glanced at the video. She was something to be played with like a toy. If the thing got hurt or damaged, why should they care? An artifact could not feel.

"Is that what I am to you? To the ship? It's master?"

It was clear Rhubreak did not know. Like her, he'd been caught in someone else's trap.

He must not take possession.

The ship did not want to be captured? How ironic. *Will you sacrifice me for the ship?*

The ship protects the contents.

Contents. Well, that was something.

He must not board this ship.

Arian searched for a response to this blindingly obvious remark. She massaged her temples, her mind going over the defensive moves they'd made during the battle at the array. Most of their moves had involved the deployment of weapons. But if this ship had them, it wasn't talking. Perhaps because it feared to destroy itself and its contents? They'd certainly come close to that when she used the comet drive. But...

The drive was propulsion—really fast propulsion, but in the end it was just movement. "We shouldn't have to hold out forever," she murmured, "just long enough for Coop to help us."

The ship that holds us has many defenses.

She stiffened. Of course. They were inside. "Let me see them." As she read through the list, she almost lost hope. What chance did Coop's fighters have against all this? She knew the *Phoenicopterians* had fighters. How would Coop put it? Skin in this game. They needed her. She had to hold out long enough and maybe help them from the inside.

And if they failed?

"Does this ship have a self-destruct?" She was startled at how calm she sounded. She felt the mental jerk from the ship and Rhubreak. "You said this ship must not fall into their hands."

There was a long pause.

"You are taking too long. I need answers and I need them quickly."

It does.

"Okay, so what else do you have that we can use to keep these...men...from boarding this ship?" Time. Would it work for or against them? Why did the word resonate inside her head? "I need to see anything and everything we can use to keep them out." She felt the ship's uncertainty. "Let me see all systems that require special controls. That can blow up or burn." As data began to appear on the screen, she felt Rhubreak's gaze and looked at him.

You are not an artifact to me. You are not a thing or an it.

She finally nodded. "I wish..." she stopped and turned back to her screens.

You are valuable to the master, the ship said.

"When you value someone, that involves *respect*. And true respect means you give them a choice." She pushed away the memory of choosing to board this ship and was grateful when Rhubreak did not remind her of it. There was choice and then there was *choice*. She knew the difference. Did they?

31

THE BEACON VANISHED when the bogey cloaked, and Coop cursed silently, even though he'd expected it.

"All right, let's execute Whiskey. I say again, execute Whiskey."

The ships in his squadron were assisting the *Boyington* by doing close flybys of the last known position of the bogey and also targeting possible escape vectors, hoping to pick up signs of unusual sensor data that could indicate engine thrust. If you knew what to look for, total cloaking was not possible. Based on scan data before it cloaked, they knew what to look for. The geeks on the *Boyington* were some of the best at finding crap like that. Once they had possible vectors, then they'd execute India.

By dropping their cloak, the bogey had unzipped its fly. Bogey had two options, in Coop's opinion. Try to flash out fast, which would leave a nice subspace disturbance for them to follow, or try to creep away, in hopes of minimizing subspace disruptions.

Coop's money was on the slow creep. If the bogey tried for a fast exit, well, it had to end at the weakened portion of the array. That was the only way out of this place. The Garradian shuttle was ready to do a comet drive jump to block their exit from the system. And they were prepared to harass the bogey all the way to the array.

He was assuming a fair bit, and if he was wrong—Coop's gut tightened—but he wasn't wrong. The ship must have slipped in with the storks when they breached the array. There'd been so sign of an anomaly since the *Boyington* got dumped here. The only way out was that weak point. The last question, did that bogey know how to open it up? If they did, well, the shuttle would be an unpleasant surprise. They'd be trapped between the array and the Coop's flyboys.

"Our assessment is that the bogey is playing possum, Banshee."

Coop had to agree with that assessment. The other purpose of their flybys was to lure the bogey into opening fire, which would also help expose their position. So far, the bogey was refusing to play.

"Roger that, home plate," Coop said. "Lima and Tango squads execute India. I say again, execute India."

The two squadrons of his wing began their maneuver, tracking ahead of the last known vector so they could lay down countermeasures chaff. If the bogey was attempting to creep away, it would have to change course or risk the chaff debris exposing its movement.

"Kilo and X-ray, execute India." He studied the screen. "Victor and Yankee, execute India."

These squadrons were creating what he hoped would be a 3D box of chaff, to either reveal or trap the bogey. It was out there. All they needed was—he gave a jerk when the beacon reappeared on their tracking, almost dead center of their chaff box. *Good girl*, he muttered to himself. They didn't have the fancy power-sucking weapons the storks had, but if they deployed the right weapons, at the right time, they could force the bogey to fight or be damaged. Or destroyed. He faced that. Knew it was one of the risks. But it had to be done. They couldn't risk the bogey escaping with Arian. She'd rather be dead than trapped. He may be a guy who didn't know much about women, but he knew this about her.

She was done with being trapped.

His gut clenched, he knew this in his mind and his heart. These were pirates. They would show no mercy. She'd done what had to be done during the last battle. He could do no less for her now.

———

Their tractor beam hadn't released yet.

"What range of motion can we manage?" And more importantly, "Can we fire engines, lift off at all?"

All roads of inquiry seemed to lead back to propulsion, though she did not give up hope of shaking out more than that.

The ship felt almost thoughtful at her question. *We can fire and achieve some lift. It secures us opposite of engine thrust. There are risks.*

"Really? Risks worse than being boarded by pirates?" The ship did not answer this. She activated the control to split the screen so she had a view of all angles of the hangar bay. One group of men was working on something that she assumed would be used to breach the hull. One of them, wearing protective head gear, manipulated a valve and fire shot out of the tube he held, a narrow, flexible-in-appearance tube that led back to a large tank on wheels. He began to apply this fire to the hatch seal.

A fire that could cut through metal. *Interesting.*

"They are attempting to cut through the hatch seal," she mused. She looked for and found a way to lock down bridge access. Unfortunately, the bridge hatch was not as well armored as the hull. They needed to stop them before a breach or they would not be able to escape. *Escape.* Apparently she still had hope. She finished assessing the system's file, set it aside, and pulled up a schematic of the ship. "Isn't there a release vent close to where he is working?"

The ship—she presumed—highlighted the vent on the schematic. "Okay, let's shut down all the vents but that one." The ship might have twitched again. "I know, there are risks. Flame and oxygen are unstable when combined. But if we're boarded..."

How many times was she going to have to explain this basic truth to the ship? On the feed she watched Bester pacing away, then stalking back to bark at the man trying to breach their hull. He was not a patient man. His head turned and he snapped at his...men did not seem the correct term for creatures who appeared barely human.

Scalawags?

That seemed not nearly evil enough, but it would suffice, she supposed. As Arian continued to comb through ship's systems that had been hidden from her before, she felt and saw, the sparks of light flashing and moving under the surface of her skin. Without looking at Rhubreak, she asked, "What are they?"

They are nanites. It was the ship who answered.

"Why haven't I seen them until..."

*They were dormant in your system until you **chose** to come aboard.*

Apparently, she'd hurt the ship's feelings. "Sorry, but choice comes with knowledge. A choice without that is not a real choice."

She, who had endured years of "choosing" on Bosakli, knew this better than either of them. She studied the lights, flowing along her arms and hands. It almost seemed as if they went in and out of the console, too. Items on the systems were high-lighted, as if the tiny lights had asked her, "will these cause the scalawags problems?" She half smiled. She and the nanites might get along very well. If they lived long enough.

Other than the sound of the hiss of the cutting fire outside, it was oddly quiet.

They are not fighting Banshee's ships.

Okay, why would they wait? But the answer was obvious, even to a former farmer. If they could breach the hull, they had a hostage to use to negotiate their way out of the system. The only way to help Coop right now was to not get caught.

They will breach the hull soon.

"All right, here goes...something." She looked at the broken straps, grabbed the edges and tied them together as firmly as she could. Something was better than nothing if things got bumpy. She wiggled her fingers, then settled them on the controls, watching for the moment Bester got close to the man with the fire. "Prepare to fire the engines on my command. Wait...wait... decompressing corridor..."

She heard the rush of air leaving the ship. A pillar of fire shot toward the upper bay, followed by a flash. The ship skidded sideways impacting with something firm. She could not be certain. The impact took out the video feed on that side.

"Fire engines." She lifted off, with a shriek of metal to metal, then slewed the rear of the ship around, aiming at the largest concentration of scalawags. Screams and yells penetrated the hull of the ship.

She skewed around the other direction, partly because of the tractor beam still holding onto the ship, her body pushing against her less than secure restraints.

Her nanites highlighted something in her systems search.

The tanks of cold sleep fluid. They, she noted, must be highly flammable. Each tank had an eject control.

That's—

"For me? Well, I won't be needing it."

The view outside showed those still standing suddenly tumbling.

This ship is under attack.

She smiled but did not speak. Because she'd noticed something else...

32

THE BOGEY DIDN'T SEEM to know the beacon exposed their position. It wasn't perfect since it didn't show the whole ship. But enemy was getting pounded as his squadrons dropped careful charges, hoping to distress, not destroy it. When would they fight back—of course. They were trying to secure a hostage. *A hostage.* His stomach clenched. What would *he* do if Arian popped up on his screen in the hands of the enemy?

"Banshee, the beacon is moving, well, erratically." Home plate sounded puzzled.

"Define erratic," Coop ordered. He pulled up his screen, but it wasn't big enough to track big movements. To him it looked like it was twitching a bit. They needed to launch the next round of depth charges. If the ship was getting ready to move—

"Our assessment is that the movement reflects beacon movement, not bogey movement."

Arian. It had to be Arian. He didn't know what she was doing, but he knew she'd be doing something, anything to keep the enemy out.

But—if they were basing their firing runs on the ship being almost stationary and it wasn't—

He shook it off. He'd already made the decision to act. They had to force the bogey to fight them or run.

"Let's do another depth charge. Victor and Yankee, you take point this time." *Make them wish they'd never ventured in here.* He called up the *Boyington*. "Sir, we're gonna need a boarding party if we crack this sucker."

"Already on the way," came Pappy's calm voice.

Tracking broke in. "Banshee, we have multiple bird squadrons closing on your position."

That was good, but was it weird to feel like he'd wandered into the final battle of *Lord of the Rings*?

————

The bay hatch opened and more scalawags pulled in a device that was probably a weapon. A type of projectile launcher, she guessed, based on its configuration.

"Do we have shields?" she asked. They'd had shields before. Had she repaired them?

Minimal shields.

Minimal would have to do. She brought them online just in time. All the scalawags but one retreated. He did something to the device, then darted for cover. Flames flared from the projectile and it launched. The video feed flickered but did not go dark.

The shields held. This time.

The force of the impact sent them dancing on the line that was the tractor beam. Much shrieking metal and crunching sounds. Arian felt her restraints giving way and grabbed at the arms. She managed to catch herself before she hit the deck. They rebounded as the tractor beam pulled them back in the other direction. With a painful yank to her shoulder, she staggered into a line of panels. She dove for her seat before the next bounce on the line. Then clambered into her seat and retied the restraints as the rebounds diminished.

The view from her videos had been dizzying, so she had looked away. Seated once more, she studied the feeds that remained active. Bodies were strewn about the decking. The feeds still shuddered. She wasn't causing it, so Coop's ship must still be firing on the scalawags. Some lifted heads as if they did not wish to rise. Others stirred in a way that indicated returning awareness and possibly injuries. One managed to get to his feet on the shuddering deck, his feet widely planted, his expression enraged.

Bester. Blood ran down the side of his face.

More scalawags poured into the hangar bay. How many more men did this ship have on board? Several of them carried long tubes with what she assumed were projectile weapons hanging from their belts.

"Are they planning to blow us up—" If they blew up her ship, they would lose a substantial portion of their ship.

Best estimate is that projectiles are armor piercing. They will breach the hatch and allow them to board. Or inject disabling gases.

Why would they wait until now—because each level of weapon increased their risk and the risk of damaging...the contents of this ship.

"Can our shields keep them out?" And if they didn't, what would happen?

Uncertain.

She figured this must be the answer to both questions.

"We need to be free of that tractor beam," she bit her lip. It was starting to really annoy her. Was it time to go Zulu and start the self-destruct? Funny how quickly one became used to hoping and how hard it was to give up. It felt odd considering where she had grown up.

I have an idea.

Arian blinked. The ship had an idea?

You will need to hurry.

Really? Arian studied the data it presented and nodded. Not bad. Did not make up for getting them into this mess, but at least it was trying—

"What was that?" Arian asked when the video feed wavered sharply multiple times.

This ship is starting to fight back.

Yeah, she'd better hurry.

———

Finally, the bogey was shooting back. Lima's Badger took a glancing hit and spun away, but managed to regain control of his ship. "Check fire, check fire," he ordered.

The lead squadrons peeled away, drawing fire—and giving the follow-on squadrons time to get targeting solutions. Despite its best efforts, the bogey was helping them to connect the current dots with the previous scans of the bogey.

"Let's take out those weapons. On my six, Tiger." He kept a light touch on his stick. If he was steering that ship? He'd use the weapons to draw them in—and there it was. "Firing counter measures."

For what felt a long time there was a confusion of exchanged fire and then Coop and PapaOne flight were in the clear. He checked stats. Two ships damaged.

"Head back to home plate," he ordered. He frowned at the data on TangoTwo. But he couldn't worry about that now. "TangoFive, looks like TangoTwo needs a tow. Did we get any of their weapons?" His systems were still trying to collect that data.

"Near as I can tell, two of their positions went dark, PapaOne."

His gaze danced over the pieces the bogey had exposed. Beacon there. That had to be a hangar bay. How could they help her?

"All right, Victor and Yankee, I want you to lay down some depth charges along the side where the beacon is." He was still making his turn back, and they needed to pile on while the enemy was recovering. "You know the range." He hoped.

"Roger that." VictorOne sounded surprised but didn't question the order.

Coop felt sweat on his face as he watched his squads move in. He might have said a prayer as explosions sparked on his screen, one after the other.

Right about now, the captain of that ship should be thinking about making a run for it, but it would take time to overcome the inertia of coming to a dead stop. Why hadn't they got any intel from the *Boyington*? They'd had plenty of time, or it felt like plenty of time to give them something.

"Home plate, do we have any intel on where their propulsion units are located?" They hadn't been visible long, but the geeks should have something to send them. As if they'd been waiting for a request, some data began to arrive. Of course, it was all based on before the shooting started and the mysterious shift of the beacon. And if the geeks were right, the propulsion was dangerously close to the hangar bay broadcasting the beacon. And he was still too far out of position to make the run.

"Kilo and X-ray, see if you can take out their propulsion."

They acknowledged his order soberly.

The bogey, as if it knew what this run was about, launched a barrage.

"Victor and Yankee give them some help. We're coming in as fast as we can."

Kilo went in first and laid down the charges, while X-ray

provided covering fire. Just as he thought they'd done the job, his tracking lit it up with a white flash that overloaded his sensors.

———

Lifted off the decking as they were, Arian didn't feel the impacts of the ship giving and receiving fire so much as she observed the impact on the scalawags in the bay. It complicated the efforts of those seeking to fire the armor piercing projectiles at them. She saw Bester gesture and scalawags ran over to provide support.

Arian, who as far as she knew had not fired a weapon until leaving Bosakli, found herself calculating trajectories and yield. "They will have to be very precise if they don't wish to blow a hole in their own ship," she noted, feeling oddly calm under the circumstances. Perhaps when one had already faced death, it became easier? No, her mind rejected that. It was not easy. For a moment her cool faltered, but she stiffened. The resolve came from fighting hard, from doing everything one could.

"I wish I had been able to help them," she murmured.

Neither the ship nor Rhubreak asked who she meant.

It is time.

The ship was correct. The scalawag was almost stable enough to fire his weapon.

"Starting feedback," she said, pressing the controls. Her outside cameras went dark as energy crackled over the surface of her ship and—she hoped—into an overload feedback to the tractor beam. Just one of multiple things that could also cause an explosion. The feedback also took out the remaining video feeds.

We are clear.

The ship had not needed to tell her. She felt the jerk as the tractor beam failed. She brought the ship around, the turn painfully slow. Who would get off the first shot? She could not see and could not decide if it was better or worse not seeing.

Now.

She activated the eject and the tank shot out of the ship, designed to speed swiftly away in an emergency. It would not travel the safe distance before it impacted with the seam in the hangar bay doors.

She grabbed the ends of her restraint straps and held on.

The explosion propelled them into the space side of the bay. The crunch of metal to metal was not reassuring. She did not have time to assess anything as the overstressed doors blew and the bay decompressed.

———

Someone shouted for falling back. Coop's sensors hadn't cleared up when the shockwave hit, sending his *Dauntless* top over tail. He fought the stick for control and cursed the scanners that were still recovering. For the first time, he was thankful for the endless sim-drills as the spin slowed and he was able to regain control.

"Lima check in," he ordered, while he waited to get his eyes back on the situation. The report was bad, but could have been worse. He moved on to the next and by the time all his squadrons had checked in, his eyes were coming back online. His heart almost stopped when he saw debris where the bogey had been. Lots and lots of debris.

His breath stopped. His heart might have, too. He couldn't, she couldn't—

"Banshee?" It was Tiger. "I've got eyes on Alpha Sierra. Like actual eyes, because my sensors are blown."

"I got er, sir. She's dead in space, but I think I got a life sign."

I think I got a life sign.

He blew out his breath. He'd take hope over no hope.

33

ARIAN DRIFTED IN COOL SEA, the water lapping gently against her body. Overhead birds circled, graceful in flight and...pink? She blinked, and the birds banked, heading for a bright light. As the light grew, birds and ocean began to fade to white...

A voice called, insistent and worried. She knew this voice. Though the ocean began to fade away, it still felt as if she swam toward the voice, and with each stroke closer, memories began to filter in to her mind. She'd lost him, hadn't she? His name hovered just above, but with the next stroke, she knew it.

Coop.

Her husband. Her love. She broke the surface and took a deep breath.

"Coop?"

"I'm here, sweetheart."

His hand squeezed her as she ran aground. She did not know where these comparisons came from, but she knew them, knew what they meant. Her lashes fluttered and lifted, and there he was.

"You look..." she could not think of a kind word. His face was gray and red lines were tracks the white portions of his eyes.

He gave her a weary grin. "Hammered? That's because I am. You've been out for..." his voice cracked, and he had to cough to finish, "...for quite a while." A hand that trembled smoothed the hair back from her face. "Welcome back."

She turned her face into his hand, pressing her lips against his skin. "I feared I would never see you again." Her eyes closed as remembered grief flooded through her once more, then she managed a smile for him. "I am not sure I did not die. I thought we would. The explosion was quite large."

"Yes," Coop said, his voice a bit unsteady, "it was...large."

She had many questions, but the act of assembling them exhausted her. "This is like the first time...we met," she murmured. "Softer though."

"You're in the infirmary, though the fact that you are alive at all is amazing, according to the docs."

It was true she did not feel much pain, she was just very tired.

Coop's finger trailed down her arm. "Rhubreak says it is the nanites that protected you and healed you."

Nanites. That's right. The lights. Her lashes lifted again.

"Do they bother you?"

He shook his head. "They saved you. We're buds."

She chuckled. "Is Rhubreak all right?" Did she wish to know if the ship was all right? She was still very angry with it for kidnapping her.

"Rhubreak says they are all well."

His gaze held curiosity and worry.

"He was pretty worried about you."

"I should have fixed my seat restraints and not the engines," she said, with a wry grin.

Coop chuckled and then seemed surprised by that.

She studied his face with hungry eyes. And perhaps other hungry parts. "When can I leave this place for ours?" she asked.

"I feel—" she caught sight of someone out of the corner of her eye and said, "—not dead."

The heat that flared in his eyes told her he'd figured out what she didn't say. He didn't care about that other person, and he pulled her into his embrace and laughed. And then he kissed her.

————

Arian wished never to be in the same bay with the ship again. She would never board it again, that she knew. She was grateful when Coop came with her to face it. Would it answer her questions? She did not know. She did know it knew more than Rhubreak.

When she saw it, she felt her anger fading. It had, as Coop put it, taken a beating. She walked to the front, not because she knew that's where its intelligence was centered, but because it seemed appropriate. Perhaps some of the formality of Bosakli lingered in her veins.

She gripped Coop's hand tightly. *You should release them.*

The ship did ask who she meant, but she felt its resistance.

They deserve to be free.

With a sort of grumble, it responded. *They are not like you.*

How are they different?

They are empty.

Empty? Arian frowned. *What is their purpose?*

The ship did not want to respond. She felt this. *Why wasn't I frozen?*

You were primary.

Primary. And they were what? Replacements if she failed to...become. *You are becoming*, it had said. Becoming what?

Meta.

The third.

You are too damaged to return to the master, she told it.

There is not a single path to the master.

She didn't like the sound of that. *I have not become what the master wished.*

Haven't you?

I am not her, whoever I was fashioned to be.

You were not created to be her. You were created to become you.

With the abilities of the meta.

If you **choose.**

And if I don't choose?

It didn't answer. It didn't have to. If she didn't choose, she could not keep either of her promises. She looked at Coop. Would she lose him? As if he heard or knew, he faced her, taking her in his arms.

"We will not lose each other again, Arian."

She leaned her cheek on his shoulder, felt his arms around her, felt all the pieces of her coming together, the new she'd felt from their marriage, but also her past, all of it melding into *Arian. Meta. The third. Lover of Coop.*

"Yes," she said. "Let's go take a look at that clock."

He sighed. "I was afraid you'd say that."

———

This time Pappy went with them to the bird planet, not even a hint of expression on his face as they made their way to the bird fountain, where he paused to look around. The birds waited patiently while Hoteimai had shown them where their DNA had been added to the wall art. After getting permission, Pappy had touched it, tracing the lines of the double helix. He glanced at Coop and given him a "who knew" look. When Pappy was ready, their entourage led them toward the dining room with the Urclock. Might be the same guards going with them. It was hard to say. They all looked alike to him. Except for Hoteimai. This time the main bird walked next to them, exchanging—well, it wasn't small talk—but it chatted with Pappy, who had donned the communication bracelet without comment or hesitation.

A real man, he told himself, can wear anything. But Coop still pushed his under the cuff of his uniform jacket. Arian had suppressed a smile when he did it, then had slid her hand into his. It wasn't regulation, but neither was being lost in space with a bunch of birds. He wasn't sure he could ever let go of her hand again. They might have to modify his *Dauntless* for her. Even stranger, Pappy had not been bothered by her nanites.

"We ran into them on the Garradian outpost." His smile had been grim, his gaze abstracted. "I'm not supposed to know about them. I know they can heal injuries." Pappy seemed a lot less negative about Arian and her chances of getting them home. Coop wouldn't call him optimistic yet, but he'd toned down the pessimism and the skepticism.

As for him, the nanites had saved her life after they pulled her from the ship near death, so they were all buds—as long as they played least in sight when they were making love. As if she heard that thought, he saw her lips curve up in that way they did when he moved in for some loving. Now he knew why dudes tried to write poetry after they fell in love—not that he'd tried. But he did find his thoughts straying to flowers opening in the sun and crap like that. Because that's what it felt like Arian was doing. Opening to him. And he was opening to her. And he didn't mind one bit. Now he understood what his married buddies meant when they'd told him to "wait until it happens to you." He didn't mind if he sometimes had a stupid smile on his face. Or he'd rather be with Arian than with them. If his buddies wanted time with him, they had to take Arian. They were a team now.

Not that any of his buddies seemed to mind. They'd fought

with him to rescue her, and now they were happy for him. It was all good.

Well, except for the part where they were still lost in space.

Did Arian know her clasp tightened as they got closer to that dining room with the stopped clock?

The big doors swung wide. The table was gone. Birds, the guard kind, lined each side, like an honor guard for the clock. It looked bigger than he remembered and closer to their level. Arian drew a deep breath and then approached it, pulling him with her. Without touching it, her hand hovered above it, her fingers extended.

"Can you start it?" Hoteimai asked.

Arian gave the bird a "who knows" look, but Coop wasn't sure the bird realized it.

Carefully, lightly, Arian touched a spot, and the glass front swung open. Still without touching the clock face, she pointed at each of the seven symbols. Her finger shifted back until it hovered over just one symbol. Coop tipped his head to the side. The symbols sort of reminded him of *kanji*, the written form of Japanese. He'd learned a bit when he'd been stationed there.

He saw her take a breath, felt her tension through her hand. She reached out and touched the symbol with the tip of her finger.

He wasn't sure where the light started, with her or with the clock. Maybe it flowed both directions. Into the clock and through her, lighting up her skin so that she glowed.

Meta.

He wasn't sure why he heard the word. Her hand felt the same, maybe he felt a kind of tingle, but that was all. Still had to keep himself from shifting uncomfortably. But he didn't, he wouldn't let go. Ever. Whoever, whatever she was, they were a team, a couple, lovers. All he had to do was hold on.

And then, in the deep silence, he heard it.

Ticking.

No one spoke. It seemed to Coop that Hoteimai stared at the clock as the ticking, slow at first, began to increase.

Then one of the other symbols began to glow.

"The tangram is forming." Hoteimai lifted its head and honked once.

Coop considered this for several seconds. "So that's a good thing?"

Arian half shrugged, but there was a little "I hope so" in her eyes.

He looked at Pappy. "We'll be home for Christmas, sir. No problem."

CHAPTER 34

XADDEK SAT UNMOVING in the low light most suited to his species, several of his legs resting on his work station. At his feet was the crewman who had brought him the report on Trajan Bester. He should have transmitted the report. He was new and did not know. Now he would never know.

So Trajan Bester had missed his date for delivery of the item. There were rumors he was dead. If he weren't, he would be.

Of more concern was the loss of the item. It was relatively rare. Possibly irreplaceable.

Was the disappearance random? The arrival of the ship indicated competition for the item, but he had not sensed other interest when he carefully and quietly began assembling this particular collection. Of course, there were always those who watched him. They knew he sought only the most interesting, the rarest pieces for his collection.

The loss of the item on Bosakli had caused him to restart his research. Why had it been warm? The pieces he'd acquired so far were all in cold sleep. What did it mean that one was aware? Did that mean others out there were, too? Could the items in cold sleep be backups? Or, troubling thought, decoys?

His legs curled in frustration. Documentation about the items was as rare as they were. And in the fragments of data he'd found, the important information had been in code. The holder of the key to the code had been most reluctant to give it up, but being slowly eaten...

Xaddek smiled, all his eyes soft with remembered pleasure. A most tasty species.

It was only later he had cause to wonder if the holder had held something back.

He pulled up the data, deeply hidden and code-protected. The only thing new was the anomaly that had snatched the item from Bester's incompetent grasp.

It had most unusual properties, not the least, the inability of anyone to track its movement. Its movement was not as random as most believed. Was he the only one who knew this?

Who else knew that the items were pieces of a puzzle that once solved, would lead to great power?

All eight of his legs curled in longing.

There was nothing he desired more than great power.

———

Thank you for reading *Found Girl*. I'm working on the next book in the series! While you're waiting, I hope you'll check out my other books. And there is a connected Project Enterprise story called *Time Trap*.

To find out about all my releases, be sure to sign up for my New Release eZine and get a free eBook!

Or hop over to my website and check out my series:

Project Enterprise The Big Uneasy Lonesome Lawmen

Browse my complete backlist by visiting my website. :-) I have some stand alone novels, too.

And if you want to talk books, you can find me here:

My Blog Facebook Fan Page Twitter Pinterest Goodreads

If you enjoyed this book, I hope you'll consider leaving a review. It's not just because I'm needy (even though I try not to be!). Reviews help other readers decide which books to buy. :-)

ALSO BY PAULINE BAIRD JONES

Available in print, digital and audio.

Science Fiction Romance/Paranormal

Project Universe Series:

The Key (book 1)

Girl Gone Nova (book 2)

Tangled in Time (book 3)

Steamrolled (book 4)

Kicking Ashe (book 5)

Found Girl (book 6)

Project Enterprise: The Short Stories

Time Trap: A Project Enterprise Series Short Story

Nebula Nine (time travel adventure)

Open With Care (Christmas collection that includes, "Riding For Christmas" and "Up on the House Top"

Specters in the Storm: A paranormal/steampunk/science fiction romance novella

Out of Time (World War II Time Travel Romance)

An Uneasy Future

(A science fiction romance mystery series set in future New Orleans)

Core Punch (1.0)

Sucker Punch (2.0)

One Two Punch: An Uneasy Future Bundle

Short Story Collections

Project Enterprise: The Short Stories

Do Wah Diddy Delete

Let's Fall in Love

The Real Dragon and other short stories

The Real Dragon

Romantic Suspense

The Big Uneasy Series:

Relatively Risky (1)

Family Treed (Short Story)

Dead Spaces (2.0)

Louisiana Lagniappe (3.0)

Worry Beads (4.0) Coming soon!

The Big Uneasy Bundle

Lonesome Lawmen Series:

The Last Enemy

Byte Me

Missing You

Lonesome Mama (Bonus short story)

(The *Lonesome Lawmen* is also available as a digital bundle)

Do Wah Diddy Die

The Spy Who Kissed Me

ABOUT THE AUTHOR

Award-winning, *USA Today* Bestselling author Pauline never liked reality, so she writes books. She likes to wander among the genres, rampaging like Godzilla, because she does love peril mixed in her romance.

To find out more about Pauline or her books:
http://paulinebjones.com

ACKNOWLEDGMENTS

There are a lot of people who helped make this book possible, but you've already read a long book, so I'll try to keep this short.

People who encouraged me when I was afraid I wouldn't get my writing mojo back:

* My sister, Marilyn, who kept me supplied with flamingos, food, and fun;

* My sweet husband, children, and grandchildren, who keep believing in me even when I embarrass them on Facebook;

* Alexis Glynn Latner, my first reader and wonderful editor, who holds my feet so gently to the fire that I don't feel heat—just lift off;

* Narelle Todd and S.E. Smith, who provided support in so many ways, there aren't words;

* Veronica Scott, who sailed with me in *Pets in Space,* who is willing to take that journey again in *Embrace the Romance: Pets in Space 2,* and became a dear friend and still takes my whine-one-one emails;

* Nathaniel Jones, my space battle consultant. The military missed out when they let him get away (Haha);

* My cover designer, Melody Simmons, who did the cover before the book was started and sent my imagination soaring. And to Paula Proofs for her keen eye and attention to detail.

Thank you. Thank you. And thank you.